P9-DGZ-880

ALSO BY HA JIN

Between Silences

Facing Shadows

Ocean of Words

Under the Red Flag

In the Pond

Waiting

The Bridegroom

Wreckage

The Crazed

War Trash

A Free Life

The Writer as Migrant

A Good Fall

Ha Jin

A Good Fall

Pantheon Books
New York

The following stories have been previously published: "A Pension Plan" in Asia Literary Review; *"Children as Enemies" in* flatmanCrooked; *"In the Crossfire" in* Granta; *"The Beauty" in* Michigan Quarterly Review; *"The House Behind a Weeping Cherry" in* The New Yorker; *"Temporary Love" in* Shenandoah; *"Shame" in* Weber: The Contemporary West; *and "A Composer and His Parakeets," "Choice," and "An English Professor" in* Zoetrope: All-Story. *"A Composer and His Parakeets" also appeared in* The O. Henry Prize Stories 2008, *edited by Laura Furman (New York: Anchor Books, 2008); "The House Behind a Weeping Cherry" also appeared in* The PEN/O. Henry Prize Stories 2009, *edited by Laura Furman (New York: Anchor Books, 2009).*

Library of Congress Cataloging-in-Publication Data
Jin, Ha, [date]
A good fall : stories / Ha Jin.
p. cm.
ISBN 978-0-307-37868-2
1. Chinese—United States—Fiction. 2. Flushing (New York, N.Y.)—Fiction.
I. Title.
PS3560.I6G66 2009
813'.54—dc22   2009008638

www.pantheonbooks.com
Printed in the United States of America
First Edition
9 8 7 6 5 4 3 2 1

TO LISHA

Contents

A Good Fall

The Bane of the Internet

MY SISTER YUCHIN and I used to write each other letters. It took more than ten days for the mail to reach Sichuan, and usually I wrote her once a month. After Yuchin married, she was often in trouble, but I no longer thought about her every day. Five years ago her marriage began falling apart. Her husband started an affair with his female boss and sometimes came home reeling drunk. One night he beat and kicked Yuchin so hard she miscarried. At my suggestion, she filed for divorce. Afterward she lived alone and seemed content. I urged her to find another man, because she was only twenty-six, but she said she was done with men for this life. Capable and with a degree in graphic design, she has been doing well and even bought her own apartment four years ago. I sent her two thousand dollars to help her with the down payment.

Last fall she began e-mailing me. At first it was exciting to chat with her every night. We stopped writing letters. I even stopped writing to my parents, because she lives near them and can report to them. Recently she said she wanted to buy a car. I had misgivings about that, though she had already paid off her mortgage. Our hometown is small. You can cross by bicycle in half an hour; a car was not a necessity for her. It's too expensive to keep an automobile there—the gas, the insurance, the registration, the maintenance, the tolls cost a fortune. I told her I didn't have a car even though I had to commute to work from Brooklyn to Flushing. But she got it into her head that she must have a car because most of her friends had cars. She wrote: "I want to let that man see how well I'm doing." She was referring to her ex-husband. I urged her to wipe him out of her mind as if he had never existed. Indifference is the strongest contempt. For a few weeks she didn't raise the topic again.

Then she told me that she had just passed the road test, bribing the officer with five hundred yuan in addition to the three thousand paid as the application and test fees. She e-mailed: "Sister, I must have a car. Yesterday Minmin, our little niece, came to town driving a brand-new Volkswagen. At the sight of that gorgeous machine, I felt as if a dozen awls were stabbing my heart. Everybody is doing better than me, and I don't want to live anymore!"

I realized she didn't simply want to impress her ex. She too had caught the national auto mania. I told her that was ridiculous, nuts. I knew she had some savings. She got a big bonus at the end of each year and freelanced at night. How had she become so vain and so unreasonable? I urged her to be rational. That was impossible, she claimed, because "everybody" drove a car in our hometown. I said she was not everybody and mustn't follow the trend. She wouldn't listen and asked me to remit her money as a loan. She already had a tidy sum in the bank, about eighty thousand yuan, she confessed.

Then why couldn't she just go ahead and buy a car if that was what she wanted? She replied: "You don't get it, sister. I cannot drive a Chinese model. If I did, people would think I am cheap and laugh at me. Japanese and German cars are too expensive for me, so I might get a Hyundai Elantra or a Ford Focus. Please lend me $10,000. I'm begging you to help me out!"

That was insane. Foreign cars are double priced in China. A Ford Taurus sells for 250,000 yuan in my home province of Sichuan, more than $30,000. I told Yuchin an automobile was just a vehicle, no need to be fancy. She must drop her vanity. Certainly I wouldn't lend her the money, because that might amount to hitting a dog with a meatball—nothing would come back. So I said no. As it is, I'm still renting and have to save for the down payment on a small apartment somewhere in Queens. My family always assumes that I can pick up cash right and left here. No matter how hard I explain, they can't see how awful my job at a sushi house is. I waitress ten hours a day, seven days a week. My legs are swollen when I punch out at ten p.m. I might never be able to buy an apartment at all. I'm eager to leave my job and start something of my own—a snack bar or a nail salon or a video store. I must save every penny.

For two weeks Yuchin and I argued. How I hated the e-mail exchanges! Every morning I flicked on the computer and saw a new message from her, sometimes three or four. I often thought of ignoring them, but if I did, I'd fidget at work, as if I had eaten something that had upset my stomach. If only I had pretended I'd never gotten her e-mail at the outset so that we could have continued writing letters. I used to believe that in the United States you could always reshape your relationships with the people back home—you could restart your life on your own terms. But the Internet has spoiled everything—my family is able to get hold of me whenever they like. They might as well live nearby.

Four days ago Yuchin sent me this message: "Elder sister, since you refused to help me, I decided to act on my own. At any rate, I must have a car. Please don't be mad at me. Here is a website you should take a look at . . ."

I was late for work, so I didn't visit the site. For the whole day I kept wondering what she was up to, and my left eyelid twitched nonstop. She might have solicited donations. She was impulsive and could get outrageous. When I came back that night and turned on my computer, I was flabbergasted to see that she had put out an ad on a popular site. She announced: "Healthy young woman ready to offer you her organ(s) in order to buy a car. Willing to sell any part as long as I still can drive thereafter. Contact me and let us talk." She listed her phone number and e-mail address.

I wondered if she was just bluffing. Perhaps she was. On the other hand, she was such a hothead that for a damned car she might not hesitate to sell a kidney, or a cornea, or a piece of her liver. I couldn't help but call her names while rubbing my forehead.

I had to do something right away. Someone might take advantage of the situation and sign a contract with her. She was my only sibling—if she messed up her life, there would be nobody to care for our old parents. If I was living near them, I might have called her bluff, but now there was no way out. I wrote her back: "All right, my idiot sister, I will lend you $10,000. Remove your ad from the website. Now!"

In a couple of minutes she returned: "Thank you! Gonna take it off right away. I know you're the only person I can rely on in the whole world."

I responded: "I will lend you the money I made by working

my ass off. You must pay it back within two years. I have kept a hard copy of our email exchanges, so do not assume you can write off the loan."

She came back: "Got it. Have a nice dream, sister!" She added a smile sign.

"Get out of my face!" I muttered.

If only I could shut her out of my life for a few weeks. If only I could go somewhere for some peace and quiet.

A Composer and His Parakeets

BEFORE DEPARTING for Thailand with her film crew, Supriya left in Fanlin's care the parakeet she had inherited from a friend. Fanlin had never asked his girlfriend from whom, but he was sure that Bori, the bird, used to belong to a man. Supriya must have had a number of boyfriends prior to himself. A pretty Indian actress, she always attracted admiring stares. Whenever she was away from New York, Fanlin couldn't help but fear she might hit it off with another man.

He had hinted several times that he might propose to her, but she would either dodge the subject or say her career would end before she was thirty-four and she must seize the five years left to make more movies. In fact, she had never gotten a leading part, always taking a supporting role. If only she hadn't been able to get any part at all, then she might have accepted the role of a wife and prospective mother.

Fanlin wasn't very familiar with Bori, a small pinkish parakeet with a white tail, and he had never let the bird enter his music studio. Supriya used to leave Bori at Animal Haven when she was away, though if a trip lasted just two or three days, she'd simply lock him in the cage with enough food and water. But this time she was going to stay abroad for three months, so she asked Fanlin to take care of the bird.

Unlike some other parrots, Bori couldn't talk; he was so quiet Fanlin often wondered if he was dumb. At night the bird slept near the window, in a cage held by a stand, like a colossal floor lamp. During the day he sat on the windowsill or on top of the cage, basking in the sunlight, which seemed to have bleached his feathers.

Fanlin knew Bori liked millet; having no idea where a pet store was in Flushing, he went to Hong Kong Supermarket down the street and bought a bag. At times he'd give the parakeet what he himself ate: boiled rice, bread, apples, watermelon, grapes. Bori enjoyed this food. Whenever Fanlin placed his own meal on the dining table, the bird would hover beside him, waiting for a bite. With Supriya away, Fanlin could eat more Chinese food—the only advantage of her absence.

"You want Cheerios too?" Fanlin asked Bori one morning as he was eating breakfast.

The bird gazed at him with a white-ringed eye. Fanlin picked a saucer, put a few pieces of the cereal in it, and placed it before Bori. He added, "Your mother has dumped you, and you're stuck with me." Bori pecked at the Cheerios, his eyelids flapping. Somehow Fanlin felt for the bird today, so he found a tiny wine cup and poured a bit of milk for Bori too.

After breakfast, he let Bori into his studio for the first time. Fanlin composed on a synthesizer, having no room for a piano. The bird sat still on the edge of his desk, watching him, as if able to understand the musical notes he was inscribing. Then, as Fanlin tested a tune on the keyboard, Bori began fluttering his wings and swaying his head. "You like my work?" Fanlin asked Bori.

The bird didn't respond.

As Fanlin revised some notes, Bori alighted on the keys and stomped out a few feeble notes, which encouraged him to play more. "Get lost!" Fanlin said. "Don't be in my way."

The bird flew back to the desk, again motionlessly watching the man making little black squiggles on paper.

Around eleven o'clock, as Fanlin stretched his arms and leaned back in his chair, he noticed two whitish spots beside Bori, one bigger than the other. "Damn you, don't poop on my desk!" he screamed.

At those words the parakeet darted out of the room. His escape calmed Fanlin a little. He told himself he ought to be patient with Bori, who was no different from a newborn. He got up and wiped off the mess with a paper towel.

Three times a week he gave music lessons to a group of five students. The tuition they paid was his regular income. They would come to his apartment on Thirty-seventh Avenue in the evening and stay two hours. One of the students, Wona Kernan, an angular woman of twenty-two, became quite fond of Bori and often held out her index finger to him, saying, "Come here, come here." The parakeet never responded to her coaxing, instead sitting on Fanlin's lap as if also attending the class. Wona once scooped up the bird and put him on her head, but Bori returned to Fanlin immediately. She muttered, "Stupid budgie, only know how to suck up to your boss."

Fanlin was collaborating with a local theater group on an opera based on the legendary folk musician Ah Bing. In his early years, Ah Bing, like his father, was a monk; then he lost his eyesight and was forced to leave his temple. He began to compose music, which he played on the streets to eke out a living.

Fanlin didn't like the libretto, which emphasized the chance nature of artistic creation. The hero of the opera, Ah Bing, was to claim, "Greatness in art is merely an accident." To Fanlin, that kind of logic did not explain the great symphonies of Beethoven or Tchaikovsky, which could not have existed without artistic theory, vision, or purpose. No art should be accidental.

Nevertheless, Fanlin worked hard on the music for *The Blind Musician.* According to his contract, he would get a six-thousand-dollar advance, to be paid in two installments, and twelve percent of the opera's earnings. These days he was so preoccupied with the composition that he seldom cooked. He would compose from seven a.m. to two p.m., then go out for lunch, often taking Bori along. The bird perched on his shoulder, and Fanlin would feel Bori's claws scratching his skin as he walked.

One afternoon at the Taipan Café on Roosevelt Avenue, after paying at the counter for lunch, Fanlin returned to his seat to finish his tea. He put a dollar tip on the table, which Bori picked up and dropped back in Fanlin's hand.

"Wow, he knows money!" a bulging-eyed waitress cried. "Don't steal my money, little thief!"

That night on the phone, Fanlin told Supriya about Bori's feat. She replied, "I never thought you'd like him. He wouldn't get money for me, that's for sure."

"I'm just his caretaker. He's yours," Fanlin said. He had expected she'd be more enthusiastic, but her voice sounded as usual, mezzo-soprano and a little sleepy. He refrained from telling her that he missed her, often touching her clothes in the closet.

• • •

It was a rainy morning. Outside, the drizzle swayed in the wind like endless tangled threads; traffic rumbled in the west. Lying in bed with a sheet crumpled over his belly, Fanlin was thinking of Supriya. She always dreamed of having children, and her parents in Calcutta had urged her to marry. Still, Fanlin felt he might be just her safety net—a fallback in case she couldn't find a more suitable man. He tried not to think too many negative thoughts and recalled those passionate nights that had thrilled and exhausted both of them. He missed her, a lot, but he knew that love was like another person's favor: one might fall out of it at any time.

Suddenly a high note broke from his studio—Bori on the synthesizer. "Stop it!" Fanlin shouted to the bird. But the note kept tinkling. He got out of bed and made for the studio.

Passing through the living room, its window somehow open and its floor scattered with sheets of paper fluttering in a draft, he heard another noise, then caught sight of a shadow slipping into the kitchen. He hurried in pursuit and saw a teenage boy crawling out the window. Fanlin, not fast enough to catch him, leaned over the sill and yelled at the burglar bolting down the fire escape, "If you come again, I'll have you arrested. Damn you!"

The boy jumped to the pavement below, his legs buckling, but he picked himself up. The seat of his jeans was dark-wet. In a flash he veered into the street and disappeared.

When Fanlin returned to the living room, Bori whizzed over and landed on his chest. The bird looked frightened, his wings quivering. With both hands Fanlin held the parakeet up and kissed him. "Thank you," he whispered. "Are you scared?"

• • •

Bori usually relieved himself in the cage, the door of which remained open day and night. Every two or three days Fanlin would change the newspaper on the bottom to keep the tiny aviary clean. In fact, the whole apartment had become an aviary of sorts, since Bori was allowed to go anywhere, including the studio. When he wasn't sleeping, the bird seldom stayed in the cage, inside which stretched a plastic perch. Even at night he avoided the perch, sleeping with his claws clutching the side of the cage, his body suspended in the air. Isn't it tiring to sleep like that? Fanlin thought. No wonder Bori often looks torpid in the daytime.

One afternoon as the parakeet nestled on his elbow, Fanlin noticed that one of Bori's feet was thicker than the other. He turned the bird over. To his surprise, he saw a blister on Bori's left foot in the shape of half a soybean. He wondered if the plastic perch was too slippery for the parakeet to hold, and if the wire cage the bird gripped instead while sleeping had blistered his foot. Maybe he should get a new cage for Bori. He flipped through the yellow pages to locate a pet store.

That evening as he was strolling in the Queens Botanical Garden, he ran into Elbert Chang, the director of the opera project. Elbert had been jogging, and as he stopped to chat with Fanlin, Bori took off for an immense cypress tree, flitting into its straggly crown before landing on a branch.

"Come down," Fanlin called, but the bird wouldn't budge. He just clasped the declining branch and looked at the men.

"That little parrot is so homely," observed Elbert. He blew his nose, brushed his sweatpants with his fingers, and jogged away, the flesh on his nape trembling a little. Beyond him a young couple walked a dachshund on a long leash.

Fanlin turned as if he were leaving, and Bori swooped down and alighted on his head. Fanlin settled the bird on his arm. "Afraid I'm going to leave you behind, eh?" he asked. "If you don't listen to me, I won't take you out again, understood?" He patted Bori's head.

The parakeet just blinked at him.

Fanlin realized that Bori must like the feel of the wooden perch. He looked around and found a branch under a tall oak and brought it home. He dismantled the plastic bar, whittled a new perch out of the branch, cut a groove on either end, and fixed it in the cage. From then on, Bori slept on the branch every night.

Proudly Fanlin told Supriya about the new perch, but she was too preoccupied to get excited. She sounded tired and merely said, "I'm glad I left him with you." She didn't even thank him. He had planned to ask her about the progress of the filming, but refrained.

The composition for the opera was going well. When Fanlin handed in the first half of the music score—132 pages in total—Elbert Chang was elated, saying he had worried whether Fanlin had embarked on the project. Now Elbert could relax—everything was coming together. Several singers had signed up. It looked like they could stage the opera the next summer.

Puffing on a cigar in his office, Elbert gave a nervous grin and told Fanlin, "I'm afraid I cannot pay you the first half of the advance now."

"Why not? Our contract states that you must."

"I know, but we just don't have the cash on hand. I'll pay you early next month when we get the money."

Fanlin's face fell, his mothy eyebrows tilting upward. He was too deep into the project to back out, yet he feared he might have more difficulty getting paid in the future. He had never worked for Elbert Chang before.

"The bird looks uglier today," Elbert said, pointing his cigar at Bori, who was standing on the desk, between Fanlin's hands.

At those words, the parakeet whooshed up and landed on Elbert's shoulder. "Hey, hey, he likes me!" cried the man. He took Bori down, and the bird fled back to Fanlin in a panic.

Fanlin noticed a greenish splotch on Elbert's jacket, on the shoulder. He stifled the laughter rising in his throat.

"Don't worry about the payment," Elbert assured him, his fingers drumming on the desktop. "You have a contract and can sue me if I don't pay you. This time is just an exception. The money is already committed by the donors. I promise this won't happen again."

Feeling better, Fanlin shook hands with the man and stepped out of the office.

Upon signing the contract for *The Blind Musician* three months earlier, the librettist, an exiled poet living on Staten Island, had insisted that the composer mustn't change a single word of the libretto. The writer, Benyong, didn't understand that, unlike poetry, opera depends on collaborative efforts. Elbert Chang liked the libretto so much he conceded to the terms the author demanded. This became a problem for Fanlin, who had in mind a musical structure that didn't always agree with the verbal text. Furthermore, some words were unsingable, such as "smoothest" and "feudalism." He had to replace them, ideally with words ending with open vowels.

One morning Fanlin set out for Staten Island to see Benyong, intending to get permission to change some words. He didn't plan to take Bori along, but the second he stepped out of his apartment, he heard the bird bump against the door repeatedly, scratching the wood. He unlocked the door and said, "Want to come with me?" The parakeet leapt to his chest, clutching his T-shirt and uttering tinny chirps. Fanlin caressed Bori and together they headed for the train station.

It was a fine summer day, the sky washed clean by a shower the previous night. On the ferryboat Fanlin stayed on the deck all the way, watching seabirds wheel around. Some strutted or scurried on the bow, where two small girls were tossing bits of bread at them. Bori joined the other birds, picking up food but not eating any. Fanlin knew the parakeet was doing that just for fun, yet no matter how he called, the bird wouldn't come back to him. So he stood by, watching Bori walking excitedly among gulls, terns, petrels. He was amazed that Bori wasn't afraid of the bigger birds and wondered if the parakeet was lonely at home.

Benyong received Fanlin warmly, as if they were friends. In fact, they'd met only twice, on both occasions for business. Fanlin liked this man who, already forty-three, hadn't lost the child in him and often threw his head back and laughed aloud.

Sitting on a sofa in the living room, Fanlin sang some lines to demonstrate the cumbersomeness of the original words. He had an ordinary voice, a bit hoarse, yet whenever he sang his own compositions, he was confident and expressive, with a vivid face and vigorous gestures, as if he were oblivious of anyone else's presence.

While he was singing, Bori frolicked on the coffee table, flapping his wings and wagging his head, his hooked bill opening and closing and emitting happy but unintelligible cries. Then the bird paused to tap his feet as if beating time, which delighted the poet.

"Can he talk?" Benyong asked Fanlin.

"No, he can't, but he's smart and even knows money."

"You should teach him how to talk. Come here, little fellow." Benyong beckoned to the bird, who ignored his outstretched hand.

Without difficulty, Fanlin got the librettist's agreement, on the condition that they exchange views before Fanlin made any changes. For lunch they went to a small restaurant nearby and shared a Hawaiian pizza. Dabbing his mouth with a red napkin, Benyong said, "I love this place. I have lunch here five days a week. Sometimes I work on my poems in here. Cheers." He lifted his beer mug and clinked it with Fanlin's water glass.

Fanlin was amazed by what the poet said. Benyong didn't hold a regular job and could hardly have made any money from his writing; few people in his situation would dine out five times a week. In addition, he enjoyed movies and popular music; two tall shelves in his apartment were loaded with CDs, more with DVDs. Evidently the writer was well kept by his wife, a nurse. Fanlin was touched by the woman's generosity. She must love poetry.

After lunch they strolled along the beach of white sand, carrying their shoes and walking barefoot. The air smelled fishy, tinged with the stink of seaweed washed ashore. Bori liked the ocean and kept flying away, skipping along the brink of the surf, pecking at the sand.

"Ah, this sea breeze is so invigorating," Benyong said as he watched Bori. "Whenever I walk here, the view of the ocean makes me think a lot. Before this immense body of water, even life and death become unimportant, irrelevant."

"What's important to you, then?"

"Art. Only art is immortal."

"That's why you've been writing full-time all along?"

"Yes, I've been making full use of artistic freedom."

Fanlin said no more, unable to suppress the image of

Benyong's self-sacrificing wife. A photo in their study showed her to be quite pretty, with a wide but handsome face. The wind increased, and dark clouds were gathering on the sea in the distance.

As the ferryboat cast off, rain clouds were billowing over Brooklyn, soundless lightning zigzagging across the sky. On deck, a man, skinny and gray-bearded, was ranting about the evildoing of big corporations. Eyes shut, he cried, "Brothers and sisters, think about who gets all the money that's yours, think about who puts all the drugs on streets to kill our kids. I know them, I see them sinning against our Lord every day. What this country needs is a revolution, so we can put every crook behind bars or ship them all to Cuba—" Fanlin was fascinated by the way words were pouring out of the man's mouth, as if the fellow were possessed by a demon, his eyes radiating a steely light. Few other passengers paid him any mind.

While Fanlin focused his attention on the man, Bori left Fanlin's shoulder and fluttered away toward the waves. "Come back, come back," Fanlin called, but the bird went on flying alongside the boat.

Suddenly a gust of wind caught Bori and swept him into the tumbling water. "Bori! Bori!" Fanlin cried, rushing toward the stern, his eyes fastened on the bird bobbing in the tumult.

He kicked off his sandals, plunged into the water, and swam toward Bori, still calling his name. A wave crashed into Fanlin's face and filled his mouth with seawater. He coughed and lost sight of the bird. "Bori, Bori, where are you?" he called, looking around frantically. Then he saw the parakeet lying supine on the slope of a swell about thirty yards away. With all his might he plunged toward the bird.

Behind him, the boat slowed and a crowd gathered on the deck. A man shouted through a bullhorn, "Don't panic! We're coming to help you!"

At last Fanlin grabbed hold of Bori, who was already motionless, his bill open. Tears gushed out of Fanlin's salt-stung eyes as he held the parakeet and looked into his face, turning him upside down to let water drain out of his crop. Meanwhile, the boat circled back and chugged toward Fanlin.

A ladder dropped from the boat. Holding Bori between his lips, Fanlin hauled himself out of the water. When he reached the deck, the gray-bearded madman stepped over and handed Fanlin his sandals without a word. People crowded around as Fanlin laid the bird on the steel deck and gently pressed Bori's chest with two fingers to pump water from his body.

Thunder rumbled in the distance and lightning cracked the city's skyline, but patches of sunlight still fell on the ocean. As the boat picked up speed heading north, the bird's knotted feet opened, then clawed the air. "He's come to!" a man exclaimed.

Sluggishly Bori opened his eyes. Cheerful cries broke out on the deck while Fanlin sobbed gratefully. A middle-aged woman took two photos of Fanlin and the parakeet, saying, "This is extraordinary."

Two days later, a short article appeared in the Metro section of *The New York Times*, reporting on the rescue of the bird. It described how Fanlin had plunged into the ocean without a second thought and patiently resuscitated Bori. The piece was brief, under two hundred words, but it created some buzz in the local community. Within a week a small Chinese-language newspaper, *The North American Tribune*, printed a long article on Fanlin and his parakeet, with a photo of them together.

Elbert Chang came one afternoon to deliver the half of the advance he'd promised. He had read about the rescue and said to Fanlin, "This little parrot is really something. He doesn't look smart but is full of tricks." He held out his hand to Bori, his fingers wiggling. "Come here," he coaxed. "You forgot crapping on me?"

Fanlin laughed. Bori still didn't stir, his eyes half shut as if he were sleepy.

Elbert then asked about the progress of the composition, to which Fanlin hadn't attended since the bird's accident. The director reassured him that the opera would be performed as planned. Fanlin promised to return to his work with redoubled effort.

Despite the attention, Bori continued to wither. He didn't eat much or move around. During the day he sat on the windowsill, hiccuping frequently. Fanlin wondered if Bori had a cold or was simply getting old. He asked Supriya about his age. She had no idea but said, "He must already be senile."

"What do you mean? Like in his seventies or eighties?"

"I'm not sure."

"Can you ask his former owner?"

"How can I do that in Thailand?"

He didn't press her further, unhappy about her lack of interest in Bori. He couldn't believe that she wasn't in contact with the bird's former owner.

One morning Fanlin looked into Bori's cage and to his horror found the parakeet lying still. He picked Bori up, the lifeless body still warm. Fanlin couldn't hold back his tears while stroking the bird's feathers; he had failed to save his friend.

He laid the tiny corpse on the dining table and observed it

for a long time. The parakeet looked peaceful and must have passed in sleep. Fanlin consoled himself with the thought that Bori hadn't suffered a miserable old age.

He buried the bird under a ginkgo in the backyard. The whole day he couldn't do anything but sit absentmindedly in his studio. His students arrived that evening, but he didn't do much teaching. After they left, he phoned Supriya, who sounded harried. With a sob in his throat he told her, "Bori died early this morning."

"Gosh, you sound like you just lost a sibling."

"I feel terrible."

"I'm sorry, but don't be silly, and don't be too hard on yourself. If you really miss the budgie, you can buy another one at a pet shop."

"He was your bird."

"I know. I don't blame you. I can't talk anymore now, sweetie. I need to go."

Fanlin wasn't able to sleep until the early-morning hours. He kept reviewing his conversation with Supriya, reproaching her as if she were responsible for Bori's death. What rankled was her casual attitude. She must have put the bird out of her mind long ago. He wondered if he should volunteer to break up with her upon her return the following month, since it would be just a matter of time before they parted.

For days Fanlin canceled his class and worked intensely on the opera. The music flowed from his pen with ease, the melodies so fluent and fresh that he paused to wonder whether he had unconsciously copied them from master composers. No, every note he had put down was original.

His neglect of teaching worried his students. One afternoon they came with a small cage containing a bright yellow parakeet. "We got this for you," Wona told Fanlin.

While certain that no bird could replace Bori, Fanlin appreciated the gesture and allowed them to put the new parakeet in Bori's cage. He told them to return for class that evening.

The parakeet already had a name, Devin. Every day Fanlin left him alone, saying nothing to him, though the bird let out all kinds of words, including obscenities. He even called Wona "hooker"; that made Fanlin wonder if Devin's former owner had sold him because of his filthy mouth. At mealtimes Fanlin would put a bit of whatever he ate in Bori's saucer for Devin, yet he often kept the transom open in the hope that the bird would fly away.

The second half of the music for the opera was complete. After Elbert Chang had read the score, he phoned Fanlin and asked to see him. Fanlin went to Elbert's office the next morning, unsure what the director wanted to discuss.

The moment Fanlin sat down, Elbert shook his head and smiled. "I'm puzzled—this half is so different from the first."

"You mean better or worse?"

"That I can't say, but the second half seems to have more feelings. Sing a couple passages. Let's see what it sounds like."

Fanlin sang one passage after another, as if the music were gushing from the depths of his being. He felt the blind musician, the hero of the opera, lamenting through him the loss of his beloved, a local beauty forced by her parents to marry a general, to be his concubine. Fanlin's voice trembled with grief, which had never happened before in his demonstrations.

"Ah, it's so sad," said Elbert's assistant. "It makes me want to cry."

Somehow the woman's words cooled Fanlin some. Then he

sang a few passages from the first half of the score, which sounded elegant and lighthearted, especially the beautiful refrain that would recur five times in the opera.

Elbert said, "I'm pretty sure the second half is emotionally right. It has more soul—sorrow without anger, affectionate but not soft. I'm impressed."

"That's true," the woman chimed in.

"What should I do?" sighed Fanlin.

"Make the whole piece more consistent," Elbert suggested.

"That will take a few weeks."

"We have time."

Fanlin set about revising the score; in fact, he overhauled the first half. He worked so hard that after a week he collapsed and had to stay in bed. Even with his eyes closed, he could not suppress the music ringing in his head. The next day he resumed his writing. Despite the fatigue, he was happy, even rapturous in this composing frenzy. He ignored Devin entirely except to feed him. The parakeet came to his side from time to time, but Fanlin was too busy to pay him any attention.

One afternoon, after working for hours, he was lying in bed to rest. Devin landed beside him. The bird tossed his long blue-tipped tail, then jumped on Fanlin's chest, fixing a beady eye on him. "Ha wa ya?" the parakeet squawked. At first Fanlin didn't understand the sharp-edged words, pronounced as if Devin were short of breath. "Ha wa ya?" the bird repeated.

"Fine. I'm all right." Fanlin smiled, his eyes filling.

Devin flew away and alighted on the half-open window. The white curtain swayed in the breeze, as if about to dance; outside, sycamore leaves were rustling.

"Come back!" Fanlin called.

The Beauty

AROUND MIDAFTERNOON, the snow thinned into sleet, and some umbrellas appeared on Kissena Boulevard. When the green lights came on, pedestrians skirted or jumped across the puddles gathering at the curbs. Dan Feng stood at the window of his office gazing down at the street lined with fruit and vegetable stands under awnings. The sight reminded him of a closing market fair when people were leaving. Just now his customer had called saying she couldn't come because of the bad weather, and Dan had phoned the seller of the condo on Forty-fifth Avenue to cancel the appointment. The rest of his afternoon was free.

He looked at his watch—3:10. What should he do? Should he pick up his baby at the day-care center? No, it was too early to call it a day. He decided to drop in on his wife, Gina, at her jewelry store in Flushing Central Mall.

Main Street was bustling, the sidewalks swarming with people pouring out of the subway station, most of them bundled in coats and a few talking on cell phones. Two blond teenage girls, probably twins and each carrying a book bag, walked along hand in hand, wearing skirts that showed their lace-up boots and bare legs. A stink of rotten fruit pinched Dan's nose, and he hastened his steps and veered onto Roosevelt Avenue. At Chung Hwa Bookstore he picked up *World Journal,* and with the newspaper under his arm, he entered the mall.

"Where's Gina?" he asked Sally, the young sales assistant at the jewelry store.

"She's having her midafternoon break," she answered, her ponytail wrapped into a bun on top of her head.

"In the back?"

"No, perhaps downstairs."

Several jade tea sets and pen pots were standing on the counter, and pink-cheeked Sally had been wiping them. Besides jewelry, the store dealt in some knickknacks. Behind her, the shelves displayed crystal horses, boats, swans, lotus flowers, goldfish, various kinds of parrots, cars, airplanes. Downstairs, on the first floor, was the lobby of the Sheraton Hotel, whose bar Gina frequented. With a seething heart Dan hustled toward the escalator, knowing his wife must be with Fooming Yu, the supervisor of the daytime staff at the hotel's front desk. The lobby was quiet, and in its middle a huge vase of mixed flowers sat on a round, two-level table. The bar was in the back, its glass walls shaded by bamboo curtains. Dan stopped at the door to scan the poorly lit interior. About a dozen tables were each surrounded by chairs, and a petite young woman hunched over the counter, leafing through a magazine, probably *Vogue.* There they were—Gina was sitting with Fooming in a corner, a tiny table between them. They were the only customers, and they went on chatting without noticing Dan. Gina tittered and said, "That's really something."

Dan couldn't make out what they were talking about. As he was deciding whether to enter, Fooming said to Gina, "Another nut, please, before I go." He sounded loud and happy.

Gina tossed a cashew, which he caught in his mouth, munching noisily. They both laughed.

"Another," he begged.

"Good dog." She chucked a Brazil nut and he snapped up that one too.

Dan turned away, dragging his feet toward the front entrance. He was sure that before he and Gina married Fooming had courted her, but Dan hadn't taken that flat-faced man as a serious rival at the time. Gina was a noted beauty in Flushing, and even now some men—Asians, whites, Latinos, blacks—would stop by the jewelry store just to look at her. Once in a while someone would offer to take her out, but according to what she had told Dan, she always declined, saying her husband would get jealous like crazy if he knew. Still, why wouldn't she quit seeing Fooming Yu? "The damned beauty," Dan muttered to himself as he stepped out of the building. "She cannot change her fickle nature. Well, serves you right. You shouldn't have chased her that hard in the first place."

Instead of returning to his office, Dan went to Sunshine Bathhouse on Union Street. The sleet was over, but the weather had become windy and colder, ice crusting on the edges of thawing snowbanks. A Boeing roared overhead, descending toward LaGuardia. The sky was darkening to indigo, and more cars appeared on the street, along which neon lights started flickering. The bathhouse, set in the basement of a two-story building, had recently opened, and it offered a sauna, a steam bath, hot-towel rubdowns, massages, pedicures. Dan paid twenty dollars at the desk, took a key, and went into the locker room. He picked up a towel and held it around his neck for a while. It had just come out of the dryer and was still warm.

Having locked up his clothes and newspaper, slipped the key on his wrist, and wrapped the towel around his waist, he made for the pool. Absentmindedly he got into the warm water. He sat on the submerged step for a moment to get used to the temperature, throwing water on his neck and armpits. He was alone and sank farther—his head rested on the rounded edge of the pool, which could hold seven or eight people and was made entirely of white tiles. He disliked saunas and worried that the dry heat could shrink his facial skin, so he took only a hot bath whenever he was here. It was so relaxing to lounge in the steaming water that he felt lazy, reluctant to scrub himself. His mind was clouded with questions and doubts. How he resented the intimacy between Gina and Fooming. Ever since the birth of their daughter, Jasmine, a year ago, he had harbored misgivings about his wife's fidelity. Their baby was homely, with thin eyes and a wide mouth, and took after neither Gina nor himself. Gina was tall and lissome, having a straight nose, double-lidded eyes, a delicate mouth, and silken skin. Dan was also handsome. People often complimented him on his good looks, which boasted shiny eyes, a high nose, and a head of bushy hair. There were always envious glances at him and his wife when they were together at a public place. So how could their daughter be so plain? In his mind a voice would murmur, "She's not mine, she's not mine." Sometimes he imagined that Fooming was Jasmine's blood father; at least their small eyes and round chins resembled each other. That could also explain why Gina wouldn't stop seeing the man.

Several times Dan had urged her to steer clear of Fooming, but she always assured him that there was nothing unusual between them and that she kept up her acquaintance with Fooming only because they were both from Jinhua, a medium-size city in Zhejiang Province. "You should have a larger heart," she told Dan.

Whenever he ran into Fooming, the man would grin and narrow his eyes at him. His knowing smile unsettled Dan, as if Fooming meant to say, "I know more about your wife than you do, from head to toe. I've made you wear horns, but what can you do about me, dumb ass?"

Before Jasmine was born, Dan had never given much thought to Fooming. Dan used to view him as a no-account loser who, though four or five years his junior and just promoted to foreman in charge of three staffers, perhaps made no more than twelve dollars an hour. By contrast, Dan owned a real estate company and had a team of agents working for him. Almost thirty-seven, he was mature and steady. Experience and maturity, if not as magical as a sense of humor, could work to an older man's advantage. From the very beginning, Dan believed there'd be no chance for Fooming, and several others, to win Gina's heart as long as he himself was a competitor. Yet the scene at the bar an hour earlier had unnerved and enraged him. If only he hadn't rushed to marry Gina after she told him she was pregnant with his child. She may have lied to him.

A tubby man came into the pool room with a hand towel over his shoulder. He boomed, "Would you like to have your feet scraped and massaged, sir?"

Startled, Dan sat up. "What time is it?"

"A quarter to five."

"I need to go. Sorry, no pedicure today."

"That's all right." The man puttered to the next room to ask others.

Dan climbed out of the pool and went to take a rinsing shower. On his way back to the locker room, passing by the massage area, he heard a male voice moaning in one of the small rooms whose doors were all shut. "Oh yes, oh yes!" the man kept saying.

Then came a sugary female voice. "Feel good, right? Hmmm . . . nice . . ."

Dan wondered if the woman was giving more than a massage in there. Probably she'd also given the guy a hand job for a bigger tip. Dan glanced at the sign standing before the entrance, which said, "For massage, please make an appointment beforehand!"

He threw on his clothes and parka and left the bathhouse. He had to pick up his daughter at five.

That evening, after their baby fell asleep, Dan and Gina sat down in the living room and talked. He put his tea mug on the glass coffee table and said, "I saw you playing a doggy game with Fooming Yu in the Sheraton bar this afternoon. 'Another nut, please, before I go.' I heard him say that and saw you feed nuts to him."

Gina blushed, pursing her lips. "It wasn't even a game. There's nothing between him and me. You shouldn't make too much of it."

"How many times have I told you to avoid that man?"

"I can't just snub him. We've known each other for many years."

"Listen, I understand you had a number of boyfriends

before we married. I don't mind that as long as you remain a faithful wife."

"Are you implying I'm cheating on you?"

"Why do you still carry on with Fooming Yu? Tell me, does he have something to do with Jasmine?"

"He doesn't know her. What are you getting at?"

"That doesn't mean he couldn't father her."

"For heaven's sake, she's yours! If you don't believe me, you can give her a DNA test."

"That I won't do. It wouldn't be fair to the baby. I can accept her as my child, all right, but you mustn't humiliate me further."

"When did I ever humiliate you?"

"You keep seeing Fooming Yu."

"To be honest, I'm not interested in him, but he often drops into my store. I can't just shoo him away."

"Why not?"

"I told you over and over again, he's my townsman. This is getting nowhere." She stood up. "I have to go to bed. I'm so tired. Jasmine will wake up soon, and I'd better catch a bit of sleep when I can. Good night." She moved toward the bedroom in which their baby was sleeping.

"Night," he said blandly.

He sighed and refilled his mug with tea from a clay pot. Seated on his rattan chair, he resumed skimming some articles on a Web site where people had been arguing about whether it was appropriate for a seventy-five-year-old celebrity, a Nobel laureate in chemistry, to marry a woman of twenty-eight. Dan's mind couldn't focus on the writings. Deep down he felt unable to trust his wife, who still seemed interested in other men. She must be one of those women who couldn't enjoy life without having a few men dangling around. If only he'd kept her home. He regretted having helped her set up the jewelry store, which had cost him more than forty thousand dollars.

Most of the articles on the Web site condemned the scientist as an irresponsible old man who set a bad example for the younger generations, but some praised him for being romantic and having a youthful spirit. The two sides, somehow knowing most of the authors' real names despite the pseudonyms they used, argued furiously and dished out muck that should have remained undisturbed in the cellars of their opponents' past. Dan was not interested in their wrangling. He couldn't stop thinking about his wife. He reasoned with himself, You asked for trouble. You were too foolish, running after her like a rutting animal. Sure, you won the beauty like a trophy, but it came with a price, with endless headaches and other men's envy. Now you've lost peace of mind, just like the Nobel laureate whose fame has robbed him of his privacy.

Dan yawned and rubbed his eyes. He shut off the computer, went to brush his teeth in the bathroom, and then turned into the other bedroom. He and his wife slept separately because he often worked deep into the night and because she wanted to sleep with their baby.

The next day Dan made an appointment with Sherlock Holmes, Inc., on Fortieth Road. On the phone the agent sounded eager, saying they handled all kinds of investigations, like private property, spousal infidelity, personal histories, family backgrounds. Dan agreed to go to the office after showing a town house to an old Taiwanese couple who planned to move to Flushing from Switzerland because they could find genuine Chinese food here.

The detective agency's office was above a hair salon and

photo studio. A slight, bespectacled man received him, saying, "Well, my friend, what can I do for you?"

Dan explained the purpose of his visit. Though dubious about the scantily bearded man and his one-horse firm, he didn't know another place in Queens offering this sort of service. "How many hands do you have here, Mr. Kwan?"

"We have people all over the world. We do investigations in America, Asia, Europe, Australia, and parts of Africa, basically on every continent except for the Arctic and the Antarctic."

"Really?" Dan pulled an index card out of his hip pocket and handed it to the agent. "I want to know these two people's personal histories. They were both from Jinhua City."

Mr. Kwan looked at the card while his small hand twisted a felt-tip pen. "This shouldn't be difficult. We have connections all over China, and I can get them to look into this. Let's see, we have their names, ages, and education, but do you know their families' current addresses in Jinhua?"

"No. Gina said all her folks were dead. I doubt it, though."

"Don't worry. We'll look it up. Anything else you want to know besides their personal histories?"

"I suspect the two might be having an affair. Can you keep an eye on them? Also, get some concrete evidence if they cross the line."

"We can do that."

Mr. Kwan put the index card on his huge table, the kind advertised as "a CEO's desk," which had recently come into fashion. This one reminded Dan of a glossy coffin. The agent itemized the cost of the investigation. On top of a three-hundred-dollar retainer and a fee of fifty dollars an hour, the client was obliged to pay for transportation, hotel, drinks, meals, and any other expenditure incurred by the detective when working on the case. This was standard, he assured Dan. Dan signed the agreement and wrote him a check.

As Mr. Kwan got up to see him to the door, Dan was amazed to find him so short, barely five foot one. Isn't his small physique too eye-catching? he wondered. At most Mr. Kwan could be a featherweight sleuth. He should have been an accountant or a software specialist—a sedentary job would suit him better.

For days Jasmine had a fever. She would cry at night, which disturbed Dan and kept him awake even in his separate room. Gina had taken her to the doctor, who prescribed some drugs, but she wouldn't give them to the baby. Instead, she fed her warm water frequently, saying this was Jasmine's grandmother's remedy. Since birth, the child had run a temperature every month or two, but every time Gina had managed to make her well without using any medicine.

Jasmine had begun to walk. According to folklore, a baby's tongue follows its legs, meaning when it can walk it will start to talk. But Jasmine, already able to toddle from one end of the room to the other, could speak only one word: "Baba" (Daddy), which thrilled Dan whenever he heard her say it. He would coax her into saying it again and again. He loved her, especially when she was happy and lively, wanting to sit on his belly or ride on his back. Even so, at times he couldn't help but wonder about her paternity. In addition to her frequent fevers, Jasmine seldom slept at night and always cried or played until the small hours. Dan had once accompanied his wife to Dr. Cohen, the pediatrician, a middle-aged woman with a gaunt face. The doctor advised that they leave their daughter alone whenever she hollered and just let her bawl. Once exhausted, she would learn it was no use crying for attention and would mend her ways. This would also train her to be independent. But Gina wouldn't follow Dr. Cohen's instructions, and the moment Jasmine started crying, she'd croon, "Mummy's coming, just a second." She'd pick her up and cradle her, walking up and down the room. Sometimes she'd pace the floor for three or four hours. Her maternal patience amazed Dan, who would replace her on some nights so that she could sleep a little before daybreak. Whenever he urged her to leave the bawling baby alone, she would say, "It's too early to build her sense of independence." She was afraid their child might feel neglected and unloved.

Tonight Jasmine simply wouldn't quit crying. Neither would she let her mother sit down or stop singing nursery rhymes. In a sleepy voice Gina was humming a song Dan vaguely remembered—"Come on, Little Bunny, / Open the door to your mummy . . ." He pulled the comforter over his face, but still heard the baby bawling. Try as he might, he couldn't go to sleep.

He got up, went to the other bedroom, and said to his wife, "Can't you give her a sleeping pill or something? Just to make her stop."

"No. That might damage her brain."

"The little bitch. She wants to torture us. I have a meeting tomorrow morning, actually in a couple hours."

"I'm sorry, I have to work too."

"Damn her! She does nothing but sleep at the day care, Mrs. Espada told me. She's like a model baby there."

"She has just reversed her sense of day and night."

"Put her down! Let her cry as much as she wants."

"Honey, don't be so nasty. She'll quiet down soon."

Her gentle voice checked his temper. He closed the door and returned to his room. He used to dream of having an angelic child whose beauty would spread over everything in their home. It wouldn't matter whether the baby was a boy or girl as long as it took after Gina or himself. Now slitty-eyed Jasmine had marred his picture of the ideal family.

He kept yawning at the meeting the next morning. One of his colleagues teased him, "You must've exerted yourself too hard last night."

"Be careful, Dan," another chimed in. "You shouldn't act like a newlywed."

People at the conference table cracked up while Dan shook his head. "My daughter's ill and cried most of the night," he muttered.

Everybody turned silent at the mention of the baby. They had all seen Jasmine and some had raised the question of whom she looked like. Their silence sent a wave of resentment over Dan, but he restrained himself because they were discussing how to acquire an old warehouse in Forest Hills and convert it into condominiums. He was eager to move out of Flushing. Its public school system wasn't too bad, but the whole area was isolated culturally—it didn't even have an English bookstore. Galleries appeared and then disappeared, and there was only one small theater, managed by his friend Elbert Chang. Most immigrants here didn't bother to use English in everyday life. Anywhere you turned, you saw restaurants, beauty parlors, retail stores, travel agencies, law offices—nothing but businesses. New arrivals had made little effort to protect the environment, or perhaps they were too desperate for survival to worry about that. Dan feared that his neighborhood would deteriorate into a slum, so he was determined to see the plan for converting the warehouse succeed. He was sure that some of his colleagues also hoped to buy the condos the company wanted to build in Forest Hills.

• • •

Jasmine got well within a week, but Gina was still unhappy about Dan's suspicion. She wouldn't reproach him but avoided speaking to him. Her reticence angered him more. He thought to himself, You think you're a good woman? I know what you've been doing on the sly. Wait and see—I'm going to find out about you.

One evening Gina came home with a flushed face. At the sight of Dan with their daughter sitting on his lap, she stopped at the door for a moment, then stepped in. She hung up her navy blue coat in the closet and sat down on the sofa opposite him. "You're ridiculous," she said.

"What's that about?" he asked.

"You hired a midget to follow Fooming and me."

Abashed, Dan didn't know how to respond, but instantly he recovered his presence of mind. "If there's no monkey business between you two, why should you mind?"

"Let me tell you, your detective botched his mission. Fooming roughed him up and gave him a bloody nose."

"Damn it, it's against the law to beat a professional agent!"

"Give me a break. The man was eavesdropping on us. He violated our privacy first."

"Your privacy? What is it that's so private between Fooming Yu and you?"

"You're insane. You hired that man to make a scene in public."

"You just said it was Fooming Yu who made a display of himself. Where did this happen?"

"In Red Chopstick."

"You're a married woman, but you dined with a bachelor in a restaurant on a busy street. Who's insane?"

"How many times have I told you he and I are just friends?"

"Then neither of you should've been upset by Mr. Kwan's inquiry."

"It was foolish of you to use that man. He's too attractive—I mean he attracts too much attention."

Dan cackled. "But as your husband, I cannot hold back my curiosity."

"All right, your detective is out. Fooming threatened to strangle him if Kwan came near him again." She got up and went into the kitchen despite Jasmine's reaching out for her and crying "Mama." In no time pots, pans, and bowls began clattering in there, mixed with Gina's sobs. "I'm cursed, cursed!" she kept saying.

The baby had started to call her "Mama" two days before. When she said that for the first time, Gina couldn't help her joyous tears, but now in the kitchen, her weeping was punctuated with sniffles.

A sharp tingle ran over Dan's scalp. If only he hadn't moved in with her before he'd had to propose to her, thanks to the child she claimed was his. Marriage seemed to have trapped both of them.

Two days later Dan went to see Mr. Kwan. A pair of Band-Aids crossed each other on the agent's cheek, but he was all smiles and very effusive. Dan apologized for the trouble Mr. Kwan had run into at Red Chopstick, but the man assured him, "It's not unusual to encounter violence in my profession. No big deal."

Outside, a vehicle honked, and a policeman barked through a megaphone, "Stop! Stop right there!" Then a fire engine surged by. A toilet flushed upstairs, a pipe hissed.

Mr. Kwan resumed speaking as if thinking aloud to himself. "I'm puzzled in a way. I'm pretty sure I knew your wife—she used to be my client."

"You mean she knew you too?"

"Correct. She recognized me in the restaurant. That's how Fooming Yu figured out I was working for you. Maybe I shouldn't tell you this, but I thought you might want to know—before you two married, your bride asked me to do a background check on you."

"Did you find any dirt in my past?"

"Not really. You're a clean man. You joined the Communist Party in the mid-eighties, but when the Tiananmen Massacre happened, you renounced your Party membership publicly, in *World Journal.* That wiped your slate clean."

Dan was impressed by the accuracy of the information. He was amazed too that his renouncement fifteen years ago was still shaping his life. He felt lucky that he had washed his hands of the Communist Party, even though he still couldn't fully grasp the significance of his act. He had renounced the Party membership mainly out of indignation at the carnage of civilians. Then everything seemed to work out to his advantage—he encountered no difficulty in getting a green card, and the FBI didn't have him under surveillance. "I see," he said to the agent. "Are you still going to keep your eye on Gina and Fooming Yu for me?"

"I can't do that anymore, but someone will step into my shoes. This new guy is an ex-cop and has a black belt in karate. Even if Fooming Yu loses his head again, he won't dare to touch our man."

"Excellent. Have you found anything unusual between him and Gina?"

"Not yet. Except for the lunch date when they squabbled over something I couldn't figure out, they haven't done anything. Here's a copy of the information on your man, but for some reason our connections in China could find nothing about your wife and her family. Her personal history is a blank. This really boggles the mind. Gina is a beautiful woman. Usually such a beauty cannot live in a place without being noticed. I wonder if she's really from Jinhua. Anyhow, we've made little headway in her case, but we're still at it. I'd guess her original name was not Gina Liu."

"Why would she change her name?"

"Usually it's a way to get rid of something infamous in one's past. But your wife's case doesn't look like that. Although she must hate me, I won't say she's a bad woman. By the way, here's my report on the expenses. Believe me, I don't feel good about the lunch and the beer, but I had to hang around in Red Chopstick. Also, I bought a copy of *Forbes* while following them at a newsstand."

"Don't worry about that." Dan glanced through the figures and wrote a check for $429.58.

He picked up the brown envelope containing the report on Fooming and took his leave. Back in his office, he went through the sheets of information and was pleased by the thoroughness of the investigation. Fooming's parents were still living in a suburban village outside Jinhua, growing vegetables and raising crabs. No wonder Fooming had such a bumpkin name. The man had two sisters and a brother, who all had their own families and lived in Jinhua. Before coming to the United States seven years ago, he had worked as a mechanic at a railroad company and also headed his workshop's branch of the Communist League. Apparently he had overstayed his tourist visa but managed to become a legal resident; his status must have been established through purchasing some fake papers, though that was too complicated to prove. At the moment he was in the process of applying for a green card. This was a natural step, since the police station in Jinhua had revoked his urban residency and he couldn't go back anymore. Nothing was extraordinary in the report, yet Dan grew more curious about Fooming's political record back in China. He called Mr. Kwan, praised the quality of the information, saying it was "a CIA job," and asked him if Fooming had been a Party member. The agent said that couldn't be verified and would depend on the size of his former workshop. If the work unit was large, Fooming, as the head of its branch of the Communist League, must have been a Party member; if it was small, he didn't have to be. But his workshop had been merged with other units long ago, so it would be hard to find out its original size.

Dan leaned back in his chair and lapsed into thought. Why did Gina's past remain blank? Where was she really from? What was her true name? She might indeed have been from Jinhua if Fooming Yu was her townsman, as she had told Dan he was. She spoke Mandarin with a susurrant accent, which meant she was a southerner originally. Dan had asked her about her family before they married, but she said they had all been killed in a derailed train accident and she was left alone in this world. "Don't you feel lucky to have a wife without any family baggage?" she countered, smiling sadly. "You don't need to buy any gifts for your parents-in-law."

The more Dan brooded about Gina, the more baffled he became. He could not believe she didn't have even one relative in China or America.

Dan's business had picked up after the Spring Festival. He was busy, and every week he clinched at least one sale. The immigrants loved buying real estate, and many would pay cash since they were unable to get a mortgage from the bank; at times several people, usually family members and relatives, would pool their money to buy a place so that they could all have shelter. The spring's good start at Dan's agency might signify another banner year. Some days he couldn't leave his office until eight or nine p.m. As the head of the company, he ought to make more sales than most of the agents to justify his leadership, so he always worked hard.

One evening, at the beginning of April, he finished a little early. As he was heading toward his Buick parked under a flowering laurel magnolia behind the office building, he saw four young men, three Asians and one Latino, standing by his car. They all wore flattops, black T-shirts, olive-drab pants, and work boots. At the sight of Dan, one of them kicked the driver's-side door.

"Hey, don't damage my property!" Dan yelled.

"Is this your car?" the tallest of them asked, a half-smoked cigarette in the corner of his mouth.

"Yes. Guys, don't do this to me."

The shortest of them, whose crown showed a "landing strip" cut, booted the Buick again. Dan got furious and shouted, "Hey, hey, stop it!"

Suddenly the fierce-eyed Latino pulled a steel bar out of his pant leg and started smashing the windshield. Dan was transfixed, speechless, while the other three thugs all produced short rebars and began hitting the car. In a minute all its windows were shattered, and so were the front lights.

At last Dan regained his speech. "Guys, why do this to me? Give me a reason at least."

The tall, thin-waisted man stepped over, wagging his forefinger, and said with a lopsided smile, "You wanna know why? 'Cause you're too nosy."

"What are you talking about? This is a new car. Hey, please, no more!"

"You really didn't get it? Let me tell you, quit using a private dick. No cop's gonna save your ass."

"You got the wrong man. You can't destroy my property like this."

"Oh yeah? Damn you, this will give you a better idea." The Latino rushed up and hit Dan on the forehead with his steel bar.

Dan fell to the ground and blacked out. They each gave him a few kicks before bolting away.

When Dan came to, he found himself lying on a gurney moving down a hallway in Flushing Hospital. Two paramedics, a man and a woman, were pushing him to the ER. They walked unhurriedly, as if strolling. Dan touched his forehead, which was bandaged; he twisted his head; his neck was stiff, but his mind was clear. He realized that someone must have dialed 911, which dispatched the ambulance. Gina was walking beside him with her narrow hand on the side of the gurney. Her eyes were puffy, still tearful. "How do you feel, sweetie?" she asked.

"I'm okay." Dan sat up and huffed out a breath.

"No, lie down."

"I'm really okay."

In the ER a young woman doctor examined him briefly and found no serious injury—he didn't need stitches—so she discharged him after giving him a CAT scan and telling Gina to keep applying ice to his bruise. If he felt dizzy, she said, he must come back without delay. He promised to do that. Gina supported him as they walked out of the hospital building and flagged down a cab. Amazingly, despite the injury, he was fully alert, as wired as if he had just downed a few espressos. How odd. He hoped he could sleep well that night.

After a wonton dinner, the couple remained sitting at the table. Gina, shamefaced, held Jasmine to her breast while she listened to Dan. Now and again she sucked in her breath, her nipple bitten by the baby. Having recalled as much as he could of the incident in the parking lot behind his office building, Dan concluded, "It was Fooming Yu who sent the thugs to smash our car and attack me. Thank God my bones are strong, or they could've kicked me to pieces."

"Believe me, I had nothing to do with this. I knew he was mean, but I never thought he'd go that far. What are you going to do?"

"What do you think I should do?"

"Will you press charges?"

"With all the thugs at large, how can I prove that Fooming Yu was behind the attack? Actually, what troubles me most is not him but you."

"Me? How do you mean?"

"What's your true relationship with him?"

"He's just a fellow townsman, no more than that."

"Stop lying to me. I feel I don't know you anymore. Tell me who you are. I can no longer live with a wife who's like a stranger to me. This home is becoming a torture chamber, too much!"

A prolonged silence filled the room. Gina got up, handed him the baby, then went into her bedroom. Dan sighed and put his elbow on the table to rest his head on his hand, but the instant his forehead touched his palm, a jolt of pain forced him to sit up. Gina came back and put a small white envelope before him. She said, "Look at what's inside; you'll see the truth."

Is it a passport or a love letter? Dan wondered. To his surprise, he took out a bunch of photos of an ugly woman with beady eyes, a bulbous nose, and a broad, thick-lipped mouth. Her face was roundish, though her eyebrows curved like a pair of crescents. "Who's this?" he asked, a bit revolted.

"It was me. After I came to America I went through a series

of plastic surgeries over the years. They changed me completely, into this woman." She pointed her thumb at her chest. "They cost me every penny I made. I used to live in Chicago, and Fooming was there too and saw my gradual transformation."

For a moment Dan was too flummoxed to speak. He handed her the baby, then asked, "Are you really from Jinhua?"

"Yes. I went to the same middle school as Fooming's sister. That's how he got to know me."

"Is your family all dead?"

"Yes, except a half brother, but he lives in the countryside and we have no contact."

"You gave me a raw deal, a raw deal! No wonder Jasmine is so homely. Tell me the truth—is she my child?"

"Yes. I've always been faithful to you."

"Still, you tricked me into this marriage."

"I don't feel good about it. That's why I won't keep you in the dark anymore. Now you can do to me what you will, but please don't tell anyone my secret. This is the only favor I ask of you."

"You can't go on deceiving others. In fact, you've deceived yourself."

"No, I love my beauty. It's the best thing America gave me. Finally I have a face that matches my figure and skin."

A voice shouted in his mind, That's not beauty, that's fraudulence!—but he didn't let that out. He asked instead, "Why can't you disentangle yourself from Fooming Yu? Because he knows your past?"

"Yes. He often hints at my secret. In fact, he keeps asking me to find him a girlfriend and saying he's miserable and lonely. Sometimes I feel sorry for him. I guess he'll let me be once he has a woman. I did introduce him to Sally, but she didn't like him. For some reason no woman's interested in him. That's why he's still stuck on me."

"But you're not his girlfriend!" He got up and started pacing the floor. Now and again he giggled and sighed, shaking his head. Outside the window the sky was scattered with ragged clouds, one of which was drifting across the rusty face of the moon. Below the clouds four or five bats were doing acrobatic stunts.

Dan's walking and laughter unsettled Gina. She begged, "Stop, please! If you want a divorce, I won't be opposed to it as long as you let me keep Jasmine."

"No way. She's mine and I love her no matter how ugly she is!" He lowered his chin, his eyes flashing. He breathed, "I want to keep these photos."

"Please don't show them to others!"

"I'm not that low."

At those words Gina broke into sobs. "Dan, I love you. I know you're a true gentleman. I promise not to speak to Fooming again. I will be a good wife and make you proud."

"No pride of that sort can swell my head again. Tell me, what's your real name?"

"Lai Hsu."

"What's that? It doesn't even sound like a woman's name."

"I was born overdue, so my parents named me Lai. Together with Hsu my name means 'arrived slowly.' "

"Why did you change your name?"

"I felt I became a new person and wanted to start afresh."

"So only Fooming Yu knew your past, huh? Does he have something else on you?"

"No. He's a vampire I can't shake off of me."

Gina buried her face in her arms, weeping, while their daughter cried, "Mama, Mama." The child kept pulling her mother's ear.

. . .

The meeting between Dan and Fooming took place the next afternoon, in the bar of the Sheraton Hotel. After tea was served, Dan said to him calmly, "I want you to leave my wife alone."

"What if I don't comply?" Fooming arched an eyebrow as if in surprise.

Unhurriedly Dan took a photo of Gina out of his inside jacket pocket and put it before Fooming, who glanced at it but didn't say a word. Dan went on, "You have nothing on her now. I know how ugly she was, but I've accepted her as my wife."

"I see. What a benevolent hubby." Fooming grinned contemptuously. "I always do what I want to and nobody can push me around."

"Listen," Dan said, fighting down his temper, "I know everything about you. You worked for five years as a mechanic in Jinhua Railroad Company."

"So? Why should I be ashamed of my humble origin?"

"More than that, you headed your workshop's branch of the Communist League. That means you were a Party member." The last sentence was just a guess, but Dan said it firmly. "You know, a communist is not supposed to set foot in the U.S. unless he's a state dignitary."

Fooming swallowed. His face paled and his eyes dropped. For a while he remained mute as if striving to recall something. Sweat beaded on his pointed nose. Then he rasped, "You can't prove that."

"But the FBI can. They can also deport you."

"Don't play the superior in front of me. You were a Party member too."

"True, but I renounced my membership publicly in 1989. That made me a clean man in this country. Besides, I'm already naturalized—I'm no longer a deportable foreigner like you."

Fooming lifted his teacup, but his hand was shaking so much that a few drops fell on his lap. He put the cup down without drinking the tea. He picked up a paper napkin and dabbed the wet spots on his pants. Dan got up and left the bar without another word, knowing the man would have to sit there for a while to let his pants dry.

That night Fooming called and promised he wouldn't bother Gina anymore. He insisted that he wanted to renounce his Party membership too, but couldn't do that publicly for fear of ruining his siblings' lives in China. He begged Dan not to inform on him, which Dan agreed to.

Fooming kept his word and never turned up at the jewelry store again. Life finally became normal for Dan and Gina. However, Dan took to frequenting the bathhouse, and whenever he went there he would make an appointment with one of the pretty masseuses beforehand. Sometimes he stayed late in his office on purpose, reluctant to go home.

Choice

THE FLYER SAID, "The applicant must be able to teach various subjects, including the preparation for the SAT. Payment is most generous." I answered the ad in the morning and was told to come for an interview that evening. The woman on the phone, Eileen Min, said her daughter needed a tutor right away. At the same time, she admitted she had seen seven or eight applicants, but none of them was suitable. She would pay forty dollars an hour, which was very attractive given my other prospects.

I was being paid to do research for the professor directing my master's thesis, but I needed another job for the summer to make enough for my tuition and living expenses in the fall. Without my parents' support, I had managed to complete one year's graduate study. There was still another year to go. I had started working on my thesis, about Jacob Riis and his effort to eradicate urban slums. My mother had called a week before and said it was not too late for me to go to a professional school, for which my parents would happily pay. I had again rejected the offer, saying I intended to apply to a PhD program in American history. My father, a successful plastic surgeon in Seattle, had always opposed my plan. He urged me to go into medicine or law or even politics—clerking for a congressman—because to him history wasn't a real profession. "Anyone can be a historian if he has read enough books," he'd say. "What do you want to be, a professor? Anyone can make more than a professor." I would remain silent while he spoke, understanding that as long as I was in the humanities I would be on my own. In my heart I despised my father as a typical philistine. He was ashamed of me, and his friends talked about me as a loser. I knew he might cut me out of his will. That didn't bother me; I wouldn't mind becoming a poor scholar.

I set out at around six thirty p.m. Eileen Min lived at 48 Folk Avenue, not far from my place, about fifteen minutes' walk. There were more pedestrians in downtown Flushing since the summer started, many of them foreign tourists or visitors from the suburban towns who came to shop or to dine in the small restaurants offering the foods of their left-behind homes. The store signs, most bearing Chinese characters, reminded me of a bustling shopping district in Shenyang. So many immigrants live and work here that you needn't speak English to get around. I stopped at the newsstand manned by a Pakistani, picked up the day's *World Journal*, and then turned onto Forty-first Avenue. A scrawny teenage girl strode toward me, dragged by a Doberman. The dog stopped at a maple sapling and urinated fitfully on the box encasing the base of the tree. The girl stood by, waiting for her dog to finish. Along the sidewalk every young tree was protected by the same tall red box.

Folk Avenue was easy to find, just a few blocks from College Point Boulevard. Number 48 was a two-story brick bungalow with a glassed-in porch. Beside a two-car garage grew a large oak tree, and behind a small tool shed in the backyard stretched a high fence of wooden boards. Despite the close proximity of the downtown and the houses crowded together in the neighborhood, this property stood out idyllically. I rang the doorbell, and a slender woman of medium height in a shirtwaist dress answered. I was amazed when she introduced herself as Eileen Min and said we had spoken that morning. To my mind, it was unlikely that such a young-looking woman could have a daughter attending high school.

She led me into her house. I was impressed by the furniture in the spacious living room, all redwood, elegant and delicate in design, like antiques. A vase of stargazer lilies sat on a credenza on the far side. On the wall above it hung a photo of a lean-faced man, middle-aged with mild eyes and a jutting forehead, his hairline receded to his crown. I sat on a leather sofa, and Eileen Min told me, "That's my late husband. He died three months ago."

"I'm sorry," I said.

"Sami, pour some tea for Mr. Hong." She said this to a teenage girl who was in a corner using a computer.

"No need to trouble yourself," I said to Sami, who rose without looking our way.

The girl headed for the kitchen. She was wearing orange slippers, and her calf-length skirt showed her thin ankles. Like her mother, she was slim, but one or two inches shorter, and she too had a fine figure. She quickly returned with a cup of tea and put it beside me. "Thanks a lot," I said.

She didn't say a word but looked me in the face, her eyebrows tilting a little toward her temples as if she were being naughty. Then she turned and entered a bedroom off the hall, her slippers squeaking on the glossy wood floor. She left her door ajar, apparently to listen in on our conversation. I produced my student ID card and my GRE scores. "These are my credentials," I told Eileen.

She examined the card. "So you're a graduate student at Queens College. What's this?"

"The results of the test for graduate studies; every applicant must take it. See, I got 720 in English and 780 in math."

"What's the perfect score?"

"Eight hundred in each subject."

"That's impressive. Forgive me for asking, but if you're so strong in math, why didn't you study science?"

"Actually I was torn between history and biology during my freshman year at NYU." I told her the truth. "Then I decided on history because I wouldn't want to depend on a lab for my work. If you do history, all you need is time and a good library."

"Also brains. Is history what you're studying now?"

"Yes, American urban history." I lifted the tea and took a sip. Then I caught Sami observing us from her room, through the gap at the door. She saw me noticing her and withdrew immediately.

Eileen beamed, her face shiny with a pinkish sheen and her almond-shaped eyes glowing. She said, "I promised Sami's father that I'd help her get into a good college. Tell me, can you help my daughter score high on the SAT?"

"Sure. I tutored my cousin two years ago, and he's a freshman at Caltech now."

"That's marvelous."

She decided to hire me. I would start the next day. Since I was still taking summer courses, I could come only in the evenings. Before I left, Eileen called Sami out to greet me as her teacher. The girl came over and said with a nod of her head, "Thank you for helping me, Mr. Hong."

"Just call me Dave," I told her.

"Okay, see you tomorrow, Dave," she said pleasantly, and grinned. Her button nose crinkled.

Coming out of the Mins' house, I felt relieved. I would teach Sami five times a week, including Saturday evenings. I no longer needed to worry about my summer income.

Sami was seventeen, and not as slow as I had expected. She was bright, but her grasp of math was shaky owing to some missed classes during her sophomore year, which had left holes in her knowledge. Those holes had expanded. She had been depressed in recent months about her father's death and unable to pay attention in class. To help her better understand basic algebra and trigonometry, we reviewed the first two years of high school math. As for English, I focused on enlarging her vocabulary and teaching her how to write clearly and expressively. This was easy, since I had taught grammar and composition before. In addition, I assigned her a list of books to read, mainly novels and plays.

Sometimes Sami was quite mischievous. She'd sniff at my arm or hair, then joke, "You smell so strange, like an animal, but that's what I like about you." At first her words embarrassed me, but gradually I got used to her playfulness. She'd wink at me, her eyes rolling and her lashes fluttering, and she talked a lot about recent movies and TV shows. I treated her strictly as a pupil; to me she was a child.

When we worked, the door of her room was always open, and I occasionally noticed Eileen eavesdropping on us. I tried to act professionally. Whenever Sami was occupied with an assignment, I would go into the living room to chat a little with her mother, who was always pleased when I did. Eileen would treat me to tea, cookies, nuts, candied fruits. Sometimes I felt she was waiting for me.

I enjoyed spending time with the Mins in their warm and comforting home. My own small studio apartment was lonely. I'd sit by myself, reading or working on my thesis, wondering what sort of life this was. If I fell ill tomorrow, what would happen to me? If I died, where would I be buried? Unless my parents came to claim my body, I might be cremated and my ashes discarded God-knows-where. I had once known a young Filipino who was killed in a traffic accident. He had signed the back of his driver's license, agreeing to be an organ donor, so his body was shipped to a hospital to have the organs and tissues harvested and then it was burned and his ashes mailed to his parents in Mindanao. At least that's what I heard. I still don't know with certainty what happened.

It was difficult to date someone in Flushing, especially if you wanted a long-term, serious relationship, because most people would work here in the daytime and then return home. Those living here didn't plan to stay for long. It was as if their current residences were merely a transitory step to someplace else. I'd had two girlfriends before, but each had left me. The memories of those breakups stung me whenever I attempted to get close to another woman.

One evening I arrived at the Mins' a little early. They were just sitting down to dinner. Eileen asked me if I'd eaten. I said, "I'm fine."

My tone must have been hesitant, for she sensed my stomach was empty and beckoned to me: "Come and eat with us."

"No, I'm not hungry."

"Listen to my mom, Dave," Sami urged. "She's your boss."

Eileen went on, "Please. If you don't mind."

I stopped resisting, sat down beside Sami, and picked up the chopsticks Eileen had placed before me. Dinner was simple: chicken curry, tomato salad sprinkled with sugar, baked anchovies, and plain rice. I liked the food, though. It was the first time I'd eaten baked anchovies, which were crispy and quite salty. Eileen explained, "It's healthier to eat small fish nowadays. Big fish have too much mercury in them."

"This is really tasty," I said.

"Wait until you have it every day," Sami piped up. "It'll make you sick just to look at it."

As we ate, Eileen kept spooning chicken cubes into my bowl, which seemed to annoy Sami. "Mom," she said, "Dave's not a baby."

"Sure. I'm just happy to have someone eating with us finally." Eileen turned to me and added, "Actually, you're the first person to sit with us at this table since March."

We were quiet for a moment. Then she said, "Tell me, Dave, which one of you cooks, you or your girlfriend?"

"At the moment I don't have a girlfriend, Aunt." I called her that out of politeness, though she was just half a generation older. I felt my face burning and saw Sami's eyes suddenly gleaming. Then she gave me a smile that displayed her tiny canines.

"Don't call me 'Aunt,'" her mother said. "Just 'Eileen' is fine."

"All right."

"Then why don't you eat with us when you come to teach Sami in the evenings? That'll save you some time."

I didn't know how to respond. Sami stepped in and said, "My mom's a wonderful cook. Accept the offer, Dave."

"Thank you," I said to Eileen. "In that case, you can pay me less for teaching Sami."

"Don't be silly. It's very kind of you to agree to keep us

company. I appreciate that. But don't grumble if I cook something you don't like."

Before I could answer, Sami put in, "My mom's rich, you know."

"Sami, don't start that again," pleaded Eileen.

"Okay, okay." The girl made a face and speared a wedge of tomato with her fork. She wouldn't use chopsticks.

The next evening Eileen made taro soup with shredded pork and coriander. It was delicious; Sami said it was her mother's specialty. She ate two bowls of the soup and asked Eileen whether we could have it more often. "You used to make this every week."

Eileen soon learned I liked seafood, and she would pick up shrimp or scallops or squid. On occasion she bought fish—yellow croaker, flounder, red snapper, perch. During the day I found myself looking forward to going to the Mins', even when I was busy with other things. To distract myself from these thoughts and keep myself from gaining much weight, I often played tennis with my friend Avtar Babu, a fellow graduate student, in art history.

Sometimes I arrived early at the Mins' to give Eileen a hand in the kitchen—peeling a bulb of garlic, opening a can or bottle, crushing peppercorns in a stone mortar, replacing a trash bag. I just enjoyed hanging around. If something went wrong in the house, Eileen would tell me, and most times I could fix it. She'd be so grateful that she would insist on paying me for the work in addition to the parts, but I refused the money. The Mins treated me almost like a family member, and I was equally attached to them.

Sami made good progress in math, but her English improved slowly. She usually followed my instructions, and even tried memorizing all the words listed at the back of her English textbook, yet there were many gaps in her mastery of the subjects. Before her father died, he'd often said he hoped she could enter an Ivy League college. I never expressed my misgivings about that and always encouraged her.

As I was explaining a trigonometric function to Sami one evening, Eileen came in panting and said, "My car won't start."

"What's wrong with it?" I asked.

"I've no clue. I drove it this morning and it ran fine."

I told Sami to do a few problems in the textbook and went out with Eileen. Her blue Volvo was parked in the driveway, under the oak tree. A few caterpillars wiggled around on the pavement nearby, and Eileen avoided stepping on them as if in fear. I got into her car and turned the key in the ignition. The starter ground lazily, but the engine wouldn't catch.

"The battery must be gone," I told her. "When was the last time you had it replaced?"

"This is a new car, just three years old."

"The battery must be lousy, then."

"What should I do?" She kept rubbing her little hands together as if washing them. "I'm supposed to deliver the books to the reading." She had inherited her husband's small publishing business, and the company was holding an event that evening.

"Where's the reading?" I asked.

"At the high school."

"How many books do you have here?"

"Thirty-two copies, one full box."

The school wasn't far away, about twenty minutes' walk, so I offered to carry the books there for her. She thought about it, saying as if to herself, "Maybe I should call a cab." Then she changed her mind and asked, "Can you really carry the books for me, Dave?"

"Absolutely."

"It's so kind of you."

I went into her house and explained the situation to Sami. When I came back, Eileen was holding the handle of a maroon suitcase with wheels. "Guess what?" she said. "I found this and put all the books into it."

"Great idea." I wondered whether she still needed me since she could pull the wheeled suitcase herself, but I decided to go with her. Together we started out.

We hurried along Main Street, toward Northern Boulevard. The suitcase wasn't heavy, but I had to lift it at the curbs whenever we crossed a street. Soon I began sweating, and the back of my T-shirt became damp. I noticed people throwing glances at the two of us, probably wondering whether we might be a couple. Eileen was thirteen years older than I but looked younger than her age, her waist small, her legs shapely, her steps full of bounce. She dabbed at her face with Kleenex as we walked. I grew excited, as if this were a date, despite the bulky thing I was dragging. When we had crossed Thirty-seventh Avenue, to my surprise she said, "Let me mop your face."

I turned to let her wipe the sweat from my forehead and cheeks. It happened so naturally that it didn't feel like the first time. She smiled, her eyes alight with feeling. Then I remembered we were in the middle of a thoroughfare, in the presence of many passersby. "We'd better hurry," I said.

We hastened our steps but soon stopped again. Near Little Lamb, the Mongolian firepot place, we ran into a bent man whom Eileen called Old Feng. He had just come out of the restaurant, still chewing. Although she introduced us, the man kept glaring at me, his eyes pouchy and bloodshot, his mouth sunken. As he talked with Eileen, he went on watching me as if wary of my presence. I stood nearby, waiting. After a few moments Eileen said, "I have to run, Old Feng. Let's discuss this later, okay?"

"Sure. I'll stop by." The old man didn't look happy. He shambled away, cleaning his teeth with a toothpick.

We continued north. Eileen explained that Old Feng had been a professional writer back in China, an editor at the official magazine *The People's Arts,* before coming to the States about ten years ago. His wife, almost twenty years his junior, worked at Gold City Supermarket so that Mr. Feng could stay home and write his books. Recently he had finished a trilogy, which Eileen would publish, though she expected to lose money on the novels. Before her husband died, he had made her promise to print the three books—because he had read parts of the manuscripts and loved the writing and because Mr. Feng had been his friend. Now Eileen had to keep her word.

Her company, Everyman Press, was tiny, with only three employees, all part-timers. It survived owing mainly to the print-on-demand equipment her late husband had installed, which allowed publication of a small run of a book at little cost. He had spent more than a quarter of a million dollars on the technology, almost half his life savings. He'd been in the pharmaceutical business originally, but—obsessed with books and with magazines and newspapers—he'd started his own press to publish obscure authors, including half a dozen poets. Eileen had worked there first as an editor. Now she was its owner and manager.

As we walked along, shop signs bearing Korean words appeared, and a small building with most of its windows boarded up. Eileen told me she had just finished editing the first novel of Mr. Feng's trilogy, the one titled *Of Pigs and People.* "I don't like it. It's too tedious and repetitive," she confessed. "I cannot see how to market this one."

We reached the high school just in time. I dropped the suitcase at the entrance to the conference room and headed back to Sami. Twilight was falling; neon lights flared up one after another along the street. I indulged in thoughts of Eileen.

There were always fresh flowers in the Mins' living room; Sami said they were gifts from men pursuing her mother. A number were courting her, most in their fifties or sixties, some still married, brazen enough to think that a recent widow would make a possible mistress. Sami said one man, who had made his fortune in the undertaking business, offered her mother a piano if she agreed to date him. Eileen turned him down, saying there was no room in her home, and besides, she was too old to learn how to play it. The man then proposed to give her one of his funeral parlors. "That sounds creepy," I said. Sami giggled. "Yeah, it did give my mom goose bumps."

Eileen always told these men that she had promised her late husband to take care of their daughter, to help her do well in school. She was not interested in any man for the time being.

The next day I bought a new battery for Eileen's car. After installing it, I drove the Volvo around a little to get the battery fully charged and the electrical system in sync again. Eileen was moved by my help and wanted to pay me, but I told her, "Take it as a birthday gift, okay?"

She nodded without saying another word. For a long while she gazed at me, her eyes giving a soft light. That pleased me a lot, and for the first time I swelled with a peculiar kind of pride that arises in a man who feels useful to a worthy woman.

Eileen's forty-first birthday was approaching. Sami told me she didn't know how to celebrate it. In the past years her father would take them to an upscale restaurant, usually Ocean Jewel or East Lake, where a cake had been prepared for her mother. This year, with her dad gone, Sami had suggested that the two of them dine out, but Eileen said she preferred to have a dinner at home. This meant I would get invited. Sami wouldn't mind that as long as her mother was happy.

I was also considering what to do for Eileen. I couldn't be extravagant, but I wanted to give her something more personal than a car battery. For a few dollars I bought a pair of cloisonné earrings from a street vendor, sky blue and in the shape of an ancient bell. I knew Sami had gotten a diamond wristwatch for her mother. She said Eileen needed a good one because her current watch would stop randomly; the girl had expensive tastes.

Eileen's birthday arrived on a pleasant August day. That evening, traffic hummed faintly in the east, and the happy cries of children rose and fell behind a nearby house that provided day care. The neighborhood was alive and peaceful. Eileen had steamed a large pomfret and braised a pork tenderloin. When the table was set, we all sat down to dinner. Eileen opened a small jar of rice wine and poured us each a cup. Sami and I didn't like the wine, finding its taste medicinal, but Eileen enjoyed it and took mouthfuls, saying it would warm and protect the stomach. She had such a quaint palate. I would have preferred a beer. But I liked the dishes a lot—

especially the salad of julienned citron mixed with slivers of dried, spiced tofu—and I didn't stop Eileen from serving me more. She was in a buoyant mood, though Sami looked a bit gloomy, as if her mind were elsewhere.

Sami and I lit candles on a chocolate cake and sang "Happy Birthday." Eileen blushed and smiled wordlessly. Then Sami brought out her present. At the sight of the watch, Eileen said to her, "Thank you, dear. But you shouldn't have spent so much. This must be outrageously expensive." She didn't try it on, but instead put it aside and let it lie in the velveteen case with the lid open.

I then handed her the tiny red envelope containing the earrings. "Please take this as a token of my gratitude," I said.

"You bought this for me?" Eileen exclaimed as she opened it. "You're so kind. Thank you!" She dangled the earrings before her daughter. "Aren't they beautiful?"

"Sure they are." The girl grimaced and ducked her head to avoid seeing Eileen's happy face. She glanced at her own gift lying beyond her mother's elbow. I was embarrassed.

Color crept into Eileen's cheeks and her neck turned pinkish. For a moment her eyes wavered, then blazed at me. Her fingers never stopped fondling the earrings. I guessed that if Sami had not been there, Eileen might have tried them on, though the holes in her earlobes might no longer accommodate the wires.

"When's your birthday, Dave?" she asked.

"October twenty-third."

"Ah, just two months away. I'll mark my calendar and we'll celebrate."

Her words warmed me because they implied she would still employ me after Sami's fall semester started. I needed the income. I noticed Sami observing me intently; she must have surmised my thoughts. I said to her, "So you'll have to bear with me a little longer."

"I won't give up on you," she said, then grinned almost fiercely, her small eyeteeth sticking out.

Not knowing what to make of that, I turned to Eileen. "Please don't trouble yourself about my birthday."

"Come on, you'll help Sami go through the college applications, won't you?"

"Sure, I'll be happy to do that."

"Then you mustn't abandon us."

Sami stood and turned away as if in a sulk. Eileen grasped her daughter's wrist and asked, "Why are you leaving?"

"I have a migraine and I need to be alone." She shook off her mother's grip and with a pout made for her room.

Eileen said to me, "Don't worry. She'll be all right."

And then something—a cup or a bottle—shattered on the floor of Sami's room. The thought of her late father hadn't occurred to me until that moment.

Sami began volunteering on Friday evenings at a nursing home on Forty-fifth Avenue, doing laundry, a service project that she could include on her college applications. She said the laundry room smelled like vomit. However, the old people liked her, because unlike some of the staff members, she didn't yell at them. She often talked to me about the place and claimed she'd rather kill herself than go to a nursing home when she was old. Once, the night-shift supervisor asked her to help towel-bathe some bedridden old women. Her job was to hold their shoulders while a nurse rubbed and washed their backs, some of which were spotted with sores. One patient, shrunken like a skeleton, screamed in Cantonese, which Sami didn't need to understand to know the crone was cursing her. Another one, who had a full head of white hair, sobbed the whole time and whined, "Such a nuisance. I better die soon!" Sami held her breath against their odors of sweat and urine.

She told her mother of the same experiences. Eileen was worried, afraid that her daughter might be more upset than she acknowledged, and asked me if Sami should quit. I assured her that Sami would be all right as long as she could talk it out. In fact, the girl wasn't that fragile, though she seemed to lack willpower. I believed the service would toughen her up a little, and also she could ask the nursing home's manager for a letter of recommendation, which might help distinguish her college applications. Eileen agreed.

When one of Eileen's employees took a week off to attend his son's wedding in Minneapolis, I offered to help in the afternoons. I didn't know how to operate the printing machine or the computer programs, so I mainly did photocopying and other clerical jobs. One afternoon Mr. Feng dropped in and began to bicker with Eileen about his novel. I was collating a handout in the inner room, where the company's motto was inscribed on two scrolls hung vertically on the wall: "To Publish Books by Anyone / To Disseminate Stories of Everyman."

"No, no, the first printing should be at least one thousand copies," I heard Mr. Feng say in a raspy voice. I looked over at him and Eileen, both seated at the long table with teacups in front of them. The old man held his chin in his knotted hand, his elbow on the tabletop.

"Please be reasonable," Eileen said. "We can't possibly sell that many copies, and neither do we have the storage space for them."

"How many copies do you plan to bring out, then?"

"Two hundred at most."

"That's ridiculous."

"We've never done more than two hundred for a novel. If you want us to print more, you should deposit a sum for the production cost."

"What are you driving at?" The old man sat back as if in horror.

"You should buy the extra copies you've ordered."

"I've no cash on hand at the moment."

"Truth be told, we cannot lose too much money on this book."

Mr. Feng coughed into his fist. He sighed. "Well, I guess I must bow to reality here. I used to have eighty thousand copies for a first run."

"That was back in China. Don't be angry with me, Old Feng. If there's the need, we can always rush to print extra copies."

"All right. I'll hold you to that."

"You have my word."

With puffy cheeks, the old man slouched out the door. Eileen heaved a long sigh and massaged her temples with her thumb and forefinger. Outside, a truck was unloading steaming-hot asphalt on the street, flashing its lights and sounding warning beeps, while a worker in a hard hat directed the traffic with an orange flag.

I wondered how long Eileen could hold on to a publishing business that was unprofitable and too much for her to manage alone.

One afternoon in late September I sprained my ankle while playing tennis with Avtar. For several days I couldn't go to the Mins', so Sami came over to take her lessons. She was excited to be in my studio apartment, which in spite of its shabbiness provided an intimate setting for the two of us. Her brown eyes were often fixed on me when I spoke to her. She laughed freely and loudly. As if we had known each other for years, she would pat my arm, and once she even pinched my cheek when I called her "kiddo." She worked less than before and talked more, though time and again I managed to bring her back to her textbooks. She sniffed the air, her pinkish nostrils twitching a little, and said, "Hm. I like the smell of your room."

One night I couldn't find my black undershirt. I'd worn it three days before and had dropped it beside my laundry basket, which was overfull. Nobody but Sami had been to my apartment that week. The thought that she had taken it alarmed me, because she was just a kid, and because I'd never known any woman to be fond of my smell. My first girlfriend said I stank to high heaven and always made me shower before bed. She wouldn't even mix her laundry with mine. My second girlfriend never complained, so I seldom used deodorant.

Then Eileen phoned and said she didn't feel comfortable with her daughter away from home in the evenings. My ankle was improving, so I agreed to return our sessions to their home. I missed her cooking. But to my surprise, the next afternoon Eileen appeared at my apartment in person, carrying a basket of fruits—tangerines, plums, apples, and pears. She apologized for not warning me. I was elated; for days my mind had been straying to her. She sat as I made her herbal tea. Her face, a bit tilted, shone with happiness.

"Well, I'm so glad to see that you can move around," she said. "How worried I was!"

"About Sami or me?"

"Both." She tittered.

"I've been thinking of you," I blurted, my face hot.

At those words, she lowered her head, her complexion turning red. Then she raised her eyes to peer at my face. I touched her wrist; she placed her other hand on my chest. We fell into each other's arms.

We moved to my bed as if out of habit. In an ardent voice she confessed, "Ah, how often I dreamed of you doing this to me!" She held me tight with both her arms and her legs while I was inside her.

For the hour she was there, my studio was for the first time awash in the warmth of a home.

Smoothing the wrinkles in her dress, she said, "Please come to teach Sami in our house. I cannot have peace of mind if she's out in the evenings, especially with you. I'm sure you must attract lots of girls."

"I've already agreed. And don't worry about that; I prefer a ripe woman." I knew I wasn't attractive.

She nodded and smiled, ready to go. I lurched up to see her off, but she stopped me and walked briskly to the door. Before closing it, she wheeled around and said, "I'll miss you, and also him." Her index finger pointed at my crotch. Then she disappeared, giggling.

She left a delicate fragrance like apricot on my pillow. For a long time I fell into a reverie, my face half buried in her scent while I imagined making love to her in her home.

For a week I helped Sami with her college essays. She was a decent writer, but at times her sentences could be convoluted, built of abstract words and clichés. I encouraged her to write simply and directly, to ensure that every sentence added something to the whole piece, to view any unintended repetition as a defect. I explained that each school received thousands of applications and couldn't consider every one carefully. The readers formed their judgments by impression and interest, and their task was to determine whether the applicant could write. So as long as the writing was clear and interesting, the content was less relevant.

Eileen and I chatted briefly and eyed each other wistfully. Only on Friday evenings when Sami was away at the nursing home could we be together. I would sneak into the Mins', and we'd go to bed for two hours. I loved Eileen. With her, I felt at ease and content, as if she were a sunlit harbor where I could anchor. She made me promise never to let her daughter suspect us of the affair.

My birthday was just a week away, and Sami and Eileen had talked between themselves about what to give me. They even asked me. Sami bought a pair of tennis rackets, which I saw stowed away under her bed. I wondered if she planned to give me both or just one of them; she had once asked me to teach her how to play sometime in the spring. Her request pleased me, because it showed that she expected me to stay around.

Actually, I wasn't a good tennis player. So, anticipating that Sami would hold me to my promise, I played with Avtar more often.

I also noticed a laptop in Eileen's room, still sealed in its box. Before I left the Mins' one evening, I overheard Sami complain to her mother, "What if he's still around next year? Will you give him a car?"

"I want him to help you more," Eileen said.

She knew my monitor had recently burned out and I'd been using a computer at the library.

Three days before my birthday I again snuck over to the Mins'. It was Friday evening. Turning onto Folk Avenue, I saw Mr. Feng emerging from Eileen's front yard. He wore a windbreaker cloak-style, the sleeves dangling. I waved to greet him, and he grunted and frowned and convulsed in a fit of coughing.

Eileen answered the door and hugged me. I asked her why Mr. Feng looked so out of sorts.

"For the same old reason," she replied. "He wanted me to print five hundred copies of his novel."

We left our shoes at her bedroom door and began making love unhurriedly. The twilight deepened outside, and we sank into the king-size bed as if we had turned in for the night. No light was on, because Eileen preferred darkness. "So I can let myself go," she told me.

"Don't you want me to give you a child?" she asked.

"Sure, I'd like to father a bunch of them. How many will you give me?"

"A dozen if I could."

"I love kids."

Suddenly there was a bang at the door. I sat up, breathless, my heart kicking. Then came Sami's shrill voice. "Damn you! Shameless animals!" She hit the door again, with something rubbery this time—it must have been my shoe—and then ran away upstairs. Eileen was shaken, her face haggard and her eyes blinking in the dim light thrown by the rising moon. She urged me to leave. "You must go now, quickly!"

A sweat broke out all over me. Hurriedly I pulled on my clothes and rushed out of their house. The streetlights were swimming in my eyes as I took flight.

Eileen called the next morning. She sounded exhausted and didn't say much on the phone. Apparently she was not alone in her office. She asked me to come to her house that evening, which I agreed to do. I couldn't figure out why she had rung me up just for that; maybe she wanted to make sure I would continue to teach Sami. But how could I remain composed in the presence of both of them?

After dinner, I set off for the Mins', full of apprehension. Approaching their yard, I saw a cardboard box next to their trash can, and lying on the box was a pair of tennis rackets, with most of the strings severed. The sight wracked my heart. About twenty feet away, five or six plump sparrows bathed in a puddle of dirty rainwater, flapping their wings and pecking at their feathers, chirping happily and ignoring me. Somehow the birds cheered me.

I rang the bell. Eileen answered the door, and I entered the living room. She simply handed me a check. She said tearfully, "Dave, we don't need your help anymore. Please don't think I called you in just to humiliate you. Sami insists I must make this clear to you in front of her." Her voice wavered.

"I understand," I managed to say. "Thanks very much." I accepted the paycheck. The house was swaying.

Before I could turn to the door, Sami said, "Wait a sec. My mom has something for you, a birthday present."

"Stop it, Sami!" Eileen burst out.

"Why not let him take it home? You won't return it or smash it anyway." She indicated the laptop on the sofa. "Please take that with you." Without waiting for my response, she tore away, hand over mouth, to her room.

"Please forgive her," Eileen murmured.

"That's all right." I scanned her pallid face, her twitching cheek. Then I walked out.

The laptop was delivered to me two days later. I thought of sending it back but feared that would hurt Eileen's feelings. I missed her terribly.

• • •

In the weeks that followed, I kept running into Sami. At first I was abashed, but she would converse with me casually about various things—the recent muggings of several Asian immigrants, an edifying sermon by a Tibetan monk, the shows in celebration of the Spring Festival, Falun Gong's call to renounce Communist Party membership. She didn't tease me as before, and even called me from time to time. I told her then that I had genuine feelings for her mother and hoped she could accept our relationship. I made her mother happy, and she made me a better man.

"Forget it," Sami huffed. "She's old enough to be *your* mother. Didn't you used to call her 'Aunt'?"

"Come on, Sami, she's only thirteen years older than I am."

"You'll never marry her. Why should you toy with her heart?"

"How do you know I'll never marry her?"

"Because she cannot give you children."

"I don't care."

"You'll just have fun with her for a while, then dump her."

"Don't call me again." I hung up, dazed at the thought of Eileen's infertility.

Though upset by Sami, I believed she'd told me the truth. When we made love, Eileen had never mentioned contraceptives; I'd assumed she was on the pill. If I were to marry an infertile woman, it would devastate my parents. I'm their only son, and they expect me to carry on the family line.

Yet I couldn't drive Eileen out of my mind. I longed to sleep with her in that king-size bed, deaf to the outside world. Never had I been so hopelessly in love. I phoned her once and grew short of breath. I said I missed her; she sighed and told me not to contact her again, at least not before Sami finished her college applications. "I just don't want to disturb her at the moment." She sounded resigned, but I could tell I was on her mind too. I reminded myself to be patient.

Unlike her mother, Sami was always in contact with me, continually calling me for advice on her applications. Her SAT scores weren't high, so her chances for the Ivy League were slim. I advised her to apply to Penn and Cornell in addition to some colleges in New York City. Her ideal school was my alma mater, NYU, because she wanted to stay close to home to keep her mother company. One Saturday morning I ran into her in the public library, in a corner on the second floor, behind the book stacks. She wore knee-high suede boots and a red peacoat with enormous buttons, looking sturdy and thick but still girlish. Unconsciously her hand kept touching the single-paned window, leaving prints on it that immediately faded away. Outside, fluffy snowflakes drifted on the wind beneath patches of blue sky. As our conversation continued, Sami insinuated that I might have an eye on Eileen's money. "Of course, lots of men are interested in women of means," she said.

"Honest to God, I've no idea how rich your mother is," I protested. "And I don't care."

"Well, I'm richer than her. I have a big trust fund." She stared at me, her eyes a bit wide set. "You have to give up on screwing my mom—enough's enough."

"I love your mother, but I can't understand why you're so heartless." Exasperated, I spun around and clattered down the stairs.

When I saw her again, I tried to be friendly because I realized I could not afford to make her my enemy. If I were to see Eileen again, I had to be accepted by both daughter and mother.

• • •

For weeks I worked hard on my thesis, sharpening the argument, smoothing out the rough spots, and preparing all the footnotes. I made myself busy to quench my miserable feelings. My professor praised what I'd written and said I could graduate before summer. The rapid progress bemused me, however, confronting me with decisions about what to do after graduation.

The days were getting longer. In late March, Sami began to receive letters from colleges. Penn turned her down, but unexpectedly Cornell accepted her. She came to my place, wild with joy, and hugged me tightly, saying that now her father must be pleased underground. In her excitement her cheeks grew ruddy, and even her hair seemed glossier. I rejoiced at the news myself, though for different reasons, and said a lot of good things about Cornell.

I called Eileen to give her my congratulations. She too was enraptured. "Without your help, Sami couldn't possibly have gotten admitted by that school," she said earnestly.

"You should urge her to go to Cornell," I suggested. "It's a great place. I know some alumni. They all loved it."

"I know what's on your mind, Dave."

"I miss you, a lot."

"I miss you too," she sighed, "but we must be patient."

A few days after that conversation I saw an ad in a local newspaper, *The North American Tribune,* for an editorial assistant position at Eileen's press. It was a part-time job, twenty hours a week, offering "wages commensurate with experience." This possibility set my mind spinning, and for a whole day I vibrated with hopes. I asked Avtar whether I should apply. Dunking a tea bag in his steaming cup, he said, "Man, if I were you, I'd go for the daughter."

That evening Sami called: both NYU and Sarah Lawrence had rejected her. Quietly elated, I urged her again about Cornell. "Just imagine how that would delight your father," I said.

Two days later, I went to Everyman Press early in the morning. None of its employees had arrived yet, and Eileen was there alone. She was surprised to see me, but composed herself immediately and led me into her office. The walls were lined with slanted shelves, mostly loaded with books and brochures. She poured a cup of coffee for me. A sad smile crossed her face, which was a bit gaunt then, her chin pointed. "Hazelnut," she said. "And cream and sugar. Sorry there's no honey."

"This will do fine." I was moved that she remembered I liked hazelnut coffee with honey and cream. I told her of my interest in the job. "I'll be a good helper to you," I assured her. "Who knows, someday I may even become a big editor."

She gazed at me, her mouth parted a bit, her bottom lip slightly thicker than the top. Then she closed her mouth and her face turned calm again. "It's too late, Dave," she said.

"What do you mean? The job is filled?"

"No, we're still looking for someone, but I cannot let you work here."

"Why? I'm not qualified?"

"No, not because of that. Sami was just accepted to Queens College. She's going there."

"You mean she gave up Cornell?"

"Yes. She's afraid I'll be lonely without her. I tried my best to persuade her to go, but she wants to stay home."

"How can you be sure that's her only reason?"

"She and I had a long talk last night. We both have feelings for you, but we promised each other that neither of us would see you again."

"I see."

"Don't be mad at me, Dave. I cherish the time you spent with me and will always remember you fondly. I know that for a woman my age, I may never meet another man as good as you. But Sami just made a big sacrifice for me, and I mustn't let her down again. No matter how much I love you."

"She's lucky to have you for a mother," I muttered.

Tears welled in my eyes, and I scrambled to the door. I didn't want her to see my face. I hurried away on the street, aware of her eyes fixed on my back. It had begun drizzling, and a fine rain swirled in the air, soaking the leafing branches and my hair. I was more touched than wretched.

Children as Enemies

OUR GRANDCHILDREN HATE US. The boy and the girl, ages eleven and nine, are just a pair of selfish, sloppy brats and have no respect for old people. Their animosity toward us originated at the moment their names were changed, about three months ago.

One evening the boy complained that his schoolmates couldn't pronounce his name, so he must change it. "Lots of them call me 'Chicken,' " he said. "I want a regular name like anyone else." His name was Qigan Xi, pronounced "cheegan hsee," which could be difficult for non-Chinese to manage.

"I wanna change mine too," his sister, Hua, jumped in. "Nobody can say it right and some call me 'Wow.' " She bunched her lips, her face puffed with baby fat.

Before their parents could respond, my wife put in, "You should teach them how to pronounce your names."

"They always laugh about my silly name, Qigan," the boy said. "If I didn't come from China, I'd say 'Chicken' too."

I told both kids, "You ought to be careful about changing your names. We decided on them only after consulting a reputable fortune-teller."

"Phew, who believes in that crap?" the boy muttered.

Our son intervened, saying to his children, "Let me think about this, okay?"

Our daughter-in-law, thin-eyed Mandi, broke in. "They should have American names. Down the road there'll be lots of trouble if their names remain unpronounceable. We should've changed them long ago."

Gubin, our son, seemed to agree, though he wouldn't say it in our presence.

My wife and I were unhappy about that, but we didn't make a serious effort to stop them, so Mandi and Gubin went about looking for suitable names for the children. It was easy in the girl's case. They picked "Flora" for her, since her name, Hua, means "flower." But it was not easy to find a name for the boy. English names are simple in meaning, mostly already empty of their original senses. Qigan means "amazing bravery." Where can you find an English name that combines the import and the resonance of that? When I pointed out the difficulty, the boy blustered, "I don't want a weird and complicated name. I just need a regular name, like Charlie or Larry or Johnny."

That I wouldn't allow. Names are a matter of fortune and fate—that's why fortune-tellers can divine the vicissitudes of people's lives by reading the orders and numbers of the strokes in the characters of their names. No one should change his name randomly.

Mandi went to the public library and checked out a book on baby names. She perused the small volume and came up with "Matty" as a choice. She explained, " 'Matty' is short for

'Mathilde,' which is from Old German and means 'powerful in battle,' very close to 'Qigan' in meaning. Besides, the sound echoes 'mighty' in English."

"It doesn't sound right," I said. In the back of my mind I couldn't reconcile "Matty" with "Xi," our family name.

"I like it," the boy crowed.

He seemed determined to contradict me, so I said no more. I wished my son had rejected the choice, but Gubin didn't make a peep, just sitting in the rocking chair and drinking iced tea. The matter was settled. The boy went to school and told his teacher he had a new name—Matty.

For a week he seemed happy, but his satisfaction was short-lived. One evening he told his parents, "Matty is a girl's name, my friend Carl told me."

"Impossible," his mother said.

"Of course it's true. I asked around, and people all said it sounded girlish."

My wife, drying her hands on her apron, suggested to our son, "Why don't you look it up?"

The book on baby names was not returned yet, so Gubin looked it up and saw "f. or m." beside the name. Evidently Mandi hadn't seen that it could be both female and male. Her negligence or ignorance outraged the boy all the more.

What should we do? The eleven-year-old turned tearful, blaming his mother for giving him a name with an ambiguous gender.

Finally my son slapped his knee and said, "I have an idea. 'Matty' can also come from 'Matt.' Why not drop the letter 'y' and call yourself Matt?"

The boy brightened up and said he liked that, but I objected. "Look, this book says 'Matt' is a diminutive of 'Matthew.' It's nowhere close to the sense of 'amazing bravery.' "

"Who gives a damn about that!" the boy spat out. "I'm gonna call myself Matt."

Wordless, I felt my face tightening. I got up and went out to smoke a pipe on the balcony. My wife followed me, saying, "My old man, don't take to heart what our grandson said. He's just confused and desperate. Come back in and eat."

"After this pipe," I said.

"Don't be long." She stepped back into the apartment, her small shoulders more stooped than before.

Below me, automobiles were gliding past on the wet street like colored whales. If only we hadn't sold everything in Dalian City and come here to join our son's family. Gubin is our only child, so we'd thought it would be good to stay with him. Now I wish we hadn't moved. At our ages—my wife is sixty-three and I'm sixty-seven—and at this time it's hard to adjust to life here. In America it feels as if the older you are, the more inferior you grow.

Both my wife and I understood we shouldn't meddle with our grandchildren's lives, but sometimes I simply couldn't help offering them a bit of advice. She believed it was our daughter-in-law who had spoiled the kids and made them despise us. I don't think Mandi is that mean, though beyond question she is an indulgent mother. Flora and Matt look down on everything Chinese except for some food they like. They hated to go to the weekend school to learn to read and write the characters. Matt announced, "I've no need for that crap."

I would have to force down my temper whenever I heard him say that. Their parents managed to make them attend the weekend school, though Matt and Flora had quit inscribing the characters. They went there only to learn how to paint with a brush, taking lessons from an old artist from Taiwan. The girl, sensitive by nature and delicate in health, might have had some talent for arts, but the boy was good at nothing but daydreaming. I just couldn't help imagining that he might end up a guttersnipe. He wouldn't draw bamboos or goldfish or landscapes with a brush; instead, he produced merely bands and lines of ink on paper, calling them abstract paintings. He experimented with the shades of the ink as if it were watercolors. Sometimes he did that at home too. Seeing his chubby face and narrow eyes as he worked in dead earnest, I wanted to laugh. He once showed a piece with some vertical lines of ink on it to an art teacher at his school. To my horror, the woman praised it, saying the lines suggested a rainfall or waterfall, and that if you observed them horizontally, they would bring to mind layers of clouds or some sort of landscape.

What a crock was that! I complained to Gubin in private and urged him to pressure the children to study serious subjects, such as science, classics, geography, history, grammar, and penmanship. If Matt really couldn't handle those, in the future he should consider learning how to repair cars and machines or how to cook like a chef. Auto mechanics make good money here—I know a fellow at a garage who can't speak any English but pulls in twenty-four dollars an hour, plus a generous bonus at the end of the year. I made it clear to my son that a few tricks in "art" would never get his kids anywhere in life, so they'd better stop dabbling with a brush. Gubin said Matt and Flora were still young and we shouldn't push them too hard, but he agreed to talk to them. Unlike Gubin, Mandi aligned herself with the children, saying we ought to let them develop freely as individuals, not straitjacket them as they would back in China. My wife and I were unhappy about our daughter-in-law's position. Whenever we criticized her, our grandchildren would mock us or yell at us in defense of their mother.

I have serious reservations about elementary education in the United States. Teachers don't force their pupils to work as hard as they can. Matt had learned both multiplication and division in the third grade, but two months ago I asked him to calculate how much seventy-four percent of $1,586 was, and he had no clue how to do it. I handed him a calculator and said, "Use this." Even so, he didn't know he could just multiply the amount by 0.74.

"Didn't you learn multiplication and division?" I asked him.

"I did, but that was last year."

"Still, you should know how to do it."

"We haven't practiced division and multiplication this year, so I'm not familiar with them anymore." He offered that as an excuse. There was no way I could make him understand that once you learned something, you were supposed to master it and make it part of yourself. That's why we say knowledge is wealth. You can get richer and richer by accumulating it within.

The teachers here don't assign the pupils any real homework. Instead they give them a lot of projects, some of which seem no more than woolgathering, and tend to inflate the kids' egos. My son had to help his children with the projects, which were more like homework for the parents. Some of the topics were impossible even for adults to tackle, such as "What is culture and how is it created?" "Make your argument for or against the Iraq War," "How does the color line divide U.S. society?" and "Do you think global trade is necessary? Why?" My son had to do research online and in the public library to get the information needed for discussing those topics. Admittedly, they could broaden the pupils' minds and give them more confidence, but at their tender age they are not supposed to think like a politician or a scholar. They should be made to follow rules; that is, to become responsible citizens first.

Whenever I asked Flora how she was ranked in her class, she'd shrug and say, "I dunno."

"What do you mean you don't know?" I suspected she must be well below the average, though she couldn't be lower than her brother.

"Ms. Gillen doesn't rank us is all," came her answer.

If that was true, I was even more disappointed with the schools. How could they make their students competitive in this global economy if they didn't instill in them the sense of getting ahead of others and becoming the very best? No wonder many Asian parents viewed the public schools in Flushing unfavorably. In my honest opinion, elementary education here tends to lead children astray.

Five weeks ago, Matt declared at dinner that he must change his last name, because a substitute teacher that morning had mispronounced "Xi" as "Eleven." That put the whole class in stitches, and some students even made fun of the boy afterward, calling him "Matt Eleven." Flora chimed in, "Yeah, I want a different last name too. My friend Reta just had her family name changed to Wu. Some people couldn't pronounce 'Ng' and called her 'Reta No Good.' "

Their parents broke out laughing, but I couldn't see why that was funny. My wife said to the girl, "You'll have your husband's last name when you grow up and get married."

"I don't want no man!" the girl shot back.

"We both must have a new last name," the boy insisted.

I burst out, "You can't do that. Your last name belongs to the family, and you can't cut yourselves off from your ancestors."

"Baloney!" The boy squished up his face.

"You mustn't speak to your granddad like that," his grandmother butted in.

Mandi and my son exchanged glances. I knew they saw this matter differently from us. Maybe they had been planning to change their children's last name all along. Enraged, I dropped my bowl on the dining table and pointed my finger at Mandi. "You've tried your best to spoil them. Now you're happy to let them break away from the family tree. What kind of daughter-in-law are you? I wish I hadn't allowed you to join our family."

"Please don't blow up like this, Dad," my son said.

Mandi didn't talk back. Instead she began sobbing, wrinkling her gourd-shaped nose. The kids got angry and blamed me for hurting their mother's feelings. The more they blabbered, the more furious I became. Finally unable to hold it back anymore, I shouted, "If you two change your last name, you leave, get out of here. You cannot remain in this household while using a different last name."

"Who are you?" Matt said calmly. "This isn't your home."

"You're just our guests," added Flora.

That drove both my wife and me mad. She yelled at our granddaughter, "So we sold everything in China, our apartment and candy store, just to be your guests here, huh? Heartless. Who told you this isn't our home?"

That shut the girl up, though she kept glaring at her grandma. Their father begged no one in particular, "Please, let us finish dinner peacefully." He went on chewing a fried shrimp with his mouth closed.

I wanted to yell at him that he was just a rice barrel thinking of nothing but food, but I controlled my anger. How could we have raised such a spineless son?

To be fair, he's quite accomplished in his profession, a bridge engineer pulling in almost six figures a year, but he's henpecked and indulgent with the kids, and got worse and worse after he came to America, as if he had become a man without temper or opinions. How often I wanted to tell him point-blank that he must live like a man, at least more like his former self. Between his mother and myself, we often wondered if he was inadequate in bed; otherwise, how could he always listen to Mandi?

After that quarrel, we decided to move out. Gubin and Mandi helped us fill out an application for housing offered to the elderly by the city, which we'll have to wait a long time to get. If we were not so old and in poor health, we'd live far away from them, completely on our own, but they are the only family we have in this country, so we could move only to a nearby place. For the time being we've settled down in a one-bedroom apartment on Fifty-fourth Avenue, rented for us by Gubin. Sometimes he comes over to see if we're all right or need anything. We've never asked him what last name our grandkids use now. I guess they must have some American name. How sad it is when you see your grandchildren's names on paper but can no longer recognize them, as though your family line has faded and disappeared among the multitudes. Whenever I think about this, it stings my heart. If only I'd had second thoughts about leaving China. It's impossible to go back anymore, and we'll have to spend our remaining years in this place where even your grandchildren can act like your enemies.

Matt and Flora usually shun us. If we ran into them on the street, they would warn us not to "torture" their mother again.

They even threatened to call the police if we entered their home without permission. We don't have to be warned. We've never set foot in their home since we moved out. I've told my son that we won't accept the kids as part of the family as long as they use a different last name.

Gubin has never brought up that topic again, though I'm still waiting for an answer from him. That's how the matter stands now. The other day, exasperated, my wife wanted to go to Mandi's fortune cookie factory and raise a placard to announce: "My Daughter-in-Law Mandi Cheng Is the Most Unfilial Person on Earth!" But I dissuaded my old better half. What's the good of that? For sure Mandi's company won't fire her just because she can't make her parents-in-law happy. This is America, where we must learn self-reliance and mind our own business.

In the Crossfire

THE EMPLOYEES COULD TELL that the company was floundering and that some of them would lose their jobs soon. For a whole morning Tian Chu stayed in his cubicle, processing invoices without a break. Even at lunchtime he avoided chatting with others at length, because the topic of layoffs unnerved him. He had worked there for only two years and might be among the first to go. Fortunately, he was already a U.S. citizen and wouldn't be ashamed of collecting unemployment benefits, which the INS regards as something of a black mark against one who applies for a green card or citizenship.

Around midafternoon, as he was typing, his cell phone chimed. Startled, he pulled it out of his pants pocket. "Hello," he said in an undertone.

"Tian, how's your day there?" came his mother's scratchy voice.

"It's all right. I told you not to call me at work. People can hear me on the phone."

"I want to know what you'd like for dinner."

"Don't bother about that, Mom. You don't know how to use the stove and oven and you might set off the alarm again. I'll pick up something on my way home."

"What happened to Connie? Why can't she do the shopping and cooking? You shouldn't spoil her like this."

"She's busy, all right? I can't talk more now. See you soon." He shut the phone and stood up to see if his colleagues in the neighboring cubicles had been listening in. Nobody seemed interested.

He sat down and yawned, massaging his eyebrows to relieve the fatigue from peering at the computer screen. He knew his mother must feel lonely at home. She often complained that she had no friends here and there wasn't much to watch on TV. True, most of the shows were reruns and some were in Cantonese or Taiwanese, neither of which she could understand. The books Tian had checked out of the library for her were boring too. If only she could have someone to chitchat with. But their neighbors all went to work in the daytime, and she dared not venture out on her own because she was unable to read the street signs in English. This neighborhood was too quiet, she often grumbled. It looked as if there were more houses than people. Chimneys were here and there, but none of them puffed smoke. The whole place was deserted after nine a.m., and not until midafternoon would she see traces of others—and then only kids getting off the school buses and padding along the sidewalks. If only she could have had a grandchild to look after, to play with. But that was out of the question, since Connie Liu, her daughter-in-law, was still attending nursing school and wanted to wait until she had finished.

It was already dark when Tian left work. The wind was tossing pedestrians' clothes and hair and stirring the surfaces of slush puddles that shimmered in the neon and the streetlights. The remaining snowbanks along the curbs were black from auto exhaust and were becoming encrusted again. Tian stopped at a supermarket in the basement of a mall and picked up a stout eggplant, a bag of spinach, and a flounder. He knew that his wife would avoid going home to cook dinner because she couldn't make anything her mother-in-law would not grouch about, so these days he cooked. Sometimes his mother offered to help, but he wouldn't let her, afraid she might make something that Connie couldn't eat—she was allergic to most bean products, especially to soy sauce and tofu.

The moment he got home, he went into the kitchen. He was going to cook a spinach soup, steam the eggplant, and fry the flounder. As he was gouging out the gill of the fish, his mother stepped in. "Let me give you a hand," she said.

"I can manage. This is easy." He smiled, cutting the fish's fins and tail with a large scissor.

"You never cooked back home." She stared at him, her eyes glinting. Ever since her arrival a week earlier, she'd been nagging him about his being uxorious. "What's the good of standing six feet tall if you can't handle a small woman like Connie?" she often said. In fact, he was five foot ten.

He nudged the side of his bulky nose with his knuckle. "Mom, in America husband and wife both cook—whoever has the time. Connie is swamped with schoolwork these days, so I do more household chores. This is natural."

"No, it's not. You were never like this before. Why did you marry her in the first place if she wouldn't take care of you?"

"You're talking like a fuddy-duddy." He patted the flatfish with a paper towel to make it sputter less in the hot corn oil.

She went on, "Both your dad and I told you not to rush to marry her, but you were too bewitched to listen. We thought you must've got her in trouble and had to give her a wedding band. Look, now you're trapped and have to work both inside and outside the house."

He didn't reply, but his longish face stiffened. He disliked the way she spoke about his wife. In fact, before his mother's arrival, Connie had always come home early to make dinner. She would also wrap lunch for him early in the morning. These days, however, she'd leave the moment she finished breakfast and wouldn't return until evening. Both of them had agreed that she should avoid staying home alone with his mother, who lectured her at every possible opportunity.

Around six thirty his wife came home. She hung her parka in the closet and, stepping into the kitchen, said to Tian, "Can I help?"

"I'm almost done."

She kissed his nape and whispered, "Thanks for doing this." Then she took some plates and bowls out of the cupboard and carried them to the dining table. She glanced into the living room, where Meifen, her mother-in-law, lounged on a sofa, smoking a cigarette and watching the news aired by New Tang Dynasty TV, a remote control in her leathery hand. Connie and Tian had told her many times not to smoke in the house, but the old woman ignored them. They dared not confront her. This was just her second week here. Imagine, she was going to stay half a year!

"Mother, come and eat," Connie said pleasantly when the table was set.

"Sure." Meifen clicked off the TV, got to her feet, and scraped out her cigarette in a saucer serving as an ashtray.

The family sat down to dinner. The two women seldom

spoke to each other at the table, so it was up to Tian to make conversation. He mentioned that people in his company had been talking about layoffs. That didn't interest his mother and his wife; probably they both believed his job was secure because of his degree in accounting.

His mother grunted, "I don't like this fish. Flavorless, like egg white." She often complained that nothing here tasted right.

"It takes a while to get used to American food," Tian told her. "When I came, I couldn't eat vegetables in the first week, so I ate mainly bananas and oranges." That was long ago, twelve years exactly.

"True," Connie agreed. "I remember how rubbery bell peppers tasted to me in the beginning. I was amazed—"

"I mean this fish needs soy sauce, and so does the soup," Meifen interrupted.

"Mom, Connie's allergic to that. I told you."

"Just spoiled," Meifen muttered. "You have a bottle of Golden Orchid soy sauce in the cabinet. That's a brand-name product, and I can't see how on earth it can hurt anyone's health."

Connie's egg-shaped face fell, her eyes glaring at the old woman and then at Tian. He said, "Mom, you don't understand. Connie has a medical condition that—"

"Of course I know. I used to teach chemistry in a middle school. Don't treat me like an ignorant crone. Ours is an intellectual family."

"You're talking like an old fogey again. In America people don't think much of an intellectual family, and most kids here can go to college if they want to."

"She's hinting at my family," Connie broke in, and turned to face her mother-in-law. "True enough, neither of my parents went to college, but they're honest and hardworking. I'm proud of them."

"That explains why you're such an irresponsible wife," Meifen said matter-of-factly.

"Do you imply I'm not good enough for your son?"

"Please, let's have a peaceful dinner," Tian pleaded.

Meifen went on speaking to Connie. "So far you've been awful. I don't know how your parents raised you. Maybe they were too lazy or too ignorant to teach you anything."

"Watch it—you mustn't bad-mouth my parents!"

"I can say whatever I want to in my son's home. You married Tian but refuse to give him children, won't cook or do household work. What kind of wife are you? Worse yet, you even make him do your laundry."

"Mom," Tian said again, "I told you we'll have kids after Connie gets her degree."

"Believe me, she'll never finish school. She just wants to use you, giving you one excuse after another."

"I can't take this anymore." Connie stood and carried her bowl of soup upstairs to the master bedroom.

Tian sighed, again rattled by the exchange between the two women. If only he could make them shut up, but neither of them would give ground. His mother went on, "I told you not to break with Mansu, but you wouldn't listen. Look what a millstone you've got on your back." Mansu was Tian's ex-girlfriend. They'd broken up many years before, but somehow the woman had kept visiting his parents back in Harbin.

"Mom, don't bring that up again," he begged.

"You don't have to listen to me if you don't like it."

"Do you mean to destroy my marriage?"

At last Meifen fell silent. Tian heard his wife sniffling upstairs. He wasn't sure whether he should remain at the dining table or go join Connie. If he stayed with his mother, his wife would take him to task later on. But if he went to Connie, Meifen would berate him, saying he was spineless and daft. She used to teach him that a man could divorce his wife and marry another woman anytime, whereas he could never disown his mother. In Meifen's words: "You can always trust me, because you're part of my flesh and blood and I'll never betray you."

Tian took his plate, half loaded with rice and eggplant and a chunk of the fish, and went into the kitchen, where he perched on a stool and resumed eating. If only he'd thought twice before writing his mother the invitation letter needed for her visa. The old woman must still bear a grudge against him and Connie for not agreeing to sponsor his nephew, his sister's son, who was eager to go to Toronto for college. Perhaps that was another reason Meifen wanted to wreak havoc here.

Since his mother's arrival, Tian and his wife had slept in different rooms. That night he again stayed in the study, sleeping on a pullout couch. He didn't go upstairs to say good night to Connie. He was afraid she would demand that he send the old woman back to China right away. Also, if he shared the bed with Connie, Meifen would lecture him the next day, saying he must be careful about his health and mustn't indulge in sex. He'd heard her litany too often: some women were vampires determined to suck their men dry; this world had gone to seed—nowadays fewer and fewer young people were willing to become parents, and all avoided responsibilities; it was capitalism that corrupted people's souls and made them greedier and more selfish. Oh, how long-winded she could become! Just the thought of her prattling would set Tian's head reeling.

Before leaving for work the next morning, he drew a

map of the nearby streets for his mother and urged her to go out some so that she might feel less lonesome—"stir-crazy" was actually the word that came to his mouth, but he didn't let it out. She might like some of the shops downtown and could buy something with the eighty dollars he'd just given her. "Don't be afraid of getting lost," he assured her. She should be able to find her way back as long as she had the address he'd written down for her—someone could give her directions.

At work Tian drank a lot of coffee to keep himself awake. His scalp was numb and his eyes heavy and throbbing a little as he was crunching numbers. If only he could have slept two or three more hours a day. Ever since his mother had arrived, he'd suffered from sleep deficiency. He would wake up before daybreak, missing the warmth of Connie's smooth skin and their wide bed, but he dared not enter the master bedroom. He was certain she wouldn't let him snuggle under the comforter or touch her. She always gave the excuse that her head would go numb and muddled in class if they had sex early in the morning. That day at work, despite the strong coffee he'd been drinking, Tian couldn't help yawning and had to take care not to drop off.

Toward midmorning Bill Nangy, the manager of the company, stepped into the large, low-ceilinged room and went up to Tracy Malloy, whose cubicle was next to Tian's. "Tracy," Bill said, "can I speak to you in my office a minute?"

All the eyes turned to plump Tracy as she walked away with their boss, her head bowed a little. The second she disappeared past the door, half a dozen people stood up in their cubicles, some grinning while others shook their heads. Tracy, a good-natured thirtysomething, had started working there long before Tian. He liked her, though she talked too much.

Others had warned her to keep her mouth shut at work, but she'd never mended her ways.

A few minutes later Tracy came out, scratching the back of her ear, and forced a smile. "Got the ax," she told her colleagues, her eyes red and watery. She slouched into her cubicle to gather her belongings.

"It's a shame," Tian said to her, and rested his elbow on top of the chest-high wall, making one of his sloping shoulders higher than the other.

"I knew this was coming," she muttered. "Bill said he would allow me to stay another week, but I won't. Just sick of it."

"Don't be too upset. I'm sure more of us will go."

"Probably. Bill said there'll be more layoffs."

"I'll be the next, I guess."

"Don't jinx yourself, Tian."

Tracy put her eyeglass case beside her coffee cup. She didn't have much stuff—a few photos of her niece and nephews and of a Himalayan cat named Daffie, a half-used pack of chewing gum, a pocket hairbrush, a compact, a romance novel, a small Ziploc bag containing rubber bands, ballpoints, Post-its, dental floss, a ChapStick. Tian turned his eyes away as though the pile of her belongings, not enough to fill her tote bag, upset him more than her dismissal.

As Tracy was leaving, more people got up and some spoke to her. "Terribly sorry, Tracy." "Take care." "Good luck." "Keep in touch, Tracy." Some of the voices actually sounded relieved and even cheerful. Tracy shook hands with a few and waved at the rest while mouthing "Thank you."

The second she went out the door, George, an orange-haired man who always wore a necktie at work, said, "This is it," as if to assure everyone that they were all safe.

"I don't think so. More of us will get canned," Tian said gloomily.

Someone cackled as if Tian had cracked a joke. He didn't laugh or say another word. He sat down and tapped the spacebar on the keyboard to bring the monitor back to life.

"Oh, I never thought Flushing was such a convenient place, like a big county seat back home," his mother said to him that evening. She had gone downtown in the morning and had a wonderful time there. She tried some beef and lamb kebabs at a street corner and ate a tiny steamer of buns stuffed with chives, lean pork, and crabmeat at a Shanghai restaurant. She also bought a bag of mung bean noodles for only $1.20. "Really cheap," she said. "Now I believe it's true that all China's best stuff is in the U.S."

Tian smiled without speaking. He stowed her purchase in the cabinet under the sink because Connie couldn't eat bean noodles. He put a pot of water on the stove and was going to make rice porridge for dinner.

From that day on, Meifen often went out during the day and reported to Tian on her adventures. Before he left for work in the morning, he'd make sure she had enough pocket money. Gradually Meifen got to know people. Some of them were also from the northeast of China and were happy to converse with her, especially those who frequented the eateries that specialized in Mandarin cuisine—pies, pancakes, sauerkraut, sausages, grilled meats, moo shu, noodles, and dumplings. In a small park she ran into some old women pushing their grandchildren in strollers. She chatted with them, and found out that one woman had lived here for more than a decade and wouldn't go back to Wuhan City anymore because all her children and grandchildren were in North America now. How Meifen envied those old grandmas, she told Tian, especially the one who had twin grandkids. If only she could live a life such as theirs.

"You'll need a green card to stay here long enough to see my babies," Tian once told his mother jokingly.

"You'll get me a green card, won't you?" she asked.

Well, that was not easy, and he wouldn't promise her. She hadn't been here for three weeks yet, but already his family had become kind of dysfunctional. How simpleminded he and Connie had been when they encouraged Meifen to apply for a half-year visa. They should have limited her visit to two months or even less. That way, if she became too much of a pain in the ass, they could say it was impossible to get her visa extended, and she'd have no choice but to go back. Now, there'd be twenty-three more weeks for them to endure. How awful!

The other day Tian and Connie had talked between themselves about the situation. She said, "Well, I'll take these months as a penal term. After half a year, when the old deity has left, I hope I'll have survived the time undamaged and our union will remain unbroken." She gave a hysterical laugh, which unsettled Tian, and he wouldn't joke with her about their predicament anymore. All he could say was "I'm sorry, really sorry." Yet he wouldn't speak ill of his mother in front of his wife.

As Connie spent more time away from home, Tian often wondered what his wife was doing during the day. Judging from her appearance, she seemed at ease and just meant to avoid rubbing elbows with his mother. In a way, Tian appreciated that. Connie used to be a good helpmate by all accounts, but the old woman's presence here had transformed her. Then, who wouldn't have changed, given the circumstances? So he ought to feel for his wife.

One evening, as he was clearing the table while Connie was

doing the dishes in the kitchen, his mother said, "I ran into a fellow townswoman today, and we had a wonderful chat. I invited her to dinner tomorrow."

"Where are you going to take her?" Tian asked.

"Here. I told her you'd pick her up with your car."

Connie, having overheard their conversation, came in, holding a dish towel and grinning at Tian. Her bell cheeks were pink, while her eyes twinkled naughtily. Again Tian was amazed by her youthful face. She was a looker, six years younger than he. He was unhappy about Meifen's inviting a guest without telling him in advance, but before he could speak, Connie began, "Mother, there'll be a snowstorm tomorrow—Tian can't drive in the bad weather."

"I saw it on TV," Meifen said. "It will be just six or seven inches, no big deal. People even bike in snow back home."

Tian told her, "It's not whether I can pick up your friend or not, Mom. You should've spoken to me before you invited anyone. I'm busy all the time and must make sure my calendar allows it."

"You don't need to do anything," Meifen said. "Leave it to me. I'll do the shopping and cooking tomorrow."

"Mom, you don't get it. This is my home and you shouldn't interfere with my schedule."

"What did you say? Sure, this is your home, but who are you? You're my son, aren't you!"

Seeing a smirk cross his wife's face, Tian asked his mother, "You mean you own me and my home?"

"How can I ever disown you? Your home should also be mine. No? Oh heavens, I never thought my son could be so selfish. Once he has his bride, he wants to disown his mother!"

"You're unreasonable," he said.

"And you're heartless."

"This is ridiculous!" He turned and strode out of the dining room.

Connie put in, "Mother, just think about it—what if Tian already has another engagement tomorrow?"

"Like I said, he won't have to be around if he has something else to do. Besides, he doesn't work on Saturdays."

"Still, he'll have to drive to pick up your friend."

"How about you? Can't you do that?"

"I don't have a driver's license yet."

"Why not? You cannot let Tian do everything in this household. You must do your share."

Seeing this was getting nowhere, Connie dropped the dish towel on the dining table and went to the living room to talk with Tian.

However, Tian wouldn't discuss the invitation with Connie, knowing his mother was eavesdropping on them. Meifen, already sixty-four, still had sharp ears and eyesight. Tian grimaced at his wife and sighed. "I guess we'll have to do the party tomorrow."

She nodded. "I'll stay home and give you a hand."

It snowed on and off for a whole day. The roofs in the neighborhood blurred and lost their unkempt features, and the snow rendered all the trees and hedges fluffy. It looked clean everywhere, and even the air smelled fresher. Trucks passed by, giving out warning signals while plowing snow or spraying salt. A bunch of children were sledding on a slope, whooping lustily, and some lay supine on the sleds as they dashed down. Another pack of them were hurling snowballs at each other and shouting war cries. Tian, amused, watched them through a window. He had dissuaded his mother from giving a multiple-course dinner, saying that here food was plentiful and one could eat fish and meat quite often. Most times it was for conversation and a warm atmosphere that people went to dinner. His mother agreed to make dumplings in addition to a few cold dishes. Actually, they didn't start wrapping dumplings when the stuffing and the dough were ready, because Meifen wanted to have her friend participate in some way in preparing the dinner, to make the occasion somewhat like a family gathering.

Toward evening it resumed snowing. Tian drove to Corona to fetch the guest, Shulan, and his mother went with him, sitting in the passenger seat. The heat was on full blast, and the wipers were busy sweeping the windshield; even so, the glass frosted in spots on the outside and fogged on the inside. Time and again Tian mopped the moisture off the glass with a pair of felt gloves, but the visibility didn't improve much. "See what I mean?" he said to his mother. "It's dangerous to drive in such weather."

She made no reply, staring ahead, her beaky face as rigid as if frozen and the skin under her chin hanging in wattles. Fortunately, Shulan's place was easy to find. The woman lived in an ugly tenement about a dozen stories high and with narrow windows. She was waiting for them in the footworn lobby when they arrived. She looked familiar to Tian. Then he recognized her—this scrawny person in a dark blue overcoat was nobody but a saleswoman at the nameless snack joint on Main Street, near the subway station. He had encountered her numerous times when he went there to buy scallion pancakes or sautéed rice noodles or pork buns for lunch. He vividly remembered her red face bathed in perspiration during the dog days when she wore a white hat, busy selling food to passersby. That place was nothing but a flimsy lean-to, open to waves of heat and gusts of wind. In winter there was no need for a heater in the room because the stoves were hot and the pots sent up steam all the time, but in summer only a small fan whirred back and forth overhead. When customers were few, the salespeople would participate in making snacks, so everybody in there was a cook of sorts. Whenever Tian chanced on this middle-aged Shulan, he'd wonder what kind of tough life she must be living. What vitality, what endurance, and what sacrifice must have suffused her personal story? How often he'd been amazed by her rustic but energetic face, furrowed by lines that curved from the wings of her nose to the corners of her broad mouth. Now he was moved, eager to know more about this fellow townswoman. He was glad that his mother had invited her.

"Where's your daughter, Shulan?" Meifen asked, still holding her friend's chapped hand.

"She's upstairs doing a school project."

"Go get her. Let her come with us. Too much brainwork will spoil the girl's looks."

Tian said, "Please bring her along, Aunt."

"All right, I'll be back in a minute." Shulan went over to the elevator. From the rear she looked smaller than when she stood behind the food stand.

Tian and Meifen sat down on the lone bench in the lobby. She explained that Shulan's husband had come to the States seven years before, but had disappeared a year later. Nobody was sure of his whereabouts, though rumor had it that he was in Houston, manning a gift shop and living with a young woman. By now Shulan was no longer troubled by his absence from home. She felt he had merely used her as his cook and bed warmer, so she could manage without him.

"Mom, you were right to invite her," Tian said sincerely.

Meifen smiled without comment.

A few minutes later Shulan came down with her daughter,

a reedy, anemic fifteen-year-old wearing circular glasses and a checkered mackinaw that was too big on her. The girl looked unhappy and climbed into the car silently. As Tian drove away, he reminded the guests in the back to buckle up. Meanwhile, the snow abated some, but the flakes were still swirling around the streetlights and fluttering outside glowing windows. An ambulance howled, its strobe slashing the darkness. Tian pulled aside to let the white van pass, then resumed driving.

Tian and Connie's home impressed Shulan as Meifen gave her a tour through the two floors and the finished basement. The woman kept saying in a singsong voice, "This is a real piece of property, so close to downtown." Her daughter, Ching, didn't follow the grown-ups but stayed in the living room fingering the piano, a Steinway, which Tian had bought for Connie at a clearance sale. The girl had learned how to play the instrument before coming to the United States, though she could tickle out only a few simple tunes, such as "Jingle Bells," "Yankee Doodle Dandy," and "The Newspaper Boy Song." Even those sounded hesitant and disjointed. She stopped when her mother came back and told her not to embarrass both of them with her "clumsy fingers" anymore. The girl then sat before the TV, watching a well-known historian speaking about the recent Orange Revolution in Ukraine and its impact on the last few communist countries. Soon the four grown-ups began wrapping dumplings. Tian used a beer bottle to press the dough, having no rolling pin in the house. He was skilled but couldn't make wrappers fast enough for the three women, so Connie found a lean hot-sauce bottle and helped him with the dough from time to time. Meifen was unhappy about the lack of a real rolling pin and grumbled, "What kind of life you two have been living! You have no plan for a decent home."

Connie wouldn't talk back, just picked up a wrapper and filled it with a dollop of the stuffing, which was seasoned with sesame oil and five-spice powder. Shulan said, "If I lived so close to downtown, I wouldn't cook at all and would have no need for a rolling pin either." She kept smiling, her front teeth propping up her top lip a bit.

"Your place's pot stickers are delicious," Tian said to her to change the subject.

"I prepare the filling every day. Meifen, next time you stop by, you should try it. It tastes real good."

"Sure thing," Meifen said. "Did you already know how to make those snacks back home?"

"No way. I learned how to do that here. My boss used to be a hotel chef in Hangzhou."

"You must've gone through lots of hardships."

"I wouldn't complain. Life here is no picnic and most people work very hard."

Tian smiled quizzically, then said, "My dad retired at fifty-eight with a full pension. Every morning he carries a pair of goldfinches in a cage to the bank of the Songhua. Old people are having an easy time back home."

"Not every one of them," his mother corrected him. "Your father enjoys some leisure only because he joined the revolution early in his youth. He's entitled to his pension and free medical care."

"Matter of fact," Shulan said, "most folks are as poor as before in my old neighborhood. I have to send my parents money every two months."

"They don't have a pension?" Meifen asked.

"They do, but my mother suffers from gout and high blood pressure. My father lost most of his teeth and needed new dentures. Nowadays folks can't afford to be sick anymore."

"That's true," Tian agreed. "Most people are the have-nots."

The stout kettle whistled in the kitchen and it was time to boil the dumplings. Connie left to set the pot on, her waist-length hair swaying a little as she walked away. "You have a nice and pretty daughter-in-law," Shulan said to Meifen. "You're a lucky woman, elder sister."

"You don't know what a devil of a temper she has."

"Mom, don't start again," Tian begged.

"See, Shulan," Meifen whispered, "my son always sides with his bride. The little fox spirit really knows how to charm her man."

"This is unfair, Mom," her son objected.

Both women laughed and turned away to wash their hands.

Ten minutes later Tian went into the living room and called Ching to come over to the table, on which, besides the steaming dumplings, were plates of smoked mackerel, roast duck, cucumber and tomato salad, and spiced bamboo shoots. When they were all seated, with Meifen at the head of the rectangular table, Tian poured plum wine for Shulan and his mother. He and Connie and Ching would drink beer.

The two older women continued reminiscing about the people they both knew. To Tian's amazement, the girl swigged her glass of beer as if it were a soft drink. Then he remembered she had spent her childhood in Harbin, where even children were beer drinkers. He spoke English with her and asked her what classes she'd been taking at school. The girl seemed too introverted to volunteer any information and just answered each question with two or three words. She confessed that she hated the Sunday class, in which she had to copy the Chinese characters and memorize them.

Shulan mentioned a man nicknamed Turtle Baron, the owner of a fishery outside Harbin. "Oh, I knew of him,"

Meifen said. "He used to drive a fancy car to the shopping district every day, but he lost his fortune."

"What happened?" Shulan asked.

"He fed drugs to crayfish so they grew big and fierce, but some Hong Kong tourists got food-poisoned and took him to court."

"He was a wild man, but a filial son, blowing big money on his mother's birthdays. Where's he now?"

"In jail," Meifen said.

"Obviously that was where he was headed. The other day I met a fellow who had just come out of the mainland. He said he wouldn't eat street food back home anymore, because he couldn't tell what he was actually eating. Some people even make fake eggs and fake salt. It's mind-boggling. How can anyone turn a profit by doing that, considering the labor?"

They all cracked up except for the girl. Sprinkling a spoonful of vinegar on the three dumplings on her plate, Shulan continued, "People ought to believe in Jesus Christ. That'll make them behave better, less like animals."

"Do you often go to church?" Meifen asked, chewing the tip of a duck wing.

"Yes, every Sunday. It makes me feel calm and hopeful. I used to hate my husband's bone marrow, but now I don't hate him anymore. God will deal with him on my behalf."

Ching listened to her mother without showing any emotion, as if Shulan were speaking about a stranger. Meifen said, "Maybe I should visit your church one of these days."

"Please do. Let me know when you want to come. I'll introduce you to Brother Zhou, our pastor. He's a true gentleman. I've never met a man so kind. He used to be a doctor in Chengdu and still gives medical advice. He cured my stomach ulcer."

Connie, eating foçaccia bread instead of the dumplings that contained soy sauce, said under her breath, "Ching, do you have a boyfriend?"

Before the girl could answer, her mother cut in, pointing her chopsticks at her daughter. "I won't let her. It's just a waste of time to have a boyfriend so early. She'd better concentrate on her schoolwork."

Ching said to Connie in English, "See what a bitch my mom is? She's afraid I'll go boy-crazy like her when she was young." The girl's eyes flashed behind the lenses of her black-framed glasses.

Both Connie and Tian giggled while the two older women were bewildered, looking at them inquiringly. Tian told them, "Ching's so funny."

"Also tricky and headstrong," added her mother.

When dinner was over, Shulan was eager to leave without having tea. She said she'd forgotten to sprinkle water on the bean sprouts in her apartment, where the radiators were too hot and might shrivel the young vegetable, which she raised and would sell to a grocery store. Before they left, Connie gave the girl a book and assured her, "This is a very funny novel. I've just finished it and you'll like it."

Tian glanced at the title—*The Catcher in the Rye*—as Meifen asked, "What's it about?"

"A boy left school and goofed around in New York," Connie answered.

"So he's a dropout?"

"Kind of."

"Why give Ching such a book? It can be a bad influence. Do you mean to teach her to rebel against her mother?"

"It's a good book!" Connie spat out.

Tian said to the guests, "Let's go."

The moment they stepped out the door, he overheard his mother growl at Connie, "Don't play the scholar with me! Don't ever talk back to me in front of others!"

"You were wrong about the book," Connie countered.

Their exchange unsettled Tian, who knew they would bicker more while he was away. Outside, it got windy and the road iced over. He drove slowly. Before every intersection he placed his foot on the brake pedal to make sure he could stop the car fully if the light turned red. Ching was in the back dozing away while her mother in the passenger seat chatted to Tian without pause. She praised Meifen as an educated woman who gave no airs. How fortunate Tian must feel to have such a clearheaded and warmhearted mother, in addition to a beautiful, well-educated wife. Her words made Tian's molars itch, and he wanted to tell her to shut her trap, but he checked himself. He still felt for this woman. Somehow he couldn't drive from his mind her image behind the food stand, her face steaming with sweat and her eyes downcast in front of customers while her knotted hands were packing snacks into Styrofoam boxes.

He dropped Shulan and Ching at their building and turned back. After he exited the highway and as he was entering College Point Boulevard, a police cruiser suddenly rushed out of a narrow street and slid toward him from the side. Tian slammed on the brakes, but the heads of the two cars collided with a bang; his Volkswagen, much lighter than the bulky Ford, was thrown aside and fishtailed a few times before it stopped. Tian's head had hit the door window, and his ears were buzzing, though he was still alert.

A black policeman hopped out of the cruiser and hurried over. "Hey, man, are you okay?" he cried, and knocked on Tian's windshield.

Tian opened his door and nodded. "I didn't see you. Sorry about this, officer." He clambered out.

"I'm sorry, man." Somehow the squarish cop chuckled. "I hit you. I couldn't stop my car—the road is too damned slippery."

Tian walked around and looked at the front of his car. The glass covers of the headlight and the blinker were smashed, but somehow all the lights were still on. A dent the size of a football warped the fender. "Well, what should I do?" he wondered aloud.

The police officer grinned. "It's my fault. My car slid into the traffic. How about this—I give you a hundred bucks and you won't file a report?"

Tian peered at the officer's catlike face and realized that the man was actually quite anxious—maybe he was new here. "Okay," Tian said, despite knowing that the amount might not cover the repairs.

"You're a good guy." The policeman pulled five twenties out of his billfold. "Here you are. I appreciate it."

Tian took the money and stepped into his car. The officer shouted, "God bless you!" as Tian drove away. He listened closely to his car, which sounded noisier than before. He hoped there was no inner damage. On the other hand, this was an old car, worth less than a thousand dollars. He shouldn't worry too much about the dent.

The instant he stepped into his house, he heard his mother yell, "Oh yeah? How much have you paid for this house? This is my son's home and you should be grateful that Tian has let you live here."

"This is my home too," Connie fired back. "You're merely our guest, a visitor."

Heavens, they would never stop fighting! Tian rushed into the living room and shouted, "You two be quiet!"

But Connie turned to him and said sharply, "Tell your mother I'm a co-owner of this house."

That was true, yet his mother also knew that Connie hadn't paid a cent for it. Tian had added her name as a co-buyer because he wanted her to keep the home if something fatal happened to him.

His mother snarled at Connie, "Shameless. A typical ingrate from an upstart's family!"

"Don't you dare run down my dad! He makes an honest living." Indeed, her father in Tianjin City was just scraping by with his used-furniture business.

"Knock it off, both of you!" Tian roared again. "I just had an accident. Our car was damaged, hit by a cop."

Even that didn't impress the women. Connie cried at Meifen, "See, I told you there'd be a snowstorm, but you were too vain to cancel the dinner. Did you mean to have your son killed?"

"It was all my fault, huh? Why didn't you learn how to drive? What have you been doing all these years?"

"I've never met someone so irrational."

"I don't know anyone as rude and as brazen as you."

"Damn it, I just had an accident!" Tian shouted again.

His wife looked him up and down. "I can see you're all right. It's an old car anyway. Let's face the real issue here: I cannot live under the same roof with this woman. If she doesn't leave, I will and I'll never come back." She marched away to her own room upstairs.

As Tian was wondering whether he should follow her, his mother said, "If you're still my son, you must divorce her. Do it next week. She's a sick, finicky woman and will give you weak kids."

"You're crazy too!" he growled.

He stomped away and shut the door of the study, in which

he was to spend that night trying to figure out how to prevent Connie from walking out on him. He would lose his mind if that happened, he was sure.

On Monday morning Tian went to Bill Nangy's office. The manager looked puzzled when Tian sat down in front of him. "Well, what can I do for you, Tian?" Bill asked in an amiable voice. He waved his large hand over the steaming coffee his secretary, Jackie, had just put on the desk. His florid face relaxed some as he saw Tian still in a gentle mood.

Tian said, "I know our company has been laying off people. Can you let me go, like Tracy Malloy?" He looked his boss full in the face.

"Are you telling me you got an offer from elsewhere?"

"No. In fact, I will appreciate it if you can write me a good recommendation. I'll have to look for a job soon."

"Then why do you want to leave us?"

"For family reasons."

"Well, what can I say, Tian? You've done a crack job here, but if that's what you want, we can let you go. Keep in mind, you're not among those we plan to discharge. We'll pay you an extra month's salary, and I hope that may tide you over until you find something."

"Thanks very much."

Tian liked his job, but he had never felt attached to the company. He was pretty sure that he could find similar work elsewhere but might not get paid as much as he made now. Yet this was a step he must take. Before the noon break Jackie put a letter of recommendation on Tian's desk, together with a card from his boss that wished him all good luck.

Tian's departure was a quiet affair, unnoticed by others. He was reluctant to talk about it, afraid he might have to explain why he had quit. He just ate lunch and crunched some potato chips in the lounge with his colleagues as though he would resume working in the afternoon as usual. But before the break was over, he walked out with his stuffed bag without saying good-bye to anyone.

He didn't go home directly. Instead, he went to a KTV joint and had a few drinks—a lager, a martini, a rye whiskey on the rocks. A young woman, heavily made up and with her hair bleached blond, slid her hips onto the barstool beside him. He ordered her a daiquiri but was too glum to converse with her. Meanwhile, two other men were chattering about Uncle Benshan, the most popular comedian in China, who was coming to visit New York, but the tickets for his show were too expensive for the local immigrants, and as a result, his sponsors had been calling around to drum up an audience for him. When the woman placed her thin hand on Tian's forearm and suggested the two of them spend some time in a private room where she could cheer him up, he declined, saying he had to attend a meeting.

Afterward, he roamed downtown for a while, then went to a pedicure place to have his feet bathed and scraped. Not until the streets turned noisier and the sky darkened to indigo did he head home. But today he returned without any groceries. He went to bed directly and drew the duvet up to his chin. When his mother came in and asked what he'd like for dinner, he merely grunted, "Whatever."

"Are you ill?" She felt his forehead.

"Leave me alone," he groaned.

"You're burning hot. What happened?"

Without answering, he pulled the comforter over his head. If only he could sleep a few days in a row. He felt sorry for himself and sick of everything.

Around six his wife came back. The two women talked in the living room. Tian overheard the words "drunk," "so gruff," "terrible." Then his mother whined, "Something is wrong. He looks like he's in a daze."

A few moments later Connie came in and patted his chest. He sat up slowly. "What happened?" she asked.

"I got fired."

"What? They didn't tell you anything beforehand?"

"No. They've been issuing pink slips right and left."

"But they should've given you a warning or something, shouldn't they?"

"Come on, this is America. People lose jobs all the time."

"What are you going to do?"

"I've no clue. I'm so tired."

They continued talking for a while. Then he got out of bed, and together they went up to Meifen in the living room. His mother started weeping after hearing the bad news, while he sprawled on a sofa, his face vacant. She asked, "So you have no job anymore?" He grimaced without answering. She went on, "What does this mean? You won't have any income from now on?"

"No. We might lose the house, the car, the TV, everything. I might not even have the money for the plane fare for your return trip."

His mother shuffled away to the bathroom, wiping her eyes. Connie observed him as if in disbelief. Then she smiled, showing her tiny, well-kept teeth, and asked in an undertone, "Do you think I should look for a job?"

"Sure," he whispered. "But I shouldn't work for the time being. You know what I mean?" He winked at her, thin rays fanning out at the corners of his eyes.

She nodded and took the hint. Then she went into the

kitchen to cook dinner. She treated her mother-in-law politely at the table that evening and kept sighing, saying this disaster would ruin their life. It looked like Tian and she might have to file for Chapter 11 bankruptcy if neither of them could land a job soon.

Meifen was shaken and could hardly eat anything. After dinner, they didn't leave the table. Connie brewed tea, and they resumed talking. Tian complained that he hadn't been able to stay on top of his job because his wife and his mother quarreled all the time. That was the root of his trouble and made him too frazzled to focus on anything. In fact, he said, he had felt the disaster befalling him and mentioned it to them several times, but they'd paid no attention.

"Can you find another job?" his mother asked.

"Unlikely. There're more accountants than pets in New York—this is the world's financial center. Probably Connie can find work before I can."

"I won't do that until I finish my training," his wife said, poker-faced.

"Please, do it as a favor for me," Meifen begged her.

"No, I want to finish nursing school first. I still have two months to go."

"You'll just let this family go to pieces without lifting a finger to help?" her mother-in-law asked.

"Don't question me like that. You've been damaging this family ever since you came." Connie glanced at Tian, who showed no response. She continued, "Now your son's career is headed for a dead end. Who's to blame but yourself?"

"Is that true, Tian?" his mother asked. "I mean, your career's over?"

"Sort of. I'll have to figure out how to restart."

Meifen heaved a deep sigh. "I told your sister I shouldn't

come to America, but she was greedy and wanted me to get you to finance her son's college in Canada. She even managed to have the boy's last name changed to Chu so he could appear as your son on the papers. Now it's over. I'll call her and your father tomorrow morning and let them know I'm heading back."

Connie peered at Tian's face, which remained wooden. He stood and said, "I'm dog-tired." He left for the study.

Meifen wrapped Connie's hand in both of hers and begged, "Please help him survive this crisis! Don't you love him? Believe me, he'll do everything to make you happy if you help him get on his feet again. Connie, you're my good daughter-in-law. Please do something to save your family!"

"Well, I can't promise anything. I've never been on the job market before."

Tian smiled and shook his head as he was listening in on them from the study. He was sure that his wife knew how to seize this opportunity to send his mother home.

For a whole week Tian stayed in while Connie called around and went out job-hunting. She had several interviews. It wasn't hard for her to find work since she was already a capable nurse. The following Wednesday a hospital in Manhattan offered her a position that paid well, plus full benefits, and she persuaded the manager to postpone her start for a week. She showed the job-offer letter to her husband and mother-in-law. "Gosh," Tian said, "you'll make more than I ever can."

Meifen perused the sheet of paper. Despite not understanding a word, she saw the figure "$32." She asked in amazement, "Connie, does this mean they'll pay you thirty-two dollars an hour?"

"Yes, but I'm not sure if I should take the job."

"Don't you want to save this home?"

"This house doesn't feel like a home to me anymore."

"How can you be so coldhearted while your husband is in hot water?"

"You made me, and Tian always takes your side. So this house is no longer my home. Let the bank repossess it—I could care less."

Tian said nothing and just gazed at the off-white wall where a painting of a cloudy landscape dotted with fishing boats and flying cranes hung. His mother started sobbing again. He sighed and glanced at his wife. He knew Connie must have accepted the job. "Mom," he said, "you came at a bad time. See, I can't make you live comfortably here anymore. Who knows what will happen to me if things don't improve? I might jump in front of a train or drive into the ocean."

"Please don't think like that! You two must join hands and survive this blow."

"I've lost heart after going through so much. This blow finished me off, and I may never recover."

"Son, please pull yourself together and put up a fight."

"I'm just too heartsick to give a damn."

Connie butted in, "Mother, how about this? You go back to China next week and let Tian and me concentrate on the trouble here."

"So I'm your big distraction, huh?"

"Yes, Mom," Tian said. "You two fought and fought and fought, and that made my life unbearable. I was completely stupefied and couldn't perform well at work. That's why they terminated me."

"All right, I'll go next week, leave you two alone, but you must give me some money. I can't go back empty-handed or our neighbors will laugh at me." Her lips quivered as she spoke, her mouth as sunken as if she were toothless.

"I'll give you two thousand dollars," Connie said. "Once I start working, I'll send you more. Don't worry about the gifts for the relatives and your friends. We'll buy you some small pieces of jewelry and a couple packs of Wisconsin ginseng."

"How about a pound of vegetable caterpillars? That will help Tian's father's bad kidneys."

"That costs five thousand dollars! You can get them a lot cheaper in China. Tell you what—I can buy you five pounds of dried sea cucumbers, the Japanese type. That will help improve my father-in-law's health too."

Meifen agreed, reluctantly—the sea cucumbers were at most four hundred dollars a pound. Yet her son's situation terrified her. If he declared bankruptcy, she might get nothing from the young couple, so she'd better take the money and leave. Worse, she could see that Tian might lose his mind if Connie left him at this moment. Meifen used to brag about him as a paragon of success to her neighbors and friends. She had never imagined that his life could be so fragile that it would crumble in just one day. No wonder people always talked about stress and insecurity in America.

Connie said pleasantly, "Mother, I won't be able to take the job until I see you off at the airport. In the meantime, I'll have to help Tian get back on his feet."

"I appreciate that," Meifen said.

That night Connie asked Tian to share the master bedroom with her, but he wouldn't, saying they mustn't nettle his mother from now on. He felt sad, afraid that Meifen might change her mind. He remembered that when he was taking the entrance exam fourteen years back, his parents had stood in the rain under a shared umbrella, waiting for him with a lunch tin, sodas, and tangerines wrapped in a handkerchief. They each had half a shoulder soaked through. Oh, never could he forget their anxious faces. A surge of gratitude drove him to the brink of tears. If only he could speak freely to them again.

Shame

SOON AFTER I'D FOUND a summer job in Flushing, I received a phone call one evening. I was thrilled to hear the voice of Professor Meng, who had come to visit some U.S. universities with a delegation of educators. He used to be my teacher, an expert in American studies at my alma mater back in Nanjing. He had translated a book of short stories by Jack London and was known as a literary scholar in China.

"Where are you staying, Mr. Meng?" I asked.

"At the Chinese consulate here."

"Can I come and see you?"

"Not tonight—I'm leaving for a party. But we'll be here for a few days. Can we meet tomorrow?"

I agreed to see him the next afternoon. According to him, after New York, his delegation would head for Boston and then for Chicago and Minneapolis. Mr. Meng had taught me in 1985, for only one semester, in a course in American Jewish fiction. He was not a remarkable teacher—his voice was too flat and at times unclear—but he had a phenomenal memory and was able to give a lot of information on authors and books, some of which I suspected he hadn't read because they were unavailable in China at the time. He was then in his early fifties, but trim and agile—a fine Ping-Pong player. He often chaffed me, saying I looked already fortyish, though I was only twenty-five. I did appear much older than my age in those days, perhaps owing to my melancholy eyes and to the dull headache I used to have in the mornings. I didn't mind Mr. Meng's joking, though. In a way I felt that he treated me better than the other teachers did.

It was overcast and muggy the next morning, as if the whole city of New York were inside a bathhouse. As usual, Ah Min and I set out with a van to deliver fabrics. He was behind the wheel while I sat in the navigator's seat. We first stopped at a sweatshop on Ninth Street in Brooklyn and dropped a few bundles of cloth there. Then we drove to downtown Manhattan and unloaded the rest of the materials at a larger factory on Mott Street. Its workshop was on the third floor of a building, and it was noisy in there, the purring and humming of sewing machines accented by the thumps of pressing irons. The floor was littered with scraps of cloth, and stacks of fabrics for coats sat against the walls. Some sewers and finishers, all women, were wearing earphones while their hands were busy. Our unloading was easy, but after that, we were to send finished products to clothing stores. We had to handle the suits and dresses carefully to avoid creasing or dirtying any of them. A thin shadow of a fellow with a pallid face helped us. Together we pulled large plastic bags over the finished garments, one for each, and then hung them on racks with wheels. After that, we took the racks down by the elevator to the first floor, which was five feet above the ground. Ah

Min backed the van up to the platform of the elevator, and I put two gangplanks in place so we could pull the racks into the vehicle. The process was slow and exacting; every time it took almost two hours. We had to be very careful, because our boss, a middle-aged man from Hong Kong, would reprimand us for any damaged product, though he had never docked our wages.

Before setting out that morning, I'd spoken to our boss, who let me have the afternoon off. Ah Min dropped me at Union Square around two p.m. after we'd delivered the last batch of suits to a haberdasher's on Fifth Avenue. He was a friendly fellow with a sleepy look in his eyes and often teased me, probably because I was a temp, as yet unable to drive confidently in Manhattan, and would return to school in Wisconsin when the summer ended. Indeed, I had come to New York mainly to make some money and to see the city, which my master's thesis adviser, Professor Freeman, had said I must visit if I wanted to understand America.

When I got out of the subway, I found it had started drizzling. As I strode along Forty-second Street toward the Hudson, I regretted not having brought an umbrella with me. The neon lights, obscured some by the powdery rain, were glowing like naked limbs. They were more voluptuous than on a fine day, as if beckoning to pedestrians, but I had to hustle to avoid being drenched. Seven or eight minutes later, I got into the Chinese consulate's entryway, in which about a dozen people were waiting for the drizzle to stop. An old man with a puffy face and small eyes was in the reception office, reading the overseas edition of *The People's Daily*. I told him my teacher's name and the purpose of my visit. He picked up the phone and punched a number.

A few moments later Mr. Meng came down. He looked the

same as three years before. We shook hands; then, in spite of my wet polo shirt, we hugged. He was happy to see me, about to take me into the consulate.

"Wait, stop!" the old man cried through the window of the reception office. "You can't go in."

I produced my maroon-covered passport and opened it to show my photo. I said, "See, I'm not a foreigner."

"Makes no difference. You're not allowed to go in."

My teacher intervened. "I'm staying here. Please let us in, comrade. He was my student. We haven't seen each other for more than three years."

"Have to follow the rule—no visitor is allowed to enter this building."

My temper was rising. Just now I had seen a young woman, apparently a visitor, go in with a nod of her head at the geezer. I asked him, "Doesn't this building belong to China? As a citizen, don't I have the right to enter Chinese territory?"

"No, you don't. Stop wagging your clever tongue here. I've met lots of gasbags like you." His lackluster eyes flared.

"You make me ashamed of holding this passport," I spat out.

"Get a blue one with a big eagle on it—as if you could."

Mr. Meng said again, "We won't go upstairs. There're some chairs in the lobby; can't we just sit over there for an hour or two? We'll stay in your view."

"No, you cannot."

The entryway was so crowded by now that we couldn't chat in there, so we went out in spite of the rain. We crossed Twelfth Avenue and observed for a while the aircraft carrier *Intrepid* exhibited on the Hudson, then turned onto Forty-fourth Street, where we found a diner set near a construction site, at a corner of which stood a pair of Porta Pottis. The place offered Italian fare. Mr. Meng ordered spaghetti with meatballs and I had a small pepperoni pizza. He confessed he'd never eaten pasta before, though he had come across words like "macaroni," "tagliatelle," "vermicelli," and "linguini" in American novels and knew they were all Italian noodles. I was pleased that he enjoyed the food, especially the tomato sauce and the Parmesan cheese, to which my stomach was as yet unaccustomed. He told me, "This is so hearty and healthy. I can taste olive oil and basil." I couldn't share his enthusiasm, since I still ate Chinese food most of the time.

He went on, "New York is so rich even the air smells fatty." He lifted his Heineken and took a gulp.

After reminiscing about some of my former classmates who had recently left China, he asked me, "How much can you make a month here?" His large nose twitched as a smile came on his narrow face.

"I'm paid by the hour, five-forty an hour."

He lowered his head to do the sum. Then he raised his eyes and said, "Wow, you make at least twenty times more than I can back home. In a few years you'll be rolling in money."

I smiled without a word. He hadn't considered that I had to spend more and pay taxes. He could hardly imagine how hard I worked. A stout waitress wearing an orange apron came over and handed us the dessert menu. I recommended that we both try the crème brûlée cheesecake, and he agreed. I liked desserts, which to me were the best part of American food. Sipping his coffee, he sighed. "What I wouldn't give to be in your shoes, Hongfan."

"I'm just a student. How can you say that?" I said.

"But you're doing graduate work in the United States and will be a real scholar someday, not like my generation, ruined by political movements in our formative years. We're a true lost generation."

"But you're already a professor."

"That's just a title. What have I accomplished? Nothing

worth mentioning. So many years wasted, it's impossible to make up for the loss."

I remembered his translation of Jack London's stories, which was a respectable effort, but I didn't bring that up. I was moved in a way; few teachers at my alma mater would speak so candidly to a student. When the cheesecake had come, he asked me whether I'd like to accompany him to meet with Professor Natalie Simon at Columbia. I was reluctant, afraid I'd lose another afternoon's work, but knowing that Simon was a famous scholar in modern American literature, I agreed to go with him. I assumed I could get permission from my boss again.

After dinner, I took Mr. Meng back to the consulate and promised to meet him at one thirty the following day. The rain had let up and the clouds were breaking, but the air was still as muggy as if it were rubbing your skin. Having seen him disappear in the entryway, I turned toward the subway station.

To my relief, my boss gladly allowed me another afternoon off, saying his daughter had graduated from Barnard College, so he liked the idea that I would accompany my former teacher to visit the university. My boss was in a jolly frame of mind these days, because his daughter had just passed her bar exam. When I joined Mr. Meng outside the consulate, he was holding a shoulder bag. I wondered if I should carry that for him, but thought better of it in case it contained something valuable. Together we took the No. 3 train uptown.

Columbia's English department was easy to find, and the door of Professor Simon's office was open. She welcomed us warmly and seated us on the only sofa in the room, which had tall windows. She waved apologetically, saying, "Sorry about such a mess in here."

She was younger than I'd thought, in her late thirties and with a regal bone structure and sparkling eyes, but her face was heavily freckled and so were her arms. Mr. Meng was fluent in English, though he had studied Russian originally and switched to this language in the early 1960s when China and the former Soviet Union had fallen out. He began talking to Professor Simon about a bibliography of American literary works already translated into Chinese—a project that he had been in charge of, funded by the government. I listened without speaking. "In addition," he told her, "we have been writing a U.S. literary history, a college textbook. I will contribute two chapters."

"That's marvelous," she said. "I wish I could read Chinese. It would be interesting to see what the Chinese scholars think of our literature."

I knew that six or seven professors had been working on that book, which would be nothing but a mishmash of articles based on the summaries of some novels and plays and on rehashing official views and interpretations. Besides the censorship that makes genuine scholarship difficult, if not impossible, some of those contributors were merely dilettantes. In most cases these people didn't know American literature at all. Professor Simon had better remain ignorant of Chinese, or she would surely be underwhelmed. She lifted two books, both hardcovers, from her desk and put them on the coffee table before us. "These are my recent books," she said. "I hope you'll like them." The top one was titled *Landscapes in Modern American Fiction,* but I couldn't see the title of the other one.

Mr. Meng touched the books. "Can you sign them for me?" he asked her.

"I've done that."

"These are precious. Thank you."

To my amazement, he took a brown silk carton out of his shoulder bag and handed it to Professor Simon, saying, "Here's a little present for you."

She was pleased and opened the box. An imitation-ivory mahjong set emerged, glossy and crisp in the fluorescent light. "Oh, this is gorgeous." Despite saying that, she seemed bewildered, and her jaw dropped a bit, as if her mouth were holding something hard to swallow.

"Do you play mahjong?" asked Mr. Meng.

"I don't know how, but my mother-in-law often plays it with her friends. She's retired, so this will be perfect for her."

A sour taste seeped into my mouth as I observed my teacher putting the two books into his bag. His manner was as natural as if he were an old friend of hers. In fact, he'd told me they'd met only once.

We didn't stay longer because Professor Simon was going to teach at three. She said she'd be delighted to visit Nanjing again if she was allowed to join the U.S. delegation that would go to China the next spring.

Coming out of the building with immense columns at its portals, I said half joshingly to Mr. Meng, "How many sets of mahjong did you bring along for this trip?"

"Six, but I have some sandalwood fans with me too. I give a set of mahjong only to an important figure."

His tone of voice was so earnest that I didn't know how to continue. He had no sense of irony and couldn't see that I was troubled by the discrepancy between the two kinds of gifts exchanged between him and Natalie Simon. I remained tongue-tied as we headed for the front entrance of the campus. He knew how to get back to the consulate, saying he had a map and would like to stretch his legs a little on such a gorgeous day, so we said good-bye and I went down into the subway station alone.

• • •

June was soon over. During the day I delivered fabrics and finished garments, and at night I pored over Edward Said's *Orientalism.* I thought that Mr. Meng had left with the delegation for Boston. Maybe he was in the Midwest now. But to my surprise, one evening I got a call from him.

"Where are you?" I asked.

"Still in New York," came his soft voice.

"You mean you didn't leave with the others?" I was astonished to realize that he'd left the delegation.

"Right. I don't want to go back too soon," he said flatly.

For a moment I was too stunned to respond. Then I managed to say, "Mr. Meng, it will be very hard for someone your age to survive here."

"I know. My wife is ill and we need to pay for her medicines and hospital bills. I could never make that kind of money in China, so I decided to stay on."

I was unsure if he was telling me the truth, but it was true that his wife had been in poor health. I said, "You may never be able to go home again."

"I won't mind. A human being should live like a bird, untrammeled by any man-made borders. I can be buried anywhere when I die. The reason I'm calling is to ask you to put me up for a few days."

I knew that my accommodating him might implicate me in his defection, but he was my former teacher, someone I was obligated to help. "Okay, you're welcome," I said.

I gave him my address and the directions. I didn't feel comfortable about sharing my tiny apartment with anyone. I hoped Mr. Meng would take my place only temporarily. Two hours later he arrived with a bulky suitcase and his shoulder bag. Since he hadn't eaten dinner, I cooked a pack of instant noodles for him, adding to it two chicken legs, two eggs, and a bunch of cilantro. He enjoyed the meal, saying this was the best dinner he had eaten since he'd left home. "Better than the banquet food," he told me. I asked him where he'd been all these days, and he confessed that he had stayed with a friend in the Bronx, but that man was leaving for upstate New York for a job in a casino, and so Mr. Meng had to look for lodging elsewhere.

In a way I admired his calm, though his round eyes blazed feverishly. If I were in his position, I might have gone bonkers. But he was an experienced man, toughened by a hard life, especially by the seven years he had spent on a chicken farm in the countryside. After the meal, it was already half past ten. We sat at the shaky dining table, chatting and sharing a pack of Newports and jasmine tea. We talked and talked, and not until around two a.m. did we decide to turn in. I wanted him to use my bed, which was just a mattress on the floor, but he insisted on sleeping on the sofa.

We both believed he needed to keep a low profile for the time being lest the consulate track him down. He shouldn't go out during the day, and every morning I'd lock him in when setting out for work. I always stocked enough food and soft drinks for him, and he would cook dinner for both of us before I came back in the evening. He seemed very patient, in good spirits. Besides groceries, I also brought back Chinese-language newspapers and magazines. He devoured all of them and said he'd never thought that the news here was so different from that in mainland China. The articles revealed so many secrets of Chinese politics and gave such diverse interpretations of historical events that he often excitedly briefed me at the table about what he had read. Sometimes I was too exhausted to listen, but I wouldn't dampen his excitement.

On my way home one evening I came across a barely used mattress dumped on a sidewalk. Together Mr. Meng and I went over and carried it back. From that day on he slept in the second bed in my room. He often jabbered at night, having bad dreams. Once he woke me up and kept sputtering, "I'll get revenge! I have powerful friends at the Provincial Administration. We will wipe out you and your cronies!"

Despite that kind of disturbance, I was glad to have him here—his presence reduced my loneliness.

Two weeks later we began talking about what he should do. I had stopped locking him in and he often went out. So far, his disappearance had been kept secret by the consulate, and no newspaper had reported it. That might not be a good sign, though, and the silence unnerved us, so I felt he should remain in hiding. Yet he was eager to work to earn his keep. I advised him to wait another week, but he wouldn't listen, saying, "We're in the United States and mustn't live in fear anymore."

We both believed he shouldn't apply for political asylum right away, since that should be a last resort and would mean he might never set foot in our motherland again. It would be better if he just lived here as an illegal alien to make some money. He could try to change his status when things cooled down—once he had the wherewithal, he could hire an attorney for that. Soon he began looking for a job in Flushing, which wasn't like a city yet in the late 1980s; housing was less expensive there, and businesses had just begun moving in. Since he spoke English, it wasn't hard for him to find work. A restaurant near Queens Botanical Garden hired him to wait tables, but he persuaded its manager, Michael Chian, who was a co-owner of the place, to let him start as a dishwasher on the pretext that he had no work experience at a restaurant. His real reason was that a dishwasher spent most of his hours in the kitchen, away from the public eye. The next day he started at Panda Terrace, making $4.60 an hour. He was pleased, although when he came back around eleven at night he'd complain he was bone-tired.

He was capable, and his boss and coworkers liked him. On occasion I went to the restaurant for a bowl of noodles or fried rice. I rarely ate dinner at that place, which I frequented mainly to see how Mr. Meng was doing. To my discomfort, the waitstaff called him "professor." He'd been rash to reveal his former identity to his fellow workers, but I said nothing about it. He seemed at ease in spite of washing dishes all day long. He told me he'd been observing the staff wait tables and concluded that he could do it easily. In a month or two he might switch jobs, either working as a waiter at the same place or moving on to another restaurant.

One Sunday afternoon my coworker Ah Min and I went to Panda Terrace for a bowl of wontons. As we were eating, two white girls in their late teens pulled into the parking lot and came over to the front door. Mayling, the barrel-waisted hostess and also a co-owner of the place, went up to them and snapped, "You can't eat here, no more."

The girls stopped short in the doorway, one wearing a sky blue sarong and bra, hoop earrings, and mirror sunglasses, while the other was also in a sarong and bra, but a yellow one. They were both chewing gum. "Why? We have money," the tall one in blue said, smiling spuriously and baring her flawless teeth.

The other girl grinned with her rouged lips, her kohl-rimmed eyes flickering. She said, "We love your eggplant fries. Mmm, yummy! Your dumplings are excellent too."

"Go away. We don't serve you," said Mayling, who tended to speak English haltingly unless she was angry.

"This is America and you can't throw your customers out, d'you know?" the shorter girl kept on.

"You're not our customer. You two didn't pay last time. I follow you to parking lot, and you saw me, but you just drived away."

"How can you be so sure it was us?"

"Get outta here, thief!"

"Don't be so nasty, China lady," the tall one said, smirking while her tongue wiped her bottom lip. "How can you prove we didn't pay you? You're barking up the wrong tree."

"Don't call me dog! Go away!" The hostess flung up her hand, rattling the jade bangles around her wrist.

The girl in yellow put in, "You can't accuse us like this. See, I have money." She took out a sheaf of singles and fives and waved them in front of Mayling's face.

Purple with anger, the hostess warned, "If you don't leave now, I call police."

"Oh yeah?" the tall girl shot back. "We're the ones who can use a cop. You accuse us of theft with no evidence. D'you know what this means in America? It's called slander, a crime. We can sue you."

"Yeah, we're gonna sue your pants off," added the one in yellow.

Mayling looked confused, but Mr. Meng strolled up to them, his hands clasped behind his back. In an even voice he said to the girls, "Ladies, you mustn't take advantage of us again. Please leave."

"God, I'm so hungry! Why can't we just have a little bite?" persisted the shorter one in yellow.

Mayling roared, "Get the hell outta here, you robber! We don't want to serve you."

"How dare you call us that?"

"You are robber. You rob us. What else you are? If you want to eat here again, give us thirty-seven dollars you didn't pay."

"C'mon. Like I said, you're talking to the wrong people." The tall girl put on a suave smile. "Did you ever see this pair of sunglasses before?"

"No, but I remember your earring."

"Give me a break. Lots of women wear this type of earrings. You can get these at Macy's for eighteen bucks."

Mr. Meng said again, "We have kept a record—your car's plate number is 895 NTY, right?"

"Yes," Mayling picked up. "If you don't go away now, I call Officer Steve again, and you can't see your mama tonight."

The girls both gave a gasp. Observing them from where I sat, I wanted to laugh but checked myself. The one in yellow grasped her friend's elbow and said, "Come, let's get out of here. This is nuts."

They both went out, teetering in wedge heels toward their scarlet coupe, their purses flapping. As they were pulling away, both Ah Min and I stood to look at the license plate, which matched the number Mr. Meng had declared.

"Bravo!" my coworker cried.

"Wow, that was extraordinary," I told my teacher.

Michael Chian, Mayling's husband, had witnessed the scene, but was unable to put in a word the whole while. Now he kept saying to Mr. Meng, "Amazing. You remembered their plate number, tsk tsk tsk. I can never do that, not even if you beat me to death."

Later Mr. Meng told me in private that he had just snuck out and looked at the license plate while Mayling and the girls were quarreling. That cracked me up. Indeed, he was a clever man, worldly wise.

His resourcefulness impressed his boss so much that Michael offered him the manager's position at the new place in upper Manhattan that the Chians were about to open, but Mr. Meng said he was too old for a job like that.

One night in the following week he returned with a copy of *Big Apple Journal,* a local Chinese-language newspaper, and slapped it on the dining table. "Damn Michael, he blabbed to some reporter about the two shameless girls!"

I looked through the short article, which gave a pretty accurate account of the incident and described Mr. Meng as "Professor Liu." Lucky for him, he'd been using an alias all along. I put down the paper and said, "It's no big deal. Nobody can tell you're the wizard with an elephant's memory." I knew he feared that the consulate might pick up his trail.

He said, "You don't know how long the officials can stretch their tentacles. I've heard that this newspaper is financed by the mainland government."

"Still, it's unlikely they can connect 'Professor Liu' with you."

"I hope you're right," he sighed.

But I was not right. Three days later the phone was ringing when I came back from work. I rushed to pick it up, panting a little. The caller, in a mellifluous voice, said he was Vice Consul Gao in charge of education and cultural exchanges. He wanted me to come over to the consulate. Flabbergasted, I tried to keep a cool head, though my temples were throbbing. I told him, "When I was there last time, I was not allowed to set foot inside the building and someone on your staff even called me a gasbag. I was so mortified I thought I'd never go there again."

"Comrade Hongfan Wang, I personally invite you this time. Come and see me tomorrow."

"I'll have to work."

"How about the day after tomorrow? That's Saturday."

"I'm not sure if I can do that. I'll have to speak to my boss first. What's this about, Consul Gao?"

"We would like to know if you have some information on your teacher Fuhua Meng's whereabouts."

"What? You mean he disappeared?"

"We just want to know where he is."

"I don't have the foggiest idea. The last time I saw him was at Columbia, where we visited Professor Natalie Simon."

"That we know."

"Then I have nothing else to report, I'm sorry."

"Comrade Hongfan Wang, you must level with me, with your motherland."

"I told you the truth."

"All right, let me know when you can come."

I said I'd phone him after speaking to my boss. Hanging up, I couldn't stop fidgeting. Whenever I had to deal with those officials, I felt helpless. I knew they might view me as an accomplice in Mr. Meng's case and might give me endless trouble in the future. Perhaps I wouldn't be able to get my passport renewed.

That night when I told my teacher about the phone call, he didn't show much emotion. He merely said, "I knew all along they were on my trail. I'm sorry to have dragged you into my trouble, Hongfan. You must be careful from now on."

"I know they may have put me on their list as well. But they can't do much to me as long as I live here legally. What are you going to do?"

"I can't stay in New York anymore. In fact, I've been in

touch with a friend of mine in Mississippi. He opened a restaurant there and asked me to go down and work for him."

"That's a good idea. You should live in a remote place where the officials can't find you. At least stay there for a year or two."

"Yes, I'll live in complete obscurity, dead to the world. I won't go to Panda Terrace tomorrow. Can you return my uniform for me and tell Mayling and Michael that I'm no longer here?"

"Well, I shouldn't do that because they could easily guess I know where you are, and then the consulate might demand a tip from me."

"Right. Forget about the uniform, then."

He decided to leave for the South the next day, taking the Greyhound directly to Jackson. I supported his decision.

To my surprise, he pulled his suitcase out of the closet and opened it. He took out a big brown envelope stuffed with paper. "Hongfan," he said with feeling, "you're a good young man, one of my best students. Here are some articles on Hemingway I brought out with me. I planned to translate them into English and publish them as a book with a title like *Hemingway in China,* and to be honest, also as a way to make some money and fame. Now I'm no longer in a position to work on this project, so I'm leaving these papers with you. I'm sure you can make good use of them."

He was tearful as he placed the envelope in front of me. I put my hand on it but didn't pull out the contents. I was familiar with most of those articles published in the professional journals over the years and knew they were poorly written and ill-informed. Few of them could be called scholarly papers. Had Mr. Meng rendered them into English, they'd have amounted to an embarrassment to those so-called scholars, some of whom had never read Hemingway in the English, except for the bilingual edition of *The Old Man and the Sea.* They'd written about his fiction mainly in accordance with reviews and summaries provided by official periodicals. Few of them really understood Hemingway. Before I read *The Sun Also Rises* in the original, it had never occurred to me that Hemingway was funny, because the wordplay and jokes were lost in translation. I was positive that no publisher in the United States would be interested in bringing these useless articles out in English. It was foolish for Mr. Meng to have conceived such a secretive project and to assume that one could make fortune and fame with it. All the same, I told him, "Thank you very much for trusting me."

He then handed me a bundle of cash, more than $1,100, and asked me to send it to his wife. I promised to mail her a check in my name.

He sighed and said our paths would cross someday. He stood, then went into the bathroom to brush his teeth and wash before going to bed. The next day would be a long day for both of us.

I've never seen him again since, nor do I know where he is now. For two decades I've moved from one state to another and never returned to China. Eventually I lost those Hemingway papers. But I remember that it was on the day Mr. Meng left New York that I sat down at night and began my first novel in English.

An English Professor

FINALLY RUSHENG TANG COULD RELAX, having turned in the materials for his tenure evaluation—three large files, one for research, the second for teaching, and the third for service. To get the promotion after being an assistant professor for seven years, he had to be excellent in one of the three areas and very good in the other two. Among the three, research was the most important, though his school was basically a teaching college. He was neither an exceptional teacher nor had he done a lot of service. He'd sat on two departmental committees and each spring helped run the students' writing contest. In research he didn't excel either, but he was lucky because a manuscript of his had recently been accepted by the SUNY Press. The monograph would be a slender volume on some divisions between male and female Asian American writers. It was not a substantial piece of scholarship, but the editor at the press had written to assure him that they would bring out the book the next spring—

a year from now. Rusheng made a copy of the official letter and included it in his research file. He had already started on a second book, which was about the use of cultural heritages among Asian American authors, and he had even placed the first chapter of this project with a journal. Some of his tenured colleagues, especially the few who had begun teaching three decades before, had never published a book, and so Rusheng felt he was was in decent shape—his case should be solid.

He went to Whitney Hall, where he was teaching his immigrant literature course this semester. On this day, a Thursday, the class was discussing *America Is in the Heart,* by Carlos Bulosan. Rusheng spoke at length about the problems involved in choosing the form of fiction or that of nonfiction. Bulosan originally wrote his story as a novel, but the press persuaded him to publish it as a memoir. The same thing happened to other books by Asian American authors—for instance, Maxine Hong Kingston's *The Woman Warrior.* That was why the writer Frank Chin claimed: "The yellow autobiography is a white racist form." To what extent can Chin's assertion be justified? Rusheng asked the class. And what are the fundamental differences between the memoir and the novel? What are the advantages and disadvantages of publishing in either form? The students were stimulated by the questions and even argued with one another.

A good class was gratifying to Rusheng, but this didn't happen very often. Most times he felt as frustrated as if he were singing to the deaf. Sometimes he couldn't help but smirk cynically in class. At the end of the previous semester a student had written in a course evaluation: "Professor Tang seemed to despise us. He often laughed at us when we said something he disliked." This semester Rusheng had been more careful about his demeanor and refrained from chuckling in front of his class. He understood that a professor was like an entertainer, obliged to make his students feel good, but he had yet to learn how to please them without revealing his effort. However, he was pretty sure that his course evaluations would be better this time around. That would demonstrate to the senior faculty that he'd been making progress in teaching.

After the class, nobody showed up during his office hours, so he left work at four p.m. On his way to the subway station he ran into Nikki, a popular teacher and an advocate for his promotion in the department; a tall black woman, she always wore a checkered headscarf and gemstone earrings at work and spoke and laughed in a hearty voice. Rusheng told her that he had just submitted his materials.

"Wow, you're quick," Nikki said. "If I were you, I would've waited until the last day. But it doesn't matter, I guess. Did you go over everything a couple of times before you handed them in?"

"I did."

"No typos, no inconsistencies?" she asked half jokingly. Two dimples appeared on her cheeks.

"I proofread everything."

"Now you can relax and wait for good news."

"Thank you for all the help, Nikki."

Although he assured her that he had carefully reviewed his materials, he felt a little uneasy. He'd gone over the research and the service files three times, but he had proofread the teaching file only once. He hoped there weren't any typos or slips in it. The deadline was the next Monday, March 31, and Nikki was right about keeping everything in his hands until the very last moment. He should have waited a few extra days.

After dinner, Rusheng felt more agitated. While his wife was watching a Japanese show, *Under the Same Eaves,* he retreated into his study and put on a jazz CD. The tumbling music floated up. He flicked on his computer, accessed his teaching file, and began reviewing it. Everything was fine—the writing was not terribly brisk, but clean and lucid; he should feel confident about it. But coming to the end of the long report, he noticed the phrase "Respectly yours."

With a sagging heart he pulled one dictionary after another from his bookcase. None of them listed "respectly" as a word. *Webster's* gave "respectfully" as the right usage, and so did the *American Heritage.* How about "respectedly"? he asked himself. Can you put "Respectedly yours" at the end of a letter? That must be all right. He vaguely remembered seeing such an expression in a bilingual dictionary—but which one? He couldn't recall. That must have been the source from which he had inadvertently derived "respectly." Oh, how silly the error looked on paper!

What to do? Should he inform Nikki of this mistake? No, that would amount to advertising his stupidity and ineptitude. But what if the whole department, not to mention the college tenure committee, saw the blunder? People wouldn't treat it as a mere typo or slip. It was a glaring solecism that indicated his incompetence in English. If he were in science or sociology or even comparative literature, the consequences of the mistake would have been less dire. But for an English professor, this was unforgivable, regardless of his sophisticated use of various methodologies to analyze a literary text. People would shake their heads and say that an English professor must at least be able to write decent English.

Worse was the thought of what a spiteful colleague might do. Rusheng knew some of the other professors had had misgivings about his ability all along. He spoke English with a heavy accent and didn't know how to praise a book or an author that he didn't like. He had once offended Gary Kalbfelt, the Melville expert in the department, by saying *Moby-Dick* was as clumsy as a deformed whale. Peter Johnson, the chairman, had never liked him, perhaps because Rusheng had been hired when Johnson was on sabbatical. He had expressed his doubts about Rusheng's adequacy as a teacher at his fourth-year review. Fortunately, Nikki had stuck up for him and convinced their colleagues that he'd been making a name in the field of Asian American literary studies. That was true to some degree, since he had often given talks at conferences. But this time it would be different—Nikki was just an associate professor, not powerful enough to sway full professors in the matter of awarding tenure. Rusheng was worried that Johnson might exploit his mistake to ruin him.

He paced up and down his study for a long time, thinking about how to make amends. The jazz had stopped a while ago, but he wasn't aware of the silence. Try as he might, he couldn't come up with a solution. When he finally went into the bedroom, his wife, Sherry, was already asleep, with a comforter over her belly and her right leg on his side of the bed. Carefully he lifted her foot, with its henna-painted toenails, straightened her leg, and moved it back to her side. Then he got into bed. He exhaled a deep sigh, and she murmured something and smiled, licking her lower lip. He observed her round face, which was still youthful, her small mouth ajar. The moment he switched off the light, her hand listlessly landed on his chest. She mumbled, "Let me try that blouse on, the flowered one. So beautiful."

He removed her hand and went on thinking about his mistake. He decided to go to the department first thing the next morning to retrieve his teaching file. It should still be there. Unlike his research materials, which had to be duplicated for the many outside reviewers, the teaching file would stay in the department, because that evaluation was to be done only by his colleagues. He shut his eyes in hopes that sleep would come soon.

Sherry sensed Rusheng's gloominess the next morning. She put a bowl of steaming oatmeal before him and asked, "What's wrong? You look so down."

"I had a bad night."

Sometimes he was insomniac, so she didn't ask further. "Take a short nap in your office before you go to class, dear," she told him.

"I'll be fine. Don't worry."

"I'll be back late this evening. Molin's gonna play at Four Seas Pavilion, and I'll have to be there."

"All right. I'll pick up something for dinner for myself."

Molin was Sherry's younger brother, a clarinetist in a local band that often performed at hotels and restaurants. He was only twenty-six, five years younger than Sherry, and still trying to figure out what to do with his life. Born in Hawaii, sister and brother had grown up in Hong Kong but came to New York four years earlier, in 1993. Sherry had been instructed by their parents to take care of him. Rusheng didn't mind his wife's spending a lot of time with Molin. He liked his brother-in-law and often went to his performances, but today, even though it was Friday, he had no appetite for the wild music Molin's band played.

Done with breakfast, he set out for work. On the train he forced himself to go over his notes for the composition class, which he'd taught so many times that he could do it without much preparation. Despite his effort to concentrate, his thoughts kept moving beyond his control. He was anxious to get to the department office before the others.

But upon arriving, he found Carrie, the secretary, and Peter Johnson already there. Rusheng hurried into the small reading room where the evaluation materials were kept for the tenured professors to check out. To his horror, nothing remained on top of the metal cabinet. He came out and asked Carrie what had happened to his files. With an eye screwed up, she said, "We made copies of them for the senior faculty."

"You mean they have started reviewing them?"

"Yep. They have to do that for the meeting, you know."

A swoon almost made him fall down, but he collected himself. At this point Johnson stepped out of his office. He was a Victorianist, spindly-legged with a small paunch hanging over his belt; a colossal pair of steel-rimmed bifocals sat on his hooked nose, covering almost half his face. He greeted Rusheng and winked quizzically, but before the junior professor could say anything, the chairman was already out the door with a thick anthology tucked under his arm. Apparently he was heading for a class, yet his odd manner unnerved Rusheng, who watched the man saunter away down the hall. Rusheng's stomach fluttered. Why wouldn't Johnson speak to him? The chairman must have noticed his use of "respectly"!

Rusheng hurried to his own office and locked the door. Except for when he had to teach his composition class, he stayed in the cell-like room all day, brooding about his predicament. Now the whole department must have seen that hideous word, and he had become a laughingstock for sure. Even Nikki might not be able to defend him anymore. What should he do? Who could help him? Never had he felt so powerless.

In recent years he'd been writing a column for the Chinese-language *Global Weekly* on English grammar and usage. If denied tenure, he would become a joke, not only in the college but also to the Chinese community that knew him as an expert. His reputation would crumble. People would gloat over his misfortune, especially those who resented his negative view of contemporary Chinese arts. If only he hadn't been so careless and so impatient. How true the saying was: "Nothing but your own stupidity can undo you."

Unable to hold in the secret any longer, on Saturday he confessed to Sherry. She was unsettled, because by nature Rusheng was a careful man, sometimes even overcautious. They were seated on the sectional sofa in their living room. Molin was also there, and he was lounging on a bamboo chair in a corner. He wore cutoff jeans and a red undershirt. He was reading a comic book and eating chocolate-coated raisins. Rusheng asked Sherry, "Do you think I should talk to Nikki?"

"She must have seen it."

"I've never felt this low in my life. If only I had changed fields in '89." He was remembering the summer when he had wondered if he should abandon his dissertation and go to law or business school like many of his fellow Chinese graduate students.

"Rusheng, you worry too much," Molin jumped in, combing his dyed yellow hair with his fingers. "Look at me—I've never had a full-time job, but I'm still surviving, breathing like everyone else. You should learn how to take it easy and enjoy life."

"I'm in a different situation, Molin," Rusheng sighed. "So many people know me that it will be a scandal if I get fired. I wish I could play an instrument like you, pick up cash wherever I am."

"I just don't believe your career will be over," Sherry said. "How many people have degrees from both Beijing University and Harvard?"

"In America a degree from a top school can help you land a job or join a club, but beyond that you still have to prove yourself and work hard to succeed." He wanted to add that his degrees were in the humanities, hardly worth anything, but he checked himself, knowing that she had agreed to marry him largely because he was a rising scholar in her eyes, and that her parents had approved their marriage thanks to his two glittering diplomas, which could have been worth a lot indeed if he were in Hong Kong or mainland China.

"Look at it this way," Sherry went on. "What's tenure? It's just a work permit that allows you to make fifty grand a year."

Rusheng frowned, then conceded. "Right. I should be able to do something else for a living."

He remained preoccupied for the whole weekend, often imagining what other kind of work he might try. When he considered how he might explain his failure to his Chinese friends, who held him in respect, he found himself at a loss. Maybe the truth was best, no matter how humiliating.

Sherry had to finish sewing an opera costume for a client, but she urged him to go to the movies or have tea with a friend. Instead he stayed home, riffling through some small magazines, none of which was interesting enough to distract him from his anxieties. The Singer sewing machine whirred in the other room, and that too somehow depressed him.

It was already mid-April, only three weeks before the semester ended. But how slowly time was creeping! Rusheng was often absentminded; in class his thoughts would wander and he would fail to hear his students' questions and comments. When he responded to them, he spoke as if by rote. He no longer assigned homework. This semester could be his last: he knew that even if the school refused him tenure, he'd be permitted to teach another year, but the prospect was too humiliating. When he ran into his colleagues, he would avoid speaking with them at length; he felt as if their eyes were boring into him for all his secrets. Nikki once chuckled, "Wake up, Rusheng. Are you suffering from sleep deficiency or something?"

He replied, "I'm on a deadline for a paper and didn't hit the sack until after midnight."

He and Sherry had talked about the next year. She suggested that he look for a job at another college, but he wouldn't do that, saying he would become a kind of pariah that few schools would be interested in hiring. He preferred to do something else, even though he might have to start from scratch.

One day, while having a drink with an editor of the *Global Weekly,* Rusheng asked whether he might work for the newspaper, knowing it was advertising for an opening in its editorial department. The man, named Eujin, shook his double chin. "No, no, Rusheng, if I were you, I wouldn't even think about it."

"I'm just tired of academia. I want a change."

"People always feel that other hills are higher than the one they're sitting on. Frankly, I envy your ability to make a living with English. Unlike you, I'm trapped in Chinese. I'm a senior editor at the paper—the highest-paid editor—and I make only twenty-six thousand dollars a year." Eujin paused, then continued, "How much does an associate professor make?"

"Around fifty-five grand, I guess."

"See the difference?" Eujin put a handful of salted peanuts into his mouth, munching noisily, a bit of beer froth on his graying mustache. "Do you know how I feel about the difference between you and me?"

"I've no clue. Tell me."

"I feel I'm still in the yuan system, even though I've lived and worked in the United States for more than two decades. Rusheng, you're already in the dollar system. You mustn't think about working for any newspaper if it's not printed in English."

Rusheng couldn't explain his plight to Eujin. He promised him to continue contributing his weekly column on English idioms and pitfalls, which Eujin said people loved to read.

Early the following week Rusheng came across an advertisement for sales representatives for a publishing company. Though he didn't feel he could make a successful salesman, he called the number in the ad, and a cheerful-voiced man told him to come in for a preliminary interview on Thursday afternoon, at three.

Two days later Rusheng showed up at the office on Roosevelt Avenue. The man receiving him was thin but broad-framed, with a mop of sandy hair; he introduced himself as Alex and held out his hand, which felt flaccid when Rusheng shook it. He gave Alex his résumé, which presented him as a part-time English instructor and didn't mention his PhD from Harvard. As the man skimmed the vita, his face widened and his hazel eyes lit up. "I was an English major. I love the classics, especially *The Iliad.* I still read every new translation that comes out."

"It's a great poem," Rusheng said in surprise. Seldom had he run into a literary person outside the college, save for the editors at the *Global Weekly.* He went on, "Nowadays people talk so much about democracy and justice, but in fact most of the ideas are already in Homer."

"Exactly. What do you teach?" Alex placed the résumé on his desk.

"American literature."

"Do you teach Steinbeck?"

"Sometimes. I've taught *Of Mice and Men.*"

"I love his books, *East of Eden,* particularly." Alex's enthusiasm discomfited Rusheng—he knew that most modernists disliked Steinbeck.

Alex then said Rusheng was qualified and invited him to attend an acceptance meeting in White Plains on Saturday. The interview had lasted only about ten minutes, as apparently Alex had to meet someone else. He wished Rusheng the best of luck.

Coming out of the building, Rusheng thought about becoming a salesman. It wouldn't be bad. Alex seemed to be cheerful and had his own office in the center of Flushing, even a secretary. Maybe if he, Rusheng, worked hard, someday he too could have that kind of confident body language, minus the weak handshake. But White Plains was far away. He'd have to take the train to get there, which meant the whole day would be gone. Still, he didn't have a choice.

That night he talked to Sherry about his interview. She encouraged him to attend the meeting, saying he should try a few things to see what suited him best. He told himself a salesman could make a good living, and that this is America, where there's no high or low among all professions as long as you can draw a fat paycheck.

The daylong acceptance meeting was held at the Ramada Inn, and Rusheng arrived fifteen minutes late. About twenty applicants were present, a third of them women; and each was given a glossy blue folder containing half a dozen handouts, a pencil, and a lined notepad. The speaker was an expert salesman, round-shouldered and hawkeyed; his hips leaned against a table as he talked about how to persuade potential customers to buy the product, *The Universal Encyclopedia.* Beside him was a whole set of the books, twenty-six volumes in three stacks. Now and again he'd pick up one to show the high quality of the print. According to him, a salesperson would get paid a commission of twenty-five percent of the list price. A whole set sold for $650, which meant you could get $162.50 from every sale.

"Imagine you make five or six sales a week," the man continued. "That would be a substantial income for anyone. The beauty of this job is that you can set your own schedule and there's no boss to keep tabs on you. You can work ten hours a week, or twenty hours, or sixty hours. It's entirely up to you, although you'll need a car for transporting the product."

That wouldn't be a problem for Rusheng, since Sherry had a car. A few applicants raised questions, and the salesman told them that he had been in this business for eighteen years and loved it. As he spoke, his broad cheeks twitched as if to force down a grin. Rusheng couldn't help but wonder if the man was telling them the truth.

Since most of the attendees had come from New York City, the company offered them free lunch at the hotel. They went into the dining room, with its French doors facing onto an oval pool. A breeze crinkled the water now and again. Rusheng sat next to a short, roly-poly man named Billy. As they ate chicken breast, steamed broccoli, and whole-wheat rolls, the two of them got into a conversation. The ruddy-faced Billy said he was a pastor but enjoyed selling the encyclopedias on the side. "Actually, I sold two sets last week," he said in a warm voice.

"Did you work hard to make the sales?" Rusheng asked.

"Not really. I just brought the first volume with me when I went to visit some families in my parish. They were pleased to buy the whole set, because they have school-age kids who can use the encyclopedia for their homework. What do you do, Rusheng?"

"I teach at a college."

"Part-time or full-time?"

"Full-time." Rusheng dropped his voice a little.

"That means you're a professor."

"Sort of."

"To be honest, if I were you, I wouldn't bother with this sales job."

"How come?"

Billy burped, then lowered his voice to a whisper. "A lot of the information in the encyclopedia will be available online soon. In a couple of years nobody will want to have such a big set of books at home anymore. I bet even the publisher won't reprint the thing again. What we're selling must be the remainder. You can't take this job as a profession."

"Then why are you in it?"

"I'm doing it just for fun, to make a bit of cash for my church."

Rusheng didn't return to the afternoon session, leaving his blue folder on a coffee table in the lobby. He stepped out of the hotel and headed for the train station in the warm sun, wearing a blue T-shirt with his button-down shirt tied around his waist. His lean body cast a squat shadow at a slant.

• • •

The semester was coming to an end. Rusheng graded papers. He could hardly concentrate, but he kept reminding himself that these were the final batch. Afterward, he wouldn't have to read this sort of garbage anymore. "You'll be liberated soon," he told himself. Yet whenever the foreboding of his imminent humiliation came to mind, a pang would seize his heart. Recently he'd been thinking of the Buddhist temple near Niagara Falls, on the Canadian side. He'd visited two years before and had a wonderful time there, conversing with a short-bearded monk while drinking chrysanthemum tea and cracking spiced pumpkin seeds. The night he spent at the temple's inn was the most peaceful time in his life. It wasn't just peace that he enjoyed there—he felt clear-minded for days after. If not married, he would go there again to see if they would accept him. They might, since he could be useful, at least as an English translator and literary pundit. How he was longing to settle in some place where nobody knew about his past.

Then, one evening in mid-May, Sherry came home with shiny cheeks and smiling eyes. She waved a letter at Rusheng and trilled, "Great news!"

"What?" he grunted, not in any mood for levity.

"You got tenure."

"Really? You've got to be kidding me." He stood but didn't move, his slightly bulging eyes fixed on her.

She stepped over and handed him the letter from Peter Johnson. Rusheng skimmed through the chairman's writing, which said:

Dear Professor Rusheng Tang,

I am delighted to inform you that our department voted to promote you to associate professor with tenure.

> We appreciate your accomplishment as a scholar and your devotion to teaching, and we believe you are an invaluable asset to our department . . .

Johnson went on to explain that the promotion still must be reviewed and approved by the college, but he also said that would be a formality, because to his knowledge the dean had never overruled one of their department's tenure decisions. After reading the heartwarming letter, Rusheng was still rooted, as if in a trance. He wasn't sure if he could believe what the chairman had written.

"What's wrong?" Sherry asked. "You're not pleased?"

"If the department voted to grant me tenure, Nikki would be the first one to notify me."

"Read the letter again. They held the meeting the day before yesterday."

"Still, this information shouldn't have come from Peter Johnson first. He can't bear the sight of me. You know that."

"You're too paranoid. Johnson wouldn't dare to pull a prank like this on you. Give Nikki a call and find out if it's true."

"All right."

He dialed Nikki's number, and at the third ring her carefree voice came up. When he mentioned his misgivings, she laughed. "Of course it's true," she assured him.

He wondered why she hadn't told him, but he didn't come out and ask her. Then she added, "Peter was quick. He was supportive this time."

"Oh, I didn't expect such an upshot."

"You earned it, Rusheng. I planned to call you yesterday, but my daughter was leaving for a Scholar Bowl tournament today, so I was busy helping her pack. Then, after seeing her off this afternoon, I was stopped on the way home by a friend

I hadn't seen for years. So I came back late and meant to call you tonight. Sorry I wasn't the messenger of the good news, but I'm really, really happy for you. In fact, except for three or four people, our whole department supported you. Yours is a strong case, and I'm sure the dean will approve it. You should celebrate, Rusheng."

Before hanging up he thanked her and said he would let her know the date for his celebratory party. Finally he was convinced. Oh, sometimes even good old Homer nods—how absentminded those erudite professors could grow when they devoted themselves to their magnificent papers and books, preoccupied heart and soul with all the marvelous, cutting-edge theories, like intertexuality, polyphonic narratology, deconstruction, and new historicism. They'd never even noticed a simple wrong word, "respectly."

"I'm tenured, wow, I'm tenured!" Rusheng cried out. He rushed over to his wife and grabbed her by the waist, swinging her around and around and around.

"Put me down! Put me down!" she shrieked.

So he did. "I'm tenured. Wow, I don't have to worry about being fired anymore. I'm a real professor now! This can happen only in America!"

"And you'll get a big raise."

Suddenly he burst into laughter. He laughed and laughed until he doubled over, until Sherry began slapping his back to relieve his coughing. Then, straightening up, he broke out singing "Born to Be Wild," a song Molin's band often performed.

"Born to be wild!" Rusheng chanted, stunning his wife.

Not knowing the whole song, he went on belting out the refrain with garbled words: "Born to be happy! Born to succeed!"

"Calm down, calm down!" his wife pleaded. But he wouldn't stop giggling and kept chanting, "What a wonderful world! Born to be tenured! Born to stand out!"

Sherry picked up the phone and dialed a number. "Molin, come over quickly. Rusheng has lost his mind . . . No, he's not violent. We just heard he got tenure and he was shocked by the good news. Come and help me calm him down."

A few moments later Molin arrived. Rusheng was still singing, though he spewed out snatches of Beijing opera now: "Today I'm drinking a bowl poured by my mother / Ah, the wine makes me bold and strong . . ."

"Give him some Benadryl," Molin told Sherry. He pulled Rusheng up from the sofa and guided him away to the bedroom.

No sooner had Rusheng sat down on the bed than his wife came with a cup of warm water and two caplets. She made him swallow the soporific, then sister and brother put him into bed. A film of sweat glistened on his domed forehead. She threw a blanket over him and said, "You must have some sleep, dear."

Rusheng was still humming something, but his voice was subdued, and his exhaustion was now apparent. Sherry dimmed the light on the nightstand and went out with her brother. "What should I do if he goes hysterical again? Take him to the hospital?" she asked Molin.

"Wait and see. He may become himself again tomorrow."

"I hope so," she sighed.

A Pension Plan

IT WAS SAID that Mr. Sheng suffered from a kind of senile dementia caused by some infarction in his brain. I was sure it was neither Parkinson's nor Alzheimer's, because I had learned quite a bit about both during my training to be a health aide. He wasn't completely disabled, but he needed to be cared for during the day. I was glad to attend to him, because I'd been out of work for more than three months before this job.

Every morning I'd wash his face with a hand towel soaked with warm water, but I'd been told I mustn't shave him, which only his family members could do. He was sixty-nine, gentle by nature and soft-spoken. He'd taught physics at a middle school back in Changchun City three decades ago, but he couldn't read his old textbooks anymore and was unable to remember the formulas and the theorems. He still could recognize many words, though. He often had a newspaper on his lap when sitting alone. My job was to cook for him, feed him, keep him clean, and take him around. A young nurse came every other day to check his vital signs and give him an injection. The twentysomething told me that actually there was no cure for Mr. Sheng's illness, which the doctor could only try to keep under control and slow down his deterioration. I felt lucky that my charge wasn't violent like many victims of dementia.

Mr. Sheng's wife had died long ago, before he came to the United States, but he believed she was still alive. Oftentimes he couldn't remember her name, so every morning I let him look through an album that contained about two dozen photos of her and him together. In the pictures, they were young and appeared to be a happy couple. She was a pretty woman, the kind of beauty with glossy skin and a delicate figure you often find in the provinces south of the Yangtze River. Sometimes when I pointed at her face and asked him, "Who's this?" he'd raise his eyes and look at me, his face blank.

About a month after I started, his daughter, Minna, intervened, saying the photos might upset him and I shouldn't show them to him anymore, so I put the album away. He never complained about its absence. Minna was a little bossy, but I didn't mind. She must have loved her dad. She called me Aunt Niu. That made me uneasy, because I had just turned forty-eight, not that old.

Part of my job was to feed Mr. Sheng. I often had to cajole him into swallowing food. Sometimes he was like a sick baby who refused to hold food in its mouth for long. I made fine meals for him—chicken porridge, fish dumplings, shrimp and taro pottage, noodles mixed with shredded shiitake mushrooms, but in spite of his full set of teeth, he seemed unable to tell any difference among most of the foods. A good part of his taste buds must have been dead. When eating, he'd jabber between mouthfuls, his words by and large incomprehensible. Yet once in a while he'd pause to ask me, "See what I mean?"

I'd keep mute. If pressed further, I'd shake my head and admit, "No, I didn't follow you."

"You always space out," he'd grunt, then refuse to eat any more.

Lunch usually took more than two hours. That didn't bother me, since in essence my job was just to help him while away time. Due to his willfulness about food, I decided to eat my own meal before feeding him.

After lunch we often went out for some fresh air, to do a little shopping and get that day's *World Journal;* I pushed him in a wheelchair. Like a housewife, he was in the habit of clipping coupons. Whenever he saw something for sale, he would cut the ad out of the paper and save it for Minna. That made me feel that he must have been a considerate husband willing to share lots of things with his wife. Now, with my help, he enjoyed frequenting the stores in Flushing. For food, he claimed he liked freshwater fish, perch, carp, eel, dace, bullhead, but he wouldn't eat seafood, or anything from the sea except for scallops. The last was recommended by the young nurse because it contained little cholesterol. She also told me to give him milk and cheese, but he disliked them.

One afternoon we went out shopping again. As we were approaching a newsstand on Main Street, Mr. Sheng cried, "Halt!"

"What?" I stopped in my tracks. People were pouring out of the subway exit.

"Wait here," he told me.

"Why?"

"She's coming."

I wanted to ask him more but held back. His mind could hardly take in a regular sentence. If I asked him a question longer than ten words, he wouldn't know how to answer.

More people were passing by, and the two of us stood in the midst of the dwindling crowd. When no passengers were coming out of the exit anymore, I asked him, "Still waiting?"

"Yeah." He rested his hands on his legs. Beside him, a scrap of newspaper was taped to the top horizontal bar of the wheelchair.

"We must buy the fish, remember?" I pointed at the ad.

He looked vacant, his pupils roving from side to side. At this point the subway exit was again swarmed with people, and pedestrians were passing back and forth on the sidewalk. To my amazement, Mr. Sheng lifted his hand at a young lady wearing maroon pants, a pink silk shirt, and wire-rimmed glasses. She hesitated, then stopped. "What can I do for you, Uncle?" she said with a Cantonese accent.

"Seen my wife?" he asked.

"Who's she? What's her name?"

He remained silent and turned his worried face up to me. I stepped in and said, "Her name is Molei Wan." Not knowing how to explain further without offending him, I just winked at the woman.

"I don't know anyone who has that name." She smiled and shook her dark-complected face.

"You're lying!" he yelled.

She glared at him, her nostrils flaring. I pulled her aside and whispered, "Miss, don't take it to heart. He has a mental disorder."

"If he's a sicko, don't let him come out to make others unhappy." She shot me a dirty look and walked away, her shoulder-length hair swaying.

Annoyed, I stepped back to his chair. "Don't speak to a stranger again," I said.

He didn't seem to understand, though he looked displeased, probably because he hadn't caught sight of his wife. I pushed him away while he muttered something I couldn't catch.

The fish store was nearby, and we bought a large whitefish, a two-pounder. It was very fresh, with glossy eyes, full scales, and a firm belly. The young man behind the counter gutted it but left the head on, like I told him. By no means could Mr. Sheng eat the whole thing—I would cook only half of it and save the other half for the next day or later. On our way back, he insisted on holding the fish himself. I had tied the top of the plastic bag, so I didn't intervene when he let it lie flat on his lap. Bloody liquid seeped out and soaked the front of his khaki pants, but I didn't notice it. When we got home, I saw the wet patch and thought he had peed. Then I found that neither of his pant legs was wet. "You meant to create more work for me, eh?" I said. "Why didn't you hold the fish right?"

He looked puzzled. Yet he must have meant to be careless with the fish, peeved that I hadn't let him wait longer outside the subway terminal. I began undressing him for a shower, which I had planned to do that day anyway. As for his pants soiled by the fish blood, I'd wash them later. There was a washer upstairs on the first floor of the house, where his daughter lived with his two grandchildren and her husband, Harry, a pudgy salesman who traveled a lot and was not home most of the time.

I helped Mr. Sheng into the bathtub. He held on to a walker with its wheels locked while I was washing him. I first lathered him all over and then rinsed him with a nozzle. He enjoyed the shower and cooperated as usual, turning this way and that. He let out happy noises when I sprayed warm water on him. He should be pleased, because few health aides would bathe their patients as carefully as I did. I had once worked in a nursing home, where old people were undressed and strapped to chairs with holes in the seats when we gave them showers. We wheeled them into a machine one by one. Like in an auto bath, water would spurt at them from every direction. When we pulled them out, they'd hiccup and shiver like featherless turkeys. Some of the aides would let those they disliked stay there wet and naked for an hour or two.

After toweling off Mr. Sheng, I helped him on with clean clothes and then combed his gray hair, which was still thick and hadn't lost its sheen. I noticed that his fingernails were quite long, with dirt beneath them, but the company's regulations didn't allow me to clip them, for fear of a lawsuit if they got infected. I told him, "Be a good boy. I'm gonna make you a fish soup."

"Yummy." He clucked, showing two gold-capped teeth.

I couldn't drive, so whenever Mr. Sheng went to see the doctor in the hospital, Minna would take both of us there in her minivan. She already had her hands full with her four-year-old twin boys and her job in a bank, and had to use a babysitter. Her father didn't believe in Western medicine and became unhappy whenever we visited the hospital. He might have his reasons—according to the young nurse who came every other day, acupuncture and medicinal herbs might be more effective in treating his illness. But he would have to pay for the herbs since Medicare didn't cover them. Even so, he'd make me push him from one herbal store to another, and sometimes he went there just to see how those doctors, unlicensed here because of their poor English, treated patients—

feeling their pulses, performing cupping, giving therapeutic massages, setting bones. He couldn't afford a whole set of herbs prescribed by a doctor, usually more than a dozen per prescription, but he'd buy something from time to time, a couple of scorpions or centipedes, or a pack of ginseng beard, which is at least ten times cheaper than the roots and which he asked me to steep in piping-hot water to make a tea for him. He would also have me bake and grind the insects and promise him never to disclose his taking them to Minna, who regarded Chinese medicine as quackery. I had no idea if centipedes and scorpions could help him, but whenever he ate a few, he would grow animated for hours, his eyes shedding a tender light while color came to his face. He'd sing folk songs, one after another. He always got the lines garbled, but the melodies were there. Familiar with those songs, I often hummed along with him.

Together we'd sing: "As the limpid brook is babbling east, / I shall keep your words secret and sweet." Or, "A little pouch with a golden string, / Made for me by the village girl / Who smiles like a blooming spring."

But often I wasn't so happy with him. Most of the time he was difficult and grouchy and would throw a tantrum out of the blue. Because Medicare covered acupuncture, he went to a clinic for the treatment regularly. The only acupuncturist within walking distance and listed by the program was Dr. Li, who practiced in one of the tenements on Forty-sixth Avenue. I often missed his office when I took Mr. Sheng there because those brick buildings appeared identical. One afternoon as I was pushing him along the sidewalk shaded by maples with purple leaves, he stopped me, saying we had just passed Dr. Li's clinic. I looked around and figured that he might be correct, so we turned and headed for the right entrance.

Excited about my mistake, he told the doctor I was "a

dope." Lying on a sloping bed with needles in his feet, he pointed at his head and said, "My memory's better now."

"Indeed," Dr. Li echoed, "you've improved a lot."

I hated that donkey-faced man, who lied to him. Mr. Sheng couldn't even remember what he'd eaten for lunch. How could anyone in his right mind say his memory had gotten better? He smiled like an idiot, his face showing smugness. I was pretty sure that he had identified the right entrance only by a fluke. Outraged, I flopped down into his wheelchair and pretended to be trembling like him. I groaned, "Oh, help me! Take me to Dr. Li. I need him to stick his magic needles into my neck."

Li laughed, quacking like a duck, while Mr. Sheng fixed his eyes on me like a pair of tiny arrowheads. Red patches were appearing on his cheeks and a tuft of hair suddenly stood up on his crown. That frightened me and I got out of the chair. Even so, I couldn't help but add, "Take me back. I can't walk by myself."

I shouldn't have aped him, speaking out of turn. For the rest of the day he went on jerking his head away from me, even though I cooked his favorite food—chicken porridge with chestnuts in it. I thought he must hate me and would make endless trouble for me. But the next morning he was himself again and even gave me a smile of recognition when I stepped into his quarters in the basement.

Mr. Sheng developed a strange habit—he would prevent me from leaving him alone and want me to sit by him all the time. Even when I went upstairs to launder his clothes, he'd get impatient, making terrible noises. He just needed my attention, I guessed. When I walked out of his room, I could feel his eyes following me. And he had become more obedient at mealtimes and would swallow whatever I fed him. One morning I asked him teasingly, pointing at my nose, "What's my name?"

He managed to say, "Jufen."

I gave him a one-armed hug, thrilled that he'd remembered my name. To be honest, I liked to stay with him, not only because I got paid eight dollars an hour but also because his fondness for me made my work easier. It took less time to feed and bathe him now. He was so happy and mild these days that even his grandchildren would come down to see him. He also went up to visit them when his son-in-law wasn't home. Somehow he seemed afraid of Harry, a white man with thick shoulders, shortish legs, and intense blue eyes. Minna told me that her husband feared that Mr. Sheng might hurt their children and that, besides, Harry didn't like the old man's smell. But honest to God, in my care, my patient didn't stink anymore.

He had quite a number of friends in the neighborhood, and we often went to a small park on Bowne Street to meet them. They were all in their sixties or seventies, three or four women while the other seven or eight were men. But unlike my charge, they weren't ill; they were more clearheaded. Though Mr. Sheng could no longer chat with them, I could see that they used to be quite chummy. They'd tease him good-naturedly, but he never said anything and just smiled at them. One afternoon, Old Peng, a chunky man with a bullet-shaped head, asked him loudly, "Who's this? Your girlfriend?" He pointed his thumb at me, its nail ringwormed like a tiny hoof.

To my surprise, Mr. Sheng nodded yes.

"When are you gonna marry her?" a toothless man asked.

"Next month?" a small woman butted in, holding a fistful of pistachios.

Mr. Sheng looked muddled while his friends kept rolling,

some waving at me. My face burning, I told them, "Don't make fun of him. Shame on you!"

"She's fierce," said Old Peng.

"Like a little hot pepper," another man echoed.

"She's real good at protecting her man," added the same woman.

I realized there was no way to stop them, so I told Mr. Sheng, "Come, let's go home."

As I was pushing him away, more jesting voices rose behind us. I began to take him to the park less often; instead we'd go to the Flushing Library. He liked to thumb through the magazines there, especially those with photographs.

One morning, as I was scrubbing him in the bathtub, he grasped my hand and pulled it toward him slowly but firmly. I thought he needed me to check a spot bothering him, but to my astonishment, he pressed my hand on his hairy belly, then down to his genitals. Before I could pull it back, he began mumbling. I looked up and saw his eyes giving out a strange light, some sparks flitting in them. Wordlessly I withdrew my hand and went on spraying water on his back. He kept saying, "I love you, I love you, you know."

Hurriedly I toweled him and helped him into a change of clean clothes. I didn't say a word the whole time, but my mind was in turmoil. How should I handle this? Should I talk to his daughter about this turn of events? He wasn't a bad man, but I didn't love him. Besides our age difference, twenty-one years, I simply couldn't imagine having an intimate relationship with a man again. My ex-husband had left me eight years ago for an old flame of his, a woman entrepreneur in the porcelain business in the Bay Area, and I was accustomed to living alone and never considered remarrying. I'd been treating Mr. Sheng well mainly with an eye to making him like and trust me so my work would be easier, but now how should I cope with this madness?

Having no clue what to do, I pretended I didn't understand him. I began to distance myself from him and stay out of his way. Still, I had to take him outdoors and I had to coax him like a child at mealtimes. Also, he'd break into a cry and let loose a flood of tears if I said something harsh to him. He'd murmur my name in a soft voice—"Jufen . . . Jufen . . . ," as if chewing the word. He could have been interesting and charming if he weren't so sick. I felt sorry for him, so I tried to be patient.

About a week later, he began to touch me whenever he could. He'd pat my behind when I stood up to get something for him. He'd also rest his fingers on my forearm as if to prevent me from going away and as if I enjoyed this intimacy. Finally, one afternoon I removed his hand from the top of my thigh and said, "Take your paw off of me. I don't like it."

He was stunned, then burst out wailing. "No fun! No fun!" he cried, pushing the air with his open hand while his face twisted, his eyes shut.

Minna heard the commotion and came down, a huge bun of hair on top of her head. At the sight of her heartbroken father, she asked sharply, "Aunt Niu, what have you done to him?"

"He—he kept harassing me, making advances, so I just told him to stop."

"What? You're a liar. He can hardly know who you are, how could he do anything like that?" Her fleshy face scrunched up, showing that she resolved to defend her father's honor.

"He likes me—that's the truth."

"He's not himself anymore. How could he have normal feelings for you?"

"He said he loved me. Ask him."

She placed her hand, dimpled at the knuckles, on his bony shoulder and shook him. "Dad, tell me, do you love Jufen?"

He looked at her blankly, as if in confusion. I hated him for keeping mute and humiliating me like this.

Minna straightened up and said to me, "Obviously you are lying. You hurt him, but you pinned the blame on him."

"Damn it, I told you the truth!"

"How can you prove that?"

"If you don't believe me, all right, I quit." I was surprised by what I said; this job was precious to me, but it was too late to retract my words.

She smirked, fluttering her mascaraed eyelashes. "Who are you? You think you're so indispensable that the Earth will stop spinning without you?"

Speechless, I walked into the doorway to collect my things. It was late afternoon, almost time to call it a day. I knew Minna had befriended Ning Zhang, the owner of my agency; they both came from Nanjing. The bitch would definitely bad-mouth me to that man to make it hard for me to land another job. Even so, I had to keep up appearances and would never beg her to take me back.

I didn't eat dinner, and I wept for hours that night. Yet I didn't regret having given Minna a piece of my mind. As I anticipated, my boss, Ning Zhang, called early the next morning and told me not to go to work anymore.

For several days I stayed home watching TV. I liked Korean and Taiwanese shows, but I wanted to learn some English, so I watched soaps, *All My Children* and *General Hospital,* which I could hardly understand. Using a friend as an interpreter, I talked to Father Lorenzo of our church about my job loss; he said I shouldn't lose heart. "God will provide, and you'll find work soon," he assured me. "At the moment you should use the free time to attend an English class here."

I didn't reply and thought, Easier said than done. At my age, how can I learn another language from scratch? I couldn't even remember the order of the alphabet. If only I were thirty years younger!

Then one evening Ning Zhang called, saying he'd like to have me take care of Mr. Sheng again. Why? I wondered to myself. Didn't they send over another health aide? I asked him, "What happened? Minna's not angry with me anymore?"

"No. She just has a short temper, you know that. Truth be told, since you left, her dad often refuses to eat, sulking like a child, so we want you to go back."

"What makes you think I'll do that?"

"I know you. You're kindhearted and will never see an old man suffer and starve because of your self-pride."

That was true, so I agreed to restart the next morning. Ning Zhang thanked me and said he'd give me a raise at the end of the year.

Minna was quite friendly when I returned to work. Her father resumed eating normally, though he still wouldn't stop saying he loved me and he would touch me whenever he could. I didn't reproach him—I just avoided body contact so I might not hurt his feelings again. To be fair, he was obsessed but innocuous. It was the incurable illness that had reduced him to such a wreck; otherwise, some older woman might have married him willingly. Whenever we ran into a friend of his on the street or in the library, Mr. Sheng would say I was his girlfriend. I was embarrassed but didn't bother to correct him. There're things that the more you try to explain, the more complicated they become. I kept mum, telling myself I was only doing my job.

Once in a while he would get assertive, attempting to make

me touch his genitals when I bathed him, or trying to fondle my breasts. He even began calling me "my old woman." Irritated, I griped to Minna in private, "We have to find a way to stop him or I can't continue to work like this."

"Aunt Niu," she sighed, "let us be honest with each other. I'm terribly worried too. Tell me, do you have feelings for my dad?"

"What do you mean?" I was puzzled.

"I mean, do you love him?"

"No, I don't."

She gave me a faint smile as if to say no woman would openly admit her affection for a man. I wanted to stress that at most I might like him a little, but she spoke before I could. "How about marrying him? I mean just in appearance."

"What a silly thing to say. How could I support myself if I don't hold a job?"

"That's why I said just in appearance."

I was more baffled. "I don't get it."

"I mean, you can keep your job but live in this apartment, pretending to be his wife. Just to make him content and peaceful. I'll pay you four hundred dollars a month. Besides, you'll keep your wages."

"Well, I'm not sure." I couldn't see what she was really driving at.

She pressed on. "It will work like this—legally you're not his spouse at all. Nothing will change except that you'll spend more time with him in here."

"I don't have to share his bed?"

"Absolutely not. You can set up your own quarters in there." She pointed at the storage room, which was poky but could be turned into a cozy nest.

"So the marriage will be just in name?"

"Exactly."

"Let me think about it, okay?"

"Sure, no need to rush."

It took me two days to decide to accept the offer. I had remembered my aunt, who in her early forties had married a paraplegic nineteen years older and nursed him to his grave. She wasn't even fond of the man but took pity on him. In a way, she sacrificed herself so that her family wouldn't starve. When her husband died, she didn't inherit anything from him—he left his house to his nephew. Later she went to join her daughter from her first marriage and is still staying with my cousin in a small town on the Yellow River. Compared with my aunt, I was in a much better position, earning wages for myself. Eventually if I moved into Mr. Sheng's place, I might not have to rent my apartment anymore and plus could save eighty-one dollars a month on the subway pass. When I told Minna of my acceptance, she was delighted and said I was kindness itself.

To my surprise, she came again in the afternoon with a sheet of paper and asked me to sign it, saying this was just a statement of the terms we'd agreed on. I couldn't read English, so I wanted to see a Chinese version. I had to be careful about signing anything; four years ago I'd lost my deposit when I left Elmhurst for Corona to share an apartment with a friend—my former landlord wouldn't refund me the seven hundred dollars and showed me the cosigned agreement that stated I would give up the money if I moved out before the lease expired.

Minna said she'd rewrite the thing in Chinese. The next morning, as I was seated beside Mr. Sheng and reading a newspaper article to him, Minna stepped in and motioned for me to come into the kitchen. I went over, and she handed me the agreement. I read through it and felt outraged. It sounded like I was planning to swindle her father out of his property. The last paragraph stated: "To sum up, Jufen Niu agrees that she shall never enter into matrimony with Jinping Sheng or accept any inheritance from him. Their 'union' shall remain nominal forever."

I asked Minna, "So you think I'm a gold digger, huh? If you don't trust me, why bother about this fake marriage in the first place?"

"I do trust you, Aunt Niu, but we're in America now, where even the air can make people change. We'd better spell out everything on paper beforehand. To tell the truth, my dad owns two apartments, which he bought many years ago when real estate was cheap in this area, so we ought to prevent any trouble down the road."

"I never thought he was rich, but I won't 'marry' him, period."

She fixed her cat eyes on me and said, "Then how can you continue working here?"

"I won't."

"I didn't mean to offend you, Aunt Niu. Can't we leave this open and talk about it later when we both calm down?"

"I just don't feel I can sell myself this way. I don't love him. You know how hard it is for a woman to marry a man she doesn't love."

She smirked. I knew what she was thinking—for a woman my age, it was foolish to take love into account when offered a marriage. Indeed, love gets scarcer as we grow older. All the same, I nerved myself and said, "This is my last day."

"Well, maybe not." She turned and made for the door, her hips jiggling a little. She shouldn't have worn jeans, which made her appear more rotund.

. . .

Ning Zhang called the next day and asked me to come to his office downtown for "a heart-to-heart talk." I told him I wouldn't feel comfortable confiding anything to a thirtysomething like him. In fact, he was pushing forty and already looked middle-aged, stout in the midriff and with a shiny bald spot like a lake in the mouth of an extinct volcano. Still, he insisted that I come over, so I agreed to see him the next morning.

For a whole day I thought about what to say to him. Should I refuse to look after Mr. Sheng no matter what? I wasn't sure, because I was in Ning Zhang's clutches. He could keep me out of work for months or even for years. Should I sign the humiliating agreement with Minna? Perhaps I had no choice but to accept it. How about asking for a raise? That might be the only possible gain I could get. So I decided to bargain with my boss for a one-dollar-an-hour raise.

Before setting out the next morning, I combed my hair, which was mostly black, and I also made up my face a little. I was amazed to see myself in the mirror: jutting cheekbones, bright eyes, and a water-chestnut-shaped mouth. If twenty years younger, I could have been a looker. Better yet, I still had a small waistline and a bulging chest. I left home, determined to confront my boss.

At the subway station I chanced on a little scarecrow of a woman who pulled a baby carriage loaded with sacks of plastic bottles and aluminum cans. No doubt she was Chinese and over seventy, in brown slacks and a black short-sleeved shirt printed with yellow hibiscuses. The cloth sacks holding the containers were clean and colored like pieces of baggage. A rusty folding stool was bound to the top of the huge load. On the side of the tiny buggy hung a string pouch holding a bottle of water and a little blue bag with a red tassel, obviously containing her lunch. There were also three large sacks, trussed together, separated from the buggy-load, and holding two-liter Coke bottles. All the people on the platform kept a distance from this white-haired woman. She looked neat and gentle but restless, and went on tightening the ropes wrapped around the load. A fiftyish man passed by with two little girls sporting loopy honey-colored curls, and the kids turned to gawk at the sacks of containers and at the old woman, who waved her small hand and said to them with a timid smile, "Bye-bye." Neither of the wide-eyed girls responded.

The train came and discharged passengers. I helped the crone pull her stuff into the car. She was so desperate to get her things aboard that she didn't even thank me after the door slid shut. She was panting hard. How many bottles and cans has she here? I wondered. Probably about two hundred. She stood by the door, afraid she wouldn't be able to get all her stuff off at her destination. Time and again I glanced at her, though no one else seemed to notice her at all. She must have been a daily passenger with a similar load.

A miserable feeling was welling in me. In that withered woman I saw myself. How many years could I continue working as a health aide who was never paid overtime or provided with any medical insurance or a retirement plan? Would I ever make enough to lay aside some for my old age? How would I support myself when I could no longer attend to patients? I must do something now, or I might end up like that little crone someday, scavenging through garbage for cans and bottles to sell to a recycling shop. The more I thought about her, the more despondent I became.

The woman got off at Junction Boulevard, dragging away her load that was five times larger than her body. People hurried past her, and I was afraid she might fall at the stairs if one of her sacks snagged on something. Her flimsy sneakers seemed to be held together by threads as she shuffled away, pulling the baby carriage while the three huge sacks on her back quivered.

Ning Zhang was pleased to see me when I stepped into his office. "Take a seat, Jufen," he said. "Anything to drink?"

"No." I shook my head and sat down before his desk.

"Tell me, how can I persuade you to go back to Minna's?"

"I want a pension plan!" I said firmly.

He was taken aback, then grinned. "Are you kidding me? You know our agency doesn't offer that and can't set a precedent."

"I know. That's why I won't go look after Mr. Sheng anymore."

"But he might die soon if he continues refusing to eat."

Pity suddenly gripped my heart, but I got hold of myself. I said, "He'll get over it, he'll be fine. He doesn't really know me that well. Besides, he has a memory like a bucket riddled with holes."

"Do you understand, if you don't work for us, you may not be able to work elsewhere either?"

"I've made up my mind that from now on I'll work only for a company that provides a pension plan."

"That means you'll have to be able to speak English."

"I can learn."

"At your age? Give me a break. How many years have you been in this country? Ten or eleven? How many English sentences can you speak? Five or six?"

"From now on I'll live differently. If I can't speak enough English to work for a unionized company, I'll starve and die!"

The determination in my voice must have impressed him. He breathed a sigh and said, "Quite frankly, I admire that, that jolt of spirit, although you make me feel like a capitalist exploiter. All right, I wish you the best of luck. If I can do anything for you, let me know."

When I came out of his office, the air pulsed with the wings of seagulls and was full of the aroma of kebabs. The trees were green and sparkling with dewdrops in the sunshine. My head was a little light with the emotion still surging in my chest. To be honest, I'm not sure if I'll be able to learn enough English to live a different life, but I must try.

Temporary Love

LINA PUT A PINECONE CANDLESTICK on the dining table, then sat down on a love seat to wait for Panbin. This was the first time she had cooked dinner since they lived together. They were both married, their spouses still in China, and about a year ago she had moved into Panbin's house as his partner. They had become "a wartime couple," a term referring to those men and women who, unable to bring their spouses to America, cohabit for the time being to comfort each other and also to reduce living expenses. For some men such a relationship was just a way to sleep with women without having to pay, but Panbin had never taken advantage of Lina. He even claimed that he'd finally fallen for her and might go berserk if she left him. Still, they had separate phone lines in the house. Whenever he was speaking to his wife, he'd keep his door shut, whereas Lina wouldn't mind his listening when she called her husband.

It was sprinkling, raindrops pattering fitfully on the bay

windows. Lina was watching the evening news, but her mind hardly registered what the anchorman was saying, nor was she captivated by the horrific scene the TV was showing of the havoc wreaked by a suicide bomber at a bus stop in Mosul. Around six o'clock the door opened and Panbin stepped in. Leaving his umbrella in a corner to dry, he said, "Mm, smells good." He was a tall man of thirty-four and looked younger than his age.

Lina went over to the dining table while telling him, "I came back earlier." She lit a candle and planted it on the steel pinecone.

He scanned the meal. "What special day is today? A holiday?"

"No. I just thought we should celebrate."

"Celebrate what, the second anniversary of our friendship?" He laughed, a little embarrassed by his own joke.

"You can say that, but this is also for our parting. Come, sit down and dig in."

Having shucked off his jacket, he slumped down on a chair and picked up a pair of chopsticks. "I told you I wouldn't think of it," he said.

"Don't be silly! Zuming will be here soon and I have to move out. If he knows about our affair, I'll be in big trouble."

He sighed, chewing a piece of curried chicken pensively. He'd never met her husband, but she'd talked about Zuming so much that Panbin felt as if he'd known the man for ages. He told her, "Maybe I can speak to him after he settles in."

"No. Don't ever provoke him. He practiced kung fu for many years and might beat you up."

"So? If you want to divorce him, he'll have no choice."

"Why should I do that? Before I moved in, you and I had agreed that the moment your wife or my husband came, our partnership would end."

"Things have changed. I love you, you know."

"Don't be softheaded about this. Come, for the good time we spent together." She raised her glass of Chablis, but he shook his head and didn't touch his wine, his pale face taut.

She put down her glass, and a prolonged silence ensued.

He finished the last bit of rice on his plate, got up, and said, "Thanks for this memorable dinner." He headed away to his own room upstairs, his feet thumping up the flight of wood steps.

She expected him to come to her that night, but except for going to the bathroom to wash up and brush his teeth, he didn't step out of his room. At the same time, she was afraid he'd join her in bed, because once he took her into his arms, she might lose her head and promise him whatever he asked for, even something beyond her ability to fulfill. She remembered that he'd once made her call him *laogong* (hubby) again and again while making love to her. Afterward she had felt so guilty that she bought a digital camera and had it delivered to her husband for his birthday. Tonight, despite her fear of losing self-control, she longed to have that intense intimacy with Panbin for the last time. After Zuming came, she would have to become a faithful wife again.

When she got up the next morning, Panbin had left for work without having breakfast. Usually he would make toast, scramble eggs, and boil rice porridge or sesame gruel for both of them, but today he'd done nothing and had not even touched the leftovers from the previous evening. She knew she might have injured his feelings, but he was being unreasonable. They had a written agreement that entitled either of them to call off their relationship anytime without the other's consent. From the very beginning they'd both understood it was just for mutual convenience that they had come together.

In her tax office she was absentminded for a whole day, and even exchanged words with an old customer who complained that she had not deducted enough business expenses on the form she'd filled out for him. He was a supervisor at a warehouse but demanded almost eight thousand dollars in tax credits for things such as brand-name suits, shoes, a computer, books, magazines, floor lamps, batteries, even a pair of dumbbells. Lina said this was cheating the IRS. The bull-necked old codger flew into a rage and said he'd go to another tax office that could give him a better deal. Somehow a rush of emotion drove Lina to the brink of tears, but she took hold of herself and told him, "Okay, suit yourself." Hard as she tried, she couldn't manage a smile.

After the customer left, Lina finished up for the day. It wasn't four o'clock yet, but she planned to move out of Panbin's house today. Three days ago she had rented a place, a one-bedroom apartment on Sanford Avenue. She wondered if she should ask someone to give her a hand, but decided first to make sure she had packed everything. Perhaps, she hoped, she wouldn't have to take her belongings with her all at once. Her husband wouldn't arrive until late March, still two weeks away.

To her surprise, Panbin was at home. On the floor of the living room sat her six boxes, all opened; evidently he'd been rummaging through them. She sneered, "You want to see if I filched something?"

"No, just curious." He grinned and lifted her one-piece swimsuit. "I've never seen you wear this." He sniffed it. "May I keep it?"

"For a million dollars." She giggled. "I'm a married woman with a husband."

He dropped her swimsuit back into a box and said, "Sit

down. Let's talk. I was out of my head yesterday evening. I'm sorry about that."

His apology mollified her some, and she sat down opposite him. She said, "Please don't act like a crazy youngster."

"You know what, I feel I'm also your husband." The expression on his face was serious, almost stony.

"Where's our marriage certificate?" She giggled again, her cheeks twitching a little.

"That's just a piece of paper. I love you. I know you better, I know every part of you, I know all your likes and dislikes, and I know you love me too."

"Don't talk like that, please! We're both married and must be responsible. Can you abandon your wife and kid for another woman?"

"Well, I'm not sure."

"See, don't play the hypocrite. What we've done is wrong, and we ought to mend our ways, the sooner the better. Truth be told, I am fond of you, but I must take my heart back and tame it before Zuming comes."

"Tell me, do you still love him?"

"This has little to do with love. I'll try to be a good wife to him."

"Can't we remain friends?"

"Depends on what kind of friendship you have in mind."

"I mean, we'll meet once in a while."

"And hop into bed?"

He grinned while nodding yes, his round eyes glimmering. "Honestly, I love you more than my wife, but I can't divorce her because there's no way I can take my son away from her."

"So let's part ways now," she said, unsure if he was telling the truth. "The temporary pain will ward off all the miserable complications."

"It's not that simple. I won't let you go."

"But you cannot make me stay."

"You know, I have a mouth that can talk."

"God, are you threatening me? You will brief Zuming on our affair if I don't remain your mistress?"

He made no reply, an awkward smile breaking on his face while small fans of rays appeared at the outside corners of his eyes. He exhaled a long sigh.

Not sure if he'd just issued her a warning, she was upset and went to the kitchen to call a cab. He followed her and pressed down the switch hook of the phone, saying, "I'm still your chauffeur and coolie, you know." He grimaced and his eyes clouded over.

She wanted to say he was a free man now, but her voice failed her. Together they carried her boxes down to his SUV in the driveway.

Living alone was no longer easy for Lina. She was accustomed to Panbin's house, to its spacious living room and the big, comfortable bed, and also to the meals he'd made for both of them. When they'd been together, he wouldn't let her cook because she complained that too much exposure to kitchen grease would age her skin. He joked that she was just a lazybones, but he took over the cooking and liked it. Now, in her own apartment, she had to do everything herself. Sometimes she wouldn't make dinner and would just pick up one or two things at a delicatessen. Since moving out, she'd expected Panbin to call, but he never did. Perhaps he was still full of spleen, as the saying affirms: "You hate as much as you love." But he was not a young bachelor and shouldn't have behaved as if she'd jilted him and wasted his life. At times she wanted to phone him, just to see how he was doing, and once she even dialed his number but at the second ring hung up. If only she could shut him out of her mind. If only her workplace weren't in downtown Flushing so that every day she wouldn't have to pass the building that housed his software company. Whenever she walked on the street, she was afraid of bumping into him.

On March 24, her husband arrived. She took the subway to JFK to meet him. They hadn't seen each other for more than four years, and he'd changed quite a bit. He had gained some weight and his face looked wider, his eyes weary, probably thanks to the twenty-hour flight. When they hugged, she gave him a smack on the cheek, but he didn't kiss her back. Instead he said with a smile, "Hey, we're in public." His voice was still strong, though less hearty. She had always loved his manly voice, which often sounded fearless and even commanding. She noticed a sprinkling of gray hair behind his temples, though he was only thirty-three, two years older than she. He must have worried a lot these last few years. Together they lugged his baggage out of the terminal and joined the line for a taxi.

Lina had bought fresh, uncooked dumplings. Back from the airport, she put on a pot of water to boil them. Zuming hadn't brought much with him; at her suggestion, he had stuffed one of his two suitcases with books, which are triple-priced in the United States. She was pleased to see the brand-new dictionaries and self-help books, useful to both of them. Zuming had said several times on the phone that he would like to go to graduate school once he was here, but she had neither agreed nor disagreed about that.

In addition to the books, he'd brought along six cartons of Red Eagle cigarettes at the advice of a friend who had been to America. Zuming lit a cigarette and dragged at it ravenously, saying to Lina, "I couldn't smoke the whole way. That almost drove me crazy."

His smoking unnerved her. She wanted to tell him to smoke outside, but she stopped herself. This was his first day here, and she wanted to please him as much as possible. She poured half a cup of cold water into the boiling pot so that the stuffing inside the dumplings could get cooked some more. After replacing the lid, she turned around and smiled at him. "I'm so happy you made it to New York finally," she said. "After dinner, you should take a shower and then go to bed. You must be exhausted."

"I'm all right." He looked at her questioningly, as if wondering whether the full-size bed was big enough for both of them.

"I thought you'd need to rest well after the long flight," she explained.

"We'll see what we can do." He tilted his big head, his heavy jaw jutting to the side while his nostrils let out tentacles of smoke.

He enjoyed the chive-and-pork dumplings and ate them with raw garlic, which Lina didn't mind. For a whole year she hadn't tasted raw garlic because Panbin was a southerner, from Jiangsu Province, and couldn't stand the smell. She peeled several cloves for Zuming and also ate one herself. She found it quite tasty. She thought of reminding him to brush his teeth after eating garlic, but she decided to save that for another time. Maybe she would buy him some gum and mints.

"Do we have a drop of liquor in here?" Zuming asked, licking his teeth.

"No, only some cooking wine," she replied.

"That's no good."

"Maybe I can go down and get a bottle from a store."

"No, no, don't bother. I don't like American wine anyway."

An airliner roared by, the noise so loud that the ceiling seemed to vibrate. They both stopped talking. When the racket died down, he said, "Heavens, how can you sleep with airplanes flying right overhead?"

"They don't cross the residential area at night." She laughed.

"That makes sense."

As they ate, Zuming told her about their families. His father had just retired and might start a kindergarten with the help of his mother and some other retirees in the neighborhood. His parents had demanded that Lina give them some grandchildren. He emphasized "some," which meant they all knew there was no one-child policy in the United States. As for her parents, her mother missed her terribly and couldn't stop talking to people, even to strangers, about her, the only daughter. Her father's condition had improved a lot after the stroke, though he still couldn't drive his cab and so had to rent it to someone younger. As they talked, Lina felt rather down, not because the news was bad but because the weight of the two families, despite the distance of an ocean and a continent, came back to her all of a sudden. She was still young, yet when she thought of her family she felt aged like an old woman.

She told her husband, "We cannot afford to have kids before we settle down."

"I understand. There'll be a long haul for us."

Zuming insisted they make love that night, and she was willing. Afterward he fell asleep and left her awake for hours. She listened to his snores, which weren't loud but sounded like a broken fan.

• • •

During the next week Zuming went out every day to get to know the area. He also spent many hours in the public library gathering information on business schools. He told Lina that he wanted to do an MBA, having found out that it was easy to earn small wages but hard to make big money here. "Who knows, someday I may end up on Wall Street," he chuckled.

She was reluctant to discourage him, but she was worried. Living in Panbin's house, she had paid only two hundred dollars a month for food and utilities because he refused to take rent from her. Now her expenses were more substantial. Her job at the tax office wasn't secure; the filing season would end soon, and the summer and fall would be a lean time. How could she make enough to support both Zuming and herself?

One evening she told him, "I don't think you should go to business school this year."

"I have to." His tone, full of resolve, surprised her.

"Why? I'm not sure if I have a stable job. Where can we get the money for tuition?"

"Don't you have forty thousand in the bank?"

"Like I said, we mustn't touch that because we'll need it for the down payment on an apartment."

"Well, I'm not sure we should buy our own place here. Anyway, I must get an MBA."

"I don't think you should rush."

"I want to give it a shot this year. You owe me that."

"Why? Why are you so stubborn?"

"You still think I don't know?" His face lengthened, his eyes ablaze.

"Know what?"

"You shacked up with a man named Panbin Wang."

She was stunned, her mind whirling. How did he hear of

it? From Panbin? Who else could have given her away? "How—how did you know?" she stammered.

"Someone told me."

"Who?"

"That's not important. If you wanted to have a peaceful conscience, you should not have slept around."

She started to sob, covering her face with her narrow hand. Meanwhile, he lounged in a chair and, pencil in mouth, continued reading a dictionary. He would have to pass the TOEFL to be admitted to a business school.

Her sniveling accentuated the quietness of the room.

A few moments later she said, "Zuming, I'm very sorry. Please forgive me. I was a weak woman and needed a man to help me here. You've seen how hard life is in this place where everyone's busy and treats others like strangers. I was so miserable and so lonely that I often thought I was losing my mind. On weekends I felt worse, cooped up in a room like a sick animal. Whenever I saw children I wanted to touch them and even imagined taking them away from their mothers. I wanted to live! To have a normal life. Panbin Wang comforted and helped me, emotionally and financially. Truth be told, without him I might've gone mad or died. At least without his help I couldn't possibly have saved that amount of money for us."

He sat up and took the pencil out of his mouth. "Honest to God, I didn't touch a woman for four years, although I had opportunities. When your father had the stroke, I nursed him every night for three months, biking to the hospital through wind and snow. No matter how miserable and depressed I was, I had to take care of your family and mine. Don't use your suffering to exonerate yourself. I suffered no less than you."

Now she knew she would probably have no choice but to

let him go to business school. This meant she'd have to empty out her bank account. There wasn't another way to placate him, to prevent him from disclosing her affair to her in-laws and thus bringing her parents to shame.

That night she didn't sleep, nor did she remove his hand resting on her thigh. Despite her fear of his anger, she felt she must stay with him. She also thought of Panbin, but still felt he was too glib and too smooth. She wondered how her husband had learned of her affair. The more she mulled it over, the more she was convinced that it must have been Panbin who had told him. She recalled his words—"I have a mouth that can talk." Apparently he had betrayed her. How could he be so vengeful and so unscrupulous? He was a big liar and had lied to her about how he loved her. If he'd really cared about her, he wouldn't have stabbed her in the back.

This wasn't over. She wouldn't let him get away with it.

She phoned Panbin two days later and asked to see him in the afternoon. He sounded pleased, though his voice was languid and lukewarm. He agreed to meet her at a karaoke club on Prince Street.

He showed up first and got a booth. A couple of minutes later she arrived. At the sight of the beers, mixed nuts, and fruit salad he'd ordered, she frowned but sat down without a word. He grinned, his lips bloodless and his eyes red. "So what's up?" he asked.

"I never thought you could be so mean, disgusting."

"What are you talking about?" He stopped munching nuts to gaze at her.

"You snitched on me to my husband."

"No, I didn't!" He laced his fingers together on his lap.

"But it's all right if he knows. The truth would come out sooner or later. What are you going to do?"

"I'll have to spend all my savings for his tuition if a business school accepts him. Tell me, what did you tell him about us?"

"I don't know him. Why don't you believe me?"

"But you could call or e-mail him. I knew you were full of tricks, but I never thought you could be an informer."

"Wait a second. I've had no contact with Zuming whatsoever. Don't unload all your trouble onto me." He sighed and then went on. "Matter of fact, I'm in a fine mess too." He pulled an envelope out of his hip pocket and put it on the coffee table. He said, "A letter from my wife. She wants a divorce."

Surprised, Lina wanted to open the letter, but refrained. Now she felt he might be innocent—he was obviously tormented by his wife's demand. Lina said, "But who could have told Zuming about us?"

"We were not like some other 'wartime couples' and never bothered to conceal our relationship. Anyone who resented us being together could tattle on us. The world is never lacking in defenders of morality. My wife also knows about our affair and cited it as grounds for divorce. Apparently people back home sympathize with her, and she'll get custody of my child for sure."

Lina felt awful, knowing how he loved his six-year-old son. She was no longer interested in ferreting out the informer. Whoever that was, what was the use? The damage was already done, and they could do nothing about it.

"When did your wife find out?" she asked, taking a swig of the beer she'd just uncapped.

"Long ago, evidently. She said she'd fallen in love with an architect, who promised her to treat my child like his own.

They've been carrying on for a while. That must be why she gave me all the excuses for not coming to join me here. How long has your husband known about us?"

"He wouldn't tell me. He must've planned all his moves before he came."

"See? I told you not to try hard to bring him over."

"I meant to keep my marriage."

"You simply couldn't pull your neck out of the yoke of the past."

"Can you?"

"I would try."

She sighed. Too late for me now, she thought. She wanted to talk with Panbin some more, to get advice on how to tackle her predicament, but she restrained herself, fearing he might take advantage of the situation to wreck her marriage. In the back of her mind some misgivings about him still lingered.

For weeks Lina had been looking for a different job while her husband spent his days cramming for tests. On weekends when she was home, he would go to the library, saying he had to concentrate. He'd wrap an egg sandwich for lunch and also pocket a handful of chocolates. Back in China he'd done graduate work in economics, so he was somewhat familiar with the test subjects. His main obstacle was English, which he was determined to overcome. In a way, Lina admired his devotion to pursuing his ambition. From the very first days of going with him, she had liked his optimism and his ability to work hard. He'd once fainted in a public restroom where he studied a math formula while squatting over a toilet bowl. In his home county, he was the only one accepted by a college in Beijing that year.

As May approached, Lina landed a bookkeeping job at a

law firm. She was pleased and a bit relieved. Still, she was unsettled by Zuming's determination to go to business school despite the hardship it would cause. She was prepared to pay his tuition, even though she might have to borrow some money. But what would he do after he got his MBA? Would he still want this marriage? Anything could happen during the next two years. If he met a woman he liked and hit it off with her, he might file for divorce. He must have been waiting for such an opportunity while squeezing whatever he could out of her, his unfaithful wife. The more Lina thought about the future, the more agitated she became. Sometimes she felt sure he must despise her. Back in Beijing, she'd planned to give him a child once they settled down, but now she was no longer willing to do it.

At night they slept in the same bed, and he would make love to her once or twice a week. She didn't enjoy it, so she wouldn't mind if he left her alone. It was after the lovemaking that she'd feel miserable, listening to him snoring while she felt used. Sometimes he'd grind his teeth or whisper something she couldn't make out. She wondered if he felt she was dirty and rotten, tainted by another man's lust. Shrewd and inscrutable, Zuming must have harbored quite a few plans, which he would never confide to anyone. When they had sex, he was sometimes rough as if intending to hurt her. That would make her miss Panbin, who, when doing it, had always spent what seemed like an hour with her and kept asking how she felt this way or that. He'd made her eager to open herself and indulge her passion. Sometimes she thought of recommending to her husband a book like *The Joy of Sex* or *She Comes First,* which he could borrow from the library, but she never dared to bring that up, knowing he might think her shameless.

. . .

She suggested that they sleep separately, and Zuming didn't object. His compliance convinced her that he would leave her someday. Even so, she was willing to pay his tuition, as a way to make up to him. She didn't regret having brought him here, though she felt it might have been a mistake to have broken up with Panbin in such a rush.

Meanwhile, she'd called Panbin at work several times, but he never picked up the phone, nor had he returned her calls. Then, one day, he did answer. He was cold and businesslike, saying he had no time to talk for long and his boss was awaiting him upstairs.

"How are you?" she asked almost timidly.

"Still alive." He sounded so bitter that she felt a twinge in her chest.

As she continued talking, he cut her short. "I have to go."

"Can I call you again sometime this week?"

"Didn't you say it was over between us? I won't have a mistress anymore. I want a wife, a home."

She remained silent and knew that something had happened to his marriage. Before she could ask, he hung up. She turned tearful and went to the law firm's bathroom to compose herself.

Later, through a mutual acquaintance, she found out that Panbin had granted his wife the divorce and the custody of their child. Over the past five years he'd sent his wife more than seventy thousand dollars, which made her rich; even after paying off her mortgage, she still had a good sum in the bank. Crushed, Panbin rarely stepped out of his house these days except when he had to go to work. Lina also learned that some young women had been recommended to him, but he wouldn't meet with any of them. He just said he wouldn't date a Chinese woman again. He seemed to have changed and now avoided people he once knew.

Soon after taking all the tests, Zuming found a job at the martial arts institute called Wu Tang on Parsons Boulevard. He was hired as an assistant instructor, mainly tutoring a tai chi class. Lina was amazed, although it was a part-time job that required Zuming to mop the floors and clean the restrooms as well. He was a survivor, full of vitality.

In late June a university in Louisiana notified him that its one-year MBA program had admitted him. Lina knew he'd planned for a more expensive school, but he'd missed most of the application deadlines. He jumped at the late admission; he wanted to go. She felt he'd begun leaving her. God knew what would happen in New Orleans once he was there. After he had his degree, where would he go? Back to China, where a U.S. MBA was worth a lot and he had already built up a business network? That was unlikely. He would probably start a career here, even though Wall Street might be beyond his reach.

She felt wretched but had no one to talk to. If only Panbin were still around. He used to listen so quietly and attentively that she had often wondered if he fell asleep as she was speaking. Afterward he would help her figure out what to do and whom to see. He was full of strategies and, despite his training in computer science, loved reading practical philosophy, especially Machiavelli and a modern book on the ways of the world titled *The Art of the Shameless.*

One Saturday afternoon in early July, Lina took a shower, let her hair fall loosely on her shoulders, slipped on a pastel blue dress that highlighted her slender waist, and went to Panbin's house as if she just happened to be passing by. He answered the door and looked surprised, but let her in. He was a lot thinner, yet spirited as before.

"Tea or coffee?" he asked her when they'd entered the living room.

"Coffee, please." She sat down on the love seat, which felt as familiar as if it belonged to her. The room with bay windows was the same, except for the floor, which had been recently waxed and was shiny throughout. He seemed to be doing fine.

He put a cup of coffee in front of her and sat down. "Well, why did you come to see me?" he asked in a flat voice.

"Is it illegal?" She tilted her oval face, her chin pointed at him as she smiled, her lips curling a little.

"I thought you'd already washed your hands of me."

"I'm still worried about you."

"No need. I'm tough and I know how to get by."

"Zuming's going to New Orleans in a couple of weeks."

"So? What does that have to do with me?"

She tittered. "Didn't you used to feel you too were my husband?"

"That was four months ago when I still had my family."

"You feel differently about me now?"

"Things have changed and I've changed too. My wife found the love of her life and took my son away from me. That almost killed me, but I resurrected myself and have become a different man."

"How different?"

"I'm going to Kiev to see my girlfriend next week."

"Your girlfriend?"

"Yes, I got to know her online."

Lina couldn't help but sneer. "So you want to become an international womanizer?"

"Oh, you can call me a cosmopolitan playboy, but I don't give a damn. From now on I won't date a Chinese woman again. Just sick of it—every Chinese has so much baggage of the past, too heavy for me to share and carry. I want to live freely and fearlessly with nothing to do with the past."

"Without the past, how can we make sense of now?"

"I've come to believe that one has to get rid of the past to survive. Dump your past and don't even think about it, as if it never existed."

"How can that be possible? Where did you get that stupid idea?"

"That is the way I want to live, the only way to live. If you hadn't worried so much about all the ties to your past, you wouldn't have left me, would you? That's the reason I've been dating a Ukranian woman, who is lovely."

"She just wants to get a green card; she can't be serious about a yellow man. Even if she agrees to marry you, she might not give you children. Or maybe you'll dump her once you're done toying with her."

"That's not something for you to speculate about. Didn't you do that to me? Anyway, you mustn't think ill of my girlfriend. I believe in names. Do you know any woman named Olga who is an adventuress?"

She laughed. "You're so silly. You haven't even met her yet, but you call her your girlfriend. Doesn't she have siblings?"

"She has a younger brother, she told me."

"Doesn't she have parents?"

"She does, and grandparents."

"See, are those not a kind of baggage? The same sort of past as we have?"

Stumped, he looked at his wristwatch and stood. "I have to go to the UPS store."

She got to her feet too and refrained from saying she wished to remain his friend, but told him she missed his cooking, to which he didn't respond. She lifted the cold coffee and downed it to the last drop, then stepped out of his house without another word. She wasn't sure how serious he was about Olga or whether he'd bought the plane tickets for Kiev. Maybe he couldn't help but act out of character. Whatever he might do, she hoped he wouldn't make a fool of himself.

The House Behind a Weeping Cherry

WHEN MY ROOMMATE MOVED OUT, I was worried that Mrs. Chen might increase the rent. I had been paying three hundred dollars a month for half a room. If my landlady demanded more, I would have to look for another place. I liked this colonial house. In front of it stood an immense weeping cherry tree that attracted birds and gave a bucolic impression, though it was already early summer and the blossoming season had passed. The house was close to downtown Flushing, and you could hear the buzz of traffic on Main Street. It was also near where I worked, convenient for everything. Mrs. Chen took up the first floor; my room was upstairs, where three young women also lived. My former roommate, an apprentice to a carpenter, had left because the three female tenants were prostitutes and often received clients in the house. To be honest, I didn't feel comfortable about that either, but I had grown used to the women, and especially liked Huong, a twiggy Vietnamese in her early twenties whose parents had migrated to Cholon from China three decades ago, when Saigon fell and the real estate market there became affordable. Also, I had just arrived in New York and at times found it miserable to be alone.

As I expected, Mrs. Chen, a stocky woman with a big mole beside her nose, came up that evening. She sat down, patted her dyed hair, and said, "Wanping, now that you're using this room for yourself we should talk about the rent."

"I'm afraid I can't pay more than what I'm paying. You can get another tenant." I waved at the empty bed behind her.

"Well, I could put out an ad for that, but I have something else in mind." She leaned toward me.

I did not respond. I disliked this Fujianese woman and felt she was too smooth. She went on, "Do you have a driver's license?"

"I have one from North Carolina, but I'm not sure if I can drive here." I had spent some time delivering produce for a vegetable farm outside Charlotte.

"That shouldn't be a problem. You can change it to a New York license—easy to do. The motor registration office is very close." She smiled, revealing her gappy teeth.

"What do you want me to do?" I asked.

"I won't charge you extra rent. You can have this room to yourself, but I hope you can drive the girls around in the evenings when they have outcalls."

I tried to stay calm and answered, "Is that legal?"

She chuckled. "Don't be scared. The girls go to hotels and private homes. No cops will burst in on them—it's very safe."

"How many times a week am I supposed to drive?"

"Not very often—four or five times, tops."

"Do you pay for the girls' meals too?"

"Yes, everything but long-distance phone calls."

At last I understood why my female housemates always ate together. "All right. I can drive them around in the evenings, but only in Queens and Brooklyn. Manhattan's too scary."

She gave a short laugh. "No problem. I don't let them go that far."

"By the way, can I eat with them when I work?"

"Sure thing. I'll tell them."

"Thank you." I paused. "You know, sometimes it can be lonely here."

A sly smile crossed her face. "You can spend time with the girls—they may give you a discount."

I didn't know how to respond. Before leaving, she made it clear that I must keep everything confidential and that she had asked me to help mainly because she wanted the women to feel safe when they went out. Johns would treat a prostitute better if they knew she had a chauffeur at her disposal. I had seen the black Audi in the garage. I hadn't driven for months and really missed the feeling of freedom that an automobile used to give me, as though I could soar in the air if there weren't cars in front of me on the highway. I looked forward to driving the women around.

After my landlady left, I stood before the window of my room, which faced the street. The crown of the weeping cherry, motionless and more than forty feet high, was a feathery mass against a sky strewn with stars. In the distance, a plane, a cluster of lights, was sailing noiselessly east through a few rags of clouds. I knew Mrs. Chen's offer might implicate me in something illicit, but I wasn't worried. I was accustomed to living among the prostitutes. When I first figured out what they did for a living, I had wanted to move out right away, like my former roommate, but I couldn't find a place close to my job—I was a presser at a garment factory downtown. Also, once I got to know the women a little better, I realized that they were not "bloodsuckers," as people assumed. Like everyone else, they had to work to survive.

I too was selling myself. Every weekday I stood at the table ironing the joining lines of cut pieces, the waists of pants, the collars and cuffs of shirts. It was sultry in the basement, where the air conditioner was at least ten years old, inefficient, and whined loudly. We were making quality clothes for stores in Manhattan, and every item had to be neatly ironed before being wrapped up for shipment.

Who would have thought I'd land in a sweatshop? My parents' last letter urged me again to go to college. But I couldn't pass the TOEFL. My younger brother had just been admitted to a veterinary school, and I'd sent back three thousand dollars for his tuition. If only I had learned a trade before coming to the United States, like plumbing, or home renovation, or Qigong. Any job would have been better than ironing clothes.

The brothel had no name. I had once come across a newspaper ad in our kitchen that read: "Angels of Your Dream—Asian Girls from Various Countries with Gorgeous Figures and Tender Hearts." It gave no contact information other than a phone number, which was the one shared by the women. I almost laughed out loud at the ad, because the three of them were all Chinese. Of course, Huong could pass for Vietnamese, speaking the language as her native tongue, and Nana could pretend to be a Malaysian or Singaporean, since she came from Hong Kong and spoke accented Mandarin. But Lili, a tall college student from Shanghai, looked Chinese through and through, even though she spoke English well. She was the one who handled the phone calls. I guessed

Lili would return to school when the summer was over, and then Mrs. Chen might hire another twentysomething who was fluent in English. I wasn't sure if my landlady was the real boss, however. The women often mentioned someone called the Croc. I had never met the man, but I learned from them that he owned some shady businesses in the area and was a coyote.

I liked having dinner with my housemates. We usually ate quite late, around eight p.m., but that was fine with me, since most days I didn't leave the factory until seven. Often I was not the only man dining with them; they offered free dinner to their clients as well. The meals were homely fare—plain rice and two or three dishes, one of which was meat while the others were vegetables. Occasionally the women would prepare a bowl of seafood in place of a vegetable dish. There would also be a soup, usually made of spinach or watercress or bamboo shoots mixed with dried shrimp, tofu or egg drops, or even rice crust. The women would take turns cooking, one person each day, unless that person was occupied with a john and another had to step in for her in the kitchen. Some of their clients enjoyed the atmosphere at the table and stayed for hours chatting.

Whenever there was another man at dinner, I would remain quiet. I'd finish eating quickly and return to my room, where I would watch TV or play solitaire or leaf through a magazine. But when I was the only man I'd stay as long as I could. The women seemed to like having me around and would even tease me. Huong was not only the prettiest but also the best cook, depending less on sauces, whereas Lili used too much sugar and Nana deep-fried almost everything. One day Huong braised a large pomfret and stir-fried slivers of potato and celery, both favorites of mine, though I hadn't told her so. None of them had a client that evening, so dinner started at seven thirty and we ate slowly.

Nana told us, "I had a guy this afternoon who said his girlfriend had just jilted him. He cried in my room—it was awful. I didn't know how to comfort him. I just said, 'You have to let it go.' "

"Did he pay you?" Lili asked.

"Uh-huh. He gave me eighty dollars without doing anything with me."

"Well, I wonder why he came here," I said.

"Maybe just to have someone to talk to," Huong said.

"I don't know," Lili pitched in. "Maybe to find out if he could still do it with another girl. Men are weak creatures and cannot survive without having a woman around."

I had never liked Lili, who would speak to me with her eyes half closed as if reluctant to pay me more mind. I said, "There're a lot of bachelors out there. Most of them are getting on all right."

"Like yourself," Nana broke in, giggling.

"I'm single because I'm too poor to get married," I confessed.

"Do you have a girlfriend?" Huong asked.

"Not yet."

"So would you go with me if I wasn't a sex worker?" Nana asked, her oval face expressionless.

"Your taste is too expensive for me," I said, laughing, though it was only partly a joke.

They all laughed. Nana continued, "Come on, I'll give you a big discount."

"I can't take advantage of you like that," I said.

That cracked them up again. I meant what I said, though. If I slept with one of them, I might have to do the same with the other two, spending a fortune. Then it would be hard to keep a balanced relationship with all of them. Besides, I wasn't sure if they were all clean and healthy. Even if they were, I disliked Lili. It was better to remain unattached.

Then the phone rang, and Lili picked it up. "Hello, honey, how may I help you?" she intoned in a sugary voice.

I resumed eating as if uninterested, but listened carefully. Lili told the caller, "We have many Asian girls here. What kind of a girl are you interested in, sir? . . . Yes, we do. . . . Of course pretty, every one of them is pretty. . . . At least one-twenty. . . . Well, that'll be between you and the girl, sir. . . . Wait, let me write it down." She grabbed a pen and began jotting down the address. Meanwhile, Huong and Nana finished their dinner, knowing that one of them would have business to take care of.

Lili said into the phone, "Got it. She'll be there within half an hour. . . . Absolutely, sir. Thank you, bye-bye."

Hanging up, Lili turned around and said, "Huong, you should go. The man's name is Mr. Han. He wants a Thai girl."

"I can't speak Thai!"

"Speak some Vietnamese to show him that you're not from China. He can't tell the difference anyway, as long as you know how to charm him."

Huong went back into her room to brush her teeth and put on some makeup, and Lili handed me the scrap of paper with our destination—a room in the Double Luck Hotel. I knew how to get there, having driven the women several times. I clapped on my brown duckbill cap, which kept my eyes hidden.

A few minutes later Huong came out, ready to go. "Wow, you're beautiful!" I said, quite amazed.

"Am I?" She lifted her arms while turning a little to let me view her from the side. Her waist was concave at the small of her back.

"Like a little fox," I said.

She slapped me on the arm. She wore a beige miniskirt and had applied lipstick, but she seemed more like a teenager who had messed up her makeup, so that her face appeared older than her petite body, which was curvaceous but tight. As she walked with her denim purse hanging from her thin shoulder, her legs and hips swayed a little as if she were about to leap. Together we went down to the garage.

The hotel was on a busy street, and two large buses stood at its front entrance, one still puffing exhaust out of its rear. Flocks of tourists were collecting their baggage, while a guide shouted to gather them for check-in. I found a quiet spot around the corner and let Huong out. "Call if you need me to come up," I told her. "I'll be waiting for you here."

"Thanks." She closed the door and strolled away, her gait as casual as if she were a guest at the hotel.

My heart sagged as I lay back in the seat to take a nap. She was young and beautiful and shouldn't be selling herself like that. For sure she had to send her parents money regularly, but there were other ways of making a living. She wasn't stupid, and she could have learned a respectable trade. She had finished high school in Vietnam and could speak some English by now. But from what I had gathered at the dining table, she was an illegal alien, whereas Nana had a Canadian green card and Lili held a student visa. They could make some money, definitely, but nothing like what the newspaper ads promised for the "massage" profession—"more than $20,000 a month." Usually, the women charged a john one hundred at the house, but they had to give Mrs. Chen forty of that. Sometimes a client would give them a tip, between twenty and sixty dollars. Nana was rawboned and on the homely side, with a slightly cavernous mouth, so her price for incalls was eighty dollars, unless the men were older and had more cash to throw around. On a good day, they could each make more than two hundred after paying our landlady. Now and then an obnoxious client would not only refuse to tip them but also walk off with their belongings. Lili had once lost a pair of silver bracelets, stolen by a man who claimed to be from Shanghai, like her.

I had asked Huong about visiting hotels and private homes. She said she could make thirty or forty dollars more per client than at the house, though there were more risks. One night I had driven her to see a john at the International Inn, but on arrival she had found two men in the suite. They dragged her in before she could back out, and worked her so hard that she felt as if her legs no longer belonged to her. She had to take off her high heels to walk back to the car. She wept all the way home. She was sick the next day but wouldn't go to a clinic, as she had no health insurance. I suggested she see Dr. Liang at Sun Garden Herbs. She paid ten dollars for a diagnosis fee. The old man put his fingers on her wrists to feel her pulse and said her kidneys were weak. Also, there was too much angry fire in her liver. He prescribed a bunch of herbs, which helped her recover. After that, I offered to accompany her into hotels and wait in the hallway, but she wouldn't let me, saying it would be too conspicuous.

I couldn't drift off to sleep in the car, thinking about Huong. What kind of man was she in there with? Was she all right? Did she like it if the john was young and handsome? Was she acting like a slut? Sometimes at night I couldn't sleep and would fantasize about her, but when I was fully awake I'd keep my distance. I knew I was just a presser in a sweatshop, gangly and nondescript, and might never be able to date a nice girl, but it would be shameful to have an easy woman as a girlfriend. At most, I could be a good friend to Huong.

Tonight she returned in less than fifty minutes, which was unusual. I was pleased to see her back all right, though her eyes were watery and shed a hard light. She slid into the passenger seat, and I pulled away from the curb. "How was it? No trouble?" I asked, afraid that the client might have discovered she wasn't Thai.

"Rotten luck again," she said.

"What happened?"

"The man's an official from Beijing. He wanted me to write him a receipt like I'd sold him medicines or something. Where could I get a receipt for him? Nuts!"

"Did he haggle with you?"

"No, but he bit my nipple so hard it must be bleeding. I'll have to put iodine on it once we're home. My clients will think I'm diseased now."

I sighed, not knowing how to respond. As we were crossing Thirty-seventh Avenue, I said, "Can't you do something less dangerous for a living?"

"You find a me a job and I'll take it."

That silenced me. She slipped a ten into my hand, which was the unspoken rule worked out by the women—every time I drove them, they tipped the same amount. Actually, only Huong and Nana did that, because Lili didn't take outcalls.

I thanked Huong and put the money into my shirt pocket.

The three women often compared notes. The best clients, they all agreed, were old men. Older johns were usually less aggressive and easier to entertain. Many of them couldn't get hard and spent more time cracking dirty jokes than doing real business. Those old goats could be more generous, having more spare cash in their "little coffers," unbeknownst to their wives. The older ones seldom ate dinner at the house. Some of them were friends of Mrs. Chen's, in which case the women would treat them like special guests, and even give them Viagra. I was surprised when I heard that.

"Viagra?" I asked Lili about Mr. Tong, a bent man in his mid-sixties. "Aren't you afraid he might have a heart attack?"

"Only half a pill, no big deal. Mrs. Chen said he always needs extra help."

"He pays you well besides," Nana said. "Lili, did he give you two hundred today?"

"One eighty," Lili replied.

"Doesn't he have a wife?" I asked.

"Not anymore. She died long ago," Huong said, cracking a spiced peanut.

"Why wouldn't he marry again?" I went on. "At least he should find someone who can take care of him."

Nana let out a sigh. "Money's the root of the trouble. He's so rich he can't find a trustworthy wife."

Huong added, "I've heard he owns a couple of restaurants."

"Also your sweatshop, Wanping." Nana looked me straight in the face, as if forcing down a laugh.

"No, he doesn't," I shot back. "My factory is owned by a girl from Hong Kong named Nini."

That had them in stitches. Actually, the owner of my garment shop was a Taiwanese man who taught college before coming to America.

Many of the johns were married men. They were reluctant

to spend time and money on a mistress for fear of complications that might destroy their marriage. So they tried to keep up appearances while indulging in a sensuous life on the sly. But there were always exceptions. One day, Huong said a middle-aged client had told her that he hadn't had sex for almost two years because his wife was too ill. Huong had advised him to come more often, at least twice a month, so that he could recover his sex life. As he was now, he was totally inadequate. "He's a good man," Huong told us. "He couldn't do anything with me at all, saying he felt guilty about his wife, but he paid me anyway."

"Then he shouldn't have come to a whorehouse in the first place," Lili said.

I could tell that Huong and Nana didn't really like Lili either. She often bitched about misplaced things, and once accused Nana of using her cell phone to call someone in San Francisco. They had a row and didn't speak to each other for days afterward.

The story about the man with a bedridden wife made me think a lot. If I were a policeman, knowing about his family situation, would I have arrested him for visiting a prostitute? Probably not. I used to believe that all johns were bad and loose men, but now I could see that some of them were nothing but wrecks with personal problems that they didn't know how to handle. They came here hoping that a prostitute might help.

I was in bed one night when a cry rose from Nana's room. At first I thought it was just an orgasmic groan she had faked to please a client. Sometimes I was unsettled by the noises the women and the men made, noises that kept me awake and fantasizing. Then Nana screamed, "Get out of here!"

I pulled on my pants and ran out of my room. The door of

Nana's room was ajar, and through the gap I saw a paunchy man of around sixty standing by the bed and madly gesticulating at Nana. This was the first time I had seen an older john make trouble. I moved closer but didn't go in. Mrs. Chen had told me to give the women a hand whenever they needed it. She hadn't made it explicit, but I'd guessed that she wanted me to provide some protection for them.

"I paid you, so I'm staying," the man barked, and flung up his hand.

"You can't make a night of it. Please go away," Nana said, her face stamped with annoyance.

I went in and asked him, "What's your problem? Didn't you already get your time with her?"

He lifted his eyes to squint at me. His face, red like a monkey's ass, showed he was drunk. In fact, the entire room reeked of alcohol. "Who are you?" he grunted. "This is none of your business. I wanna stay here tonight, and nobody can make me change my mind."

I could tell that he thought this was like China, where it's commonplace for a john to spend a night with a girl if he pays enough. "I am just a tenant," I said. "You've been kicking up such a racket that I can't sleep."

"So? Deal with it. I want my money's worth."

As he was speaking, I glanced at Nana's bed. Two wet spots stained a pink sheet, and a pair of pillows had been cast aside. On the floor was an overturned cane chair. By now both Huong and Lili were up too, but they stayed outside the door, watching. I told the man, "It's the rule here: you fire your gun and you leave. No girl is supposed to be your bed warmer."

"I paid her for what I want."

"All right, this is not my problem. I'm going to call the

police. We simply cannot sleep while you're rocking the house."

"Oh yeah? Call the cops and see who they'll haul away first." He seemed more awake now, his eyes glittering.

I pressed on. "All the tenants here will say that you broke in to assault this woman." I was surprised by what I said, and I saw Huong and Lili avert their eyes.

"Cut that shit out! I paid this ho." He pointed at Nana.

"She's not a whore. Nana, you didn't invite him here, did you?"

"Uh-uh." She shook her head.

I told him, "See, we're all her witnesses. You'd better get out of here, now."

"I can't believe this. There's no good faith in this world anymore—it's worse than China." He grabbed his walking stick and lumbered out of the room.

The three women laughed and told me that the old goat was a first-time visitor and that they felt lucky to have me living on the same floor. We were in the kitchen now, all wide awake. Nana put on a kettle to boil some water for an herbal tea called Sweet Dreams.

I wasn't pleased by what I had done. "I acted like a pimp, didn't I?"

"No, you did well," Huong replied.

"Thank God we have a man among us," Lili added.

Lili's words made me uneasy. I'm not one of you, I thought. But afterward, I felt they were more friendly than before, and even Lili started speaking to me more often and with her eyes fully open. They'd ask me what I would like for dinner, and cooked fish three or four times a week because I was fond of seafood. My factory provided steamed rice for its workers at lunch, so I just needed to bring something to go with it.

Whenever it was Huong's turn to cook, she would set aside the leftovers in a plastic container for me to take to work the next day. Nana and Lili often joked that Huong treated me as if I were her boyfriend. At first, I felt embarrassed, but little by little I got used to their teasing.

One morning in late July, I woke up feeling as if my lungs were on fire. I must have caught the flu, but I had to go to the factory, where a stack of cut pieces was waiting to be ironed. Unlike the sewing women, I couldn't sit down at the ironing table. The shop provided tea in a samovar, which tasted a little fishy, but I drank one mug after another to soothe my throat and keep my eyes open. As a result, I went to the bathroom more frequently. Some of the floorboards were crooked, and I had to be careful when walking around. By midafternoon I was sweating all over and my pulse was racing, so I decided to rest on a long bench by the wall, but I tripped and fell before I could reach it. The moment I picked myself up, my foreman, Jimmy Choi, a broad-shouldered fellow of about forty-five, came over and said, "Are you all right, Wanping?"

"I'm okay," I mumbled, brushing the dust off my pants.

"You look terrible."

"I might be running a fever."

He felt my forehead with his thick, rough hand. "You'd better go home. We're not busy today, and Danny and Marc can manage without you."

Jimmy drove me back to Mrs. Chen's in his pickup and told me not to worry about coming to work the next day if I didn't feel up to it. I said I would try my best to show up.

I felt too awful to join my housemates at dinner. Instead, I stayed in bed with my eyes closed, forcing myself not to moan. Still, I couldn't help moaning through my nose occasionally, which made me feel better. Before dark, Huong came in and put a carton of orange juice and a cup on the nightstand, saying I must drink a lot of liquid to excrete the poison from my body. "What would you like for dinner?" she asked.

"I don't want to eat."

"Come on, you must eat something to fight the illness."

"I'll be all right."

I knew she would be busy that evening, because it was Friday. After she left, I drank some orange juice and then lay back and tried to fall asleep. My throat felt slightly better, but the fever was still raging. I regretted not having gone to the herb store earlier to get some ready-made boluses. The room was quiet except for the faint drone of a mosquito. The instant it landed on my cheek, I killed it with a slap. I was miserable and couldn't help but miss home. Such a feeling hadn't visited me for a long time—I had always managed to suppress my homesickness so that I could make it through my daily routine. A busy man cannot afford to be nostalgic. But that evening the image of my mother kept coming to mind. She knew a lot of folk remedies and could easily have helped me recover in a day or two, but she would have kept me in bed for longer to ensure that I recuperated fully. When I was little, I used to enjoy being sick so she could fuss over me. I hadn't seen her for two years now. Oh, how I missed her!

As I was dozing off, someone knocked on the door. "Come in," I said.

Huong came in again, this time holding a steaming bowl. "Sit up and eat some noodles," she told me.

"You cooked this for me?" I was amazed that it was wheat noodles, made from scratch, not the rice noodles we usually ate. She must have guessed that, as a northerner, I would prefer wheat.

"Yes, for you," she said. "Eat it while it's hot. It will make you feel better."

I sat up and began eating with chopsticks and a spoon. There were slivers of chives and napa cabbage in the soup, along with some dried shrimp and three poached eggs. I was touched and turned my head away so that she wouldn't see my wet eyes. This was genuine home cooking from my province, and I hadn't tasted anything like it for two years. I wanted to ask her how she had learned to make noodles like this, but I didn't say a word; I just kept eating ravenously. Meanwhile, seated on a chair beside my bed, she watched me intently, her eyes shimmering.

"Huong, where are you?" Lili cried from the living room.

"Here, I'm here." She got up and left, leaving the door ajar.

I strained my ears to listen. Lili said, "A man at the Rainbow Inn wants a girl."

"Wanping's ill and can't drive today," Huong replied.

"The place is on Thirty-seventh Avenue, just a few steps away. You've been there."

"I don't want to go tonight."

"What do you mean, you don't want to go?"

"I should stay and take care of Wanping. Can't Nana go?"

"She's busy with someone."

"Can you do it for me?"

"Well," Lili sighed, "okay, only this once."

"Thank you."

When Huong came back, I told her, "You shouldn't spend so much time with me. You have things to do."

"Don't be silly. Here is some vitamin C and aspirin. Take two of each after the meal."

That night she checked on me from time to time to make sure I took the pills and drank enough liquid and was fully covered with a thick comforter of hers, so that I could sweat out my flu. Around midnight, I fell asleep, but I had to keep getting up to pee. Huong had left an aluminum cuspidor in my room and told me to use it instead of going to the bathroom, so that I wouldn't catch cold again.

The next morning, my fever had subsided, though I still felt weak, not as steady on my feet as before. I called Jimmy and said I would definitely come to work that day, but I didn't get there until after ten. Even so, some of my fellow workers were amazed that I had reappeared so quickly. They must have thought I had caught something more serious, like pneumonia or a venereal disease, and would remain in bed for a week or so. I was glad there was not a lot of work piled up on my ironing table.

A week later, some sewers left the factory and we all got busier. There were twenty women at the garment shop, and with two or three exceptions, they were all married and had children. Most of them were Chinese, though four were Mexican. They could come and go according to their own schedules. That was a main reason they kept their jobs, which paid by the piece, and not very much. Most of them, working full-time, made about three hundred dollars a week. Like them, I could keep a flexible schedule as long as I didn't let work accumulate on my ironing table or miss deadlines. I must admit that our boss, Mr. Fuh, was a decent man, proficient in English and knowledgeable about business management; he even provided health-care benefits for us, which was another reason some of the women worked here. Their husbands were menial workers or small-business owners and couldn't possibly get health insurance for their families. Like the other two young pressers, Marc and Danny, I didn't bother about insurance. I was strong and healthy, not yet thirty, and wouldn't spend three hundred a month on that.

We had been getting more orders for women's garments lately, so I went to work earlier, around seven. But I took long breaks during the day so that I could sit or lie down somewhere to rest my back and legs.

Our factory advertised for some sewers to replace the ones we'd lost, and one evening I brought a flyer back to the house. Lili was with a client in her room, but at dinner I showed it to Huong and Nana and said I would try to help them get the jobs if they were interested.

"How much can a sewer make?" Nana asked.

"About three hundred a week," I said.

"My, so little. Not for me."

Huong broke in. "Does your boss use people without a work permit?"

"There're some illegal workers at the factory. I can put in a word for you."

"If only I could sew!"

Her words made my heart leap. I went on, "It's not that hard to learn. There are sewing classes downtown. It takes three weeks to graduate."

"And lots of tuition too," added Nana.

"Not really—three or four hundred dollars," I said.

"I still owe the Croc a big debt, or I would've quit selling my flesh long ago," Huong muttered. Besides smuggling people, the man also operated gambling dens in Queens, one of which had recently got busted.

I said no more. For sure, a sewer made much less than a prostitute, but a sewer could live a respectable life. However, I could see Nana's logic—her work here was more lucrative. Sometimes she made three hundred dollars in a single day. My housemates spent a lot of time watching TV and listening to music when they had no clients, but how long could they continue living like that? Their youth would fade someday.

Then what would they do? I remained silent, unsure if I should tell Huong what I thought in Nana's presence.

A slightly overweight white man with wavy hair came out of Lili's room. He looked angry and muttered to himself, "Cheap Chinese stuff, fucking cheap!" Throwing a fierce glance at us, he turned and left. The women's clients were mostly Asian, and occasionally one or two Hispanics or blacks. It was rare to see a white john here.

Lili came out of her room, sobbing. She collapsed on a chair and covered her face with her long-fingered hand. Huong put a bowl of wontons in front of her, but Lili fell back on her chair, saying, "I can't eat now."

"What happened?" Nana asked.

"Another condom break," Lili said. "He got furious and said he might've caught some disease from me. He paid me only sixty dollars, saying I used a substandard rubber made in China."

"Was it really Chinese?" I asked her.

"I have no clue."

"It might be," Huong said. "Mrs. Chen always gets stuff from Silver City."

"But that's a Korean store," I said.

"I feel so awful to be Chinese here, because China always makes cheap products," Lili said. "China has degraded its people and let me down."

I didn't know what to say. How could an individual blame a country for her personal trouble?

That night, I asked Huong to come out, and together we talked under the weeping cherry. The stringy branches floated in a cool breeze, while the leaves, like a swarm of arrowheads, flickered in the soft rays cast by the streetlights. Fireworks were exploding in the west, at Shea Stadium—the

Mets must have won a game. I worked up my nerve and said to Huong, "Why can't you quit this sex work so we can be together?"

Her eyes gleamed, fastened on me. "You mean you want to be my boyfriend?"

"Yes, but I also want you to stop selling yourself."

She sighed. "I have to pay the Croc two thousand dollars a month. There's no other way I can make that kind of money."

"How much of your smuggling fee do you still owe him?"

"My parents paid up their fifteen percent in Vietnam, but I still have eighteen thousand to pay."

I paused, figuring out some numbers in my head. That was a big sum, but not impossible. "I can make more than fourteen hundred a month. After the rent and everything, I'll have about a thousand left. I can help you pay the debt if you quit your work."

"Where can I get the other thousand every month? I'd love to be a sewer, but that doesn't pay enough. I've been thinking about the job ever since you mentioned it. It would take a long time for me to get enough experience to make even three hundred a week. Meanwhile, how can I pay the Croc?" She swallowed, then continued, "I often dream of going back, but my parents won't let me. They say that my little brother will join me here eventually. They only want me to send them more money. If only I could jump ship."

We talked for more than an hour, trying to figure out a way. She seemed elated by my offer to help, but at moments her excitement unnerved me a little and made me wonder whether I was being rash. What if we didn't get along? How could we conceal her past from others? Despite my uneasiness, in my mind's eye I kept seeing her in a small white cottage stirring a pot with a large ladle while humming a song, and outside, children's voices were rising and falling. I suggested that we speak to the Croc in person and see if there was another way of paying him. Before she went back to the house, she kissed me on the cheek and said, "Wanping, I would do anything for you. You are a good man."

Great joy welled up in my heart, and I stayed in the damp air for a long time, dreaming of how we could start our life anew someday. If only I had more cash. I thought of asking Huong to share my bed, but decided not to, for fear that the other two women might inform Mrs. Chen of our relationship. A full moon was shining on the sleeping street, the walls and roofs bathed in the whitish light. Insects were chirring timidly, as if short of breath.

Two days later, I left work earlier, and Huong and I set out to meet with the Croc, who had sounded Cantonese on the phone. We crossed Northern Boulevard and headed for the area near I-678. His headquarters was on Thirty-second Avenue, in a large warehouse. Two prostitutes, one white and the other Hispanic, were loitering in front, wearing nothing but bras and frayed jean shorts. Both of them seemed high on something, and the white woman, who had tousled hair and a missing tooth, shouted at me, "Hey, can you spare a smoke?"

I shook my head. Huong and I hurried into the warehouse. Its interior was filled with large boxes of textiles and shoes. We found the office in a corner. A strapping man was sprawled in a leather chair, smoking a cigar. He sat up at the sight of us and smirked. "Take a seat," he said, pointing at a sofa.

The moment we sat down, Huong said, "This is my boyfriend, Wanping. We came to ask you a favor."

The man nodded at me. He turned to Huong. "Okay, what can I do for you?"

"I need some extra time. Can I pay you thirteen hundred a month?"

"No way." He smirked again, his ratlike eyes darting right and left.

"How about fifteen hundred?"

"I said no."

"You see, I have a medical condition and have to take a different job that doesn't pay as much."

"That's not my problem." He fingered his wispy mustache.

I stepped in. "I will help her pay you, but we simply cannot come up with two thousand a month for now. Please give us an extra half year."

"A rule is a rule. If someone breaks it with impunity, the rule will have no force anymore. We've never given anyone such an extension. So don't even try to get clever with me. If you don't pay the full amount in time, you know what we'll do." He jerked his thumb at Huong.

She looked at me, tears forming in her eyes. I patted her arm, signaling that we should leave. We got up and left the warehouse after saying we appreciated his meeting with us.

On the way back, we talked about what the consequences would be if we failed to make the monthly payment. I was pensive, knowing it was dangerous to deal with a thug like the Croc. I had heard horrifying stories of how members of the Asian Mafia punished people, especially new arrivals who had offended them. They had shoved a man into a van and shipped him to a cannery in New Jersey to make pet food of him; they had cut off a little girl's nose because her father hadn't paid them the protection fee; they had tied a middle-aged woman's hands, plugged her mouth, stuffed her into a burlap sack, and then dropped her into the ocean. The Chinese gangs spread the Mafia stories to intimidate people. Some of those tales might just be rumors, and, granted, the

Croc might not belong to the Mafia at all, but he could do Huong and me in easily. He had to be a gangster, if not the leader of a gang. Also, he likely had networks in China and Vietnam that could hurt our families.

After dinner, I went into Huong's room, which was clean and smelled of pineapple. On the windowsill sat a vase of marigolds. I said to her, "What if we just leave New York?"

"And go where?" She sounded calm, as if she too had this idea.

"Anywhere. America is a big country, and we can live in a remote town under different names, or move around, working on farms like the Mexicans. There must be some way for us to survive. First we can go to North Carolina, and from there we'll move on."

"What about my family? The Croc will hold my parents accountable."

"You shouldn't worry so much. You have to take care of yourself first."

"My parents would never forgive me if I just disappeared."

"But haven't they just been using you? You've been their cash cow."

That seemed to be sinking in. A moment later, she said, "You're right. Let's get out of here."

We decided to leave as soon as possible. She had some cash on hand, about two thousand dollars, while I still had fourteen hundred in my savings account. The next morning on the way to work I stopped at Cathay Bank and took out all the money. I felt kind of low, knowing that from now on I couldn't write to my parents, or the Croc's men might hunt us down. To my family, I would be as good as dead. In this place, we had no choice but to take loss as necessity.

That afternoon, Huong had packed a suitcase secretly and

stuffed some of my clothes into a duffel bag. I wished that I could have said good-bye to my boss and some fellow workers, and gotten my three-hundred-dollar deposit back from Mrs. Chen. At dinner, both Nana and Lili teased Huong, saying she had begun working for me, as a cleaning lady. The two of us tried to appear normal, and I even cracked a few jokes.

Fortunately, there was no outcall that night. When the other two women had gone to bed, Huong and I slipped out of the house. I carried her suitcase while she lugged my bag. The weeping cherry blurred in the haze, its crown edgeless, like a small hill. A truck was rumbling down Main Street as we strode away, arm in arm, without looking back.

A Good Fall

AGAIN GANCHIN COLLAPSED in the kung fu class he was teaching. Seated on the floor, he gasped for breath and couldn't get up. A student stepped over to give him a hand, but Ganchin waved to stop him. He forced himself to announce, "Let's call it a day. Please come back tomorrow afternoon." The seventeen boys and girls were collecting their bags in a corner and exiting the exercise hall. Some kept glancing at their teacher's contorted face.

Late that afternoon Master Zong called Ganchin into the small meditation room. They sat down on the floor, and the heavy-jawed master poured a cup of tea for him and said, "Brother, I'm afraid we have to let you go. We've tried but cannot get your visa renewed." He placed Ganchin's passport on the coffee table, beside the teacup.

Stunned, Ganchin opened his mouth, but no words came out. Indeed, he had been sick for weeks and couldn't teach the kung fu classes as well as before, yet never had he imagined that Master Zong would dismiss him before his contract expired. Ganchin said, "Can you pay me the salary the temple owes me?"

"We don't owe you anything," Zong answered, his hooded eyes glued to Ganchin's pale face.

"Our contract says clearly that you'll pay me fifteen hundred dollars a month. So far you haven't paid me a cent."

"Like I said, that was just a formality—we had to put down a figure to get the visa for you."

"Master Zong, I worked for you for more than two years and never made any trouble. Now that you fired me, you should give me at least my salary so I can go back and clear the debts I owe."

"We've provided lodging and board for you. This is New York, where everything's expensive. As a matter of fact, we paid you a lot more than fifteen hundred a month."

"But without some cash in hand I can't go home. I spent a fortune to get this teaching position, bribing the elders in charge of international exchanges at my monastery."

"We have no money for you."

"Then I cannot leave."

Zong picked up Ganchin's passport and inserted it into his robe. "I can't let you have your papers if you stay on illegally. From now on you're on your own, and you must move out tomorrow. I don't care where you go. Your visa has expired and you're already an illegal alien, a lawbreaker."

Zong got up from the floor and went out to the backyard, where his midnight blue BMW was parked. Ganchin was still sitting cross-legged in the room as the car pulled away. He knew the master was going home to Long Island, where he had recently bought a house in Syosset. Zong and his woman had just had a baby, but they couldn't marry because as the master of the temple he dared not take a wife openly. He'd kept his former residence, a town house in lower Manhattan, where he often put up his friends and the friends of his friends.

The temple felt deserted despite the tiny halos of candles on the rows of small tables in the service hall, at the end of which sat a tall statue of the Buddha smiling serenely, with his hands resting palms up on his knees. Ganchin closed the windows and bolted the front door. Since he had become ill, he had been more afraid of the night, when he felt more desolate and homesick. Originally he'd thought that by the time his three-year stint here was over he could return loaded with gifts and dollars. But now, penniless, he couldn't imagine going back. His father had written that some creditors had shown up to pester his family. The old man urged him not to rush home, not until he made enough money.

Ganchin cooked himself some rice porridge and ate it with two preserved eggs. After the meal he forced himself to drink some boiled water to keep down the acid gastric juice that was surging up into his throat. He decided to call Cindy, who had once learned martial arts from him when she visited Tianjin City, where his monastery and kung fu school were located. She was an "ABC" (American-born Chinese) but could speak Mandarin. Ever since she'd met him again in Flushing, she had been friendly and often invited him to tea downtown.

They agreed to meet at Lovely Melodies, a bar at the northern end of Alexis Street. It was an out-of-the-way place where few could recognize Ganchin as a monk of Gaolin Temple. On arrival, he didn't go in, but waited for Cindy because he had no money. Within a minute she showed up. Together they entered the bar, found a table in a corner, and ordered their drinks. There were only about a dozen customers, but the music was loud. A young man near the front was belting out a karaoke song as if heartbroken:

What I miss most is your big smile
That still sweetens my dreams.
Although I run into you all the while,
Your face no longer beams . . .

"He really meant to get rid of you?" Cindy asked Ganchin about Master Zong, sipping her margarita with a straw.

"No doubt about it. I'll have to move out tomorrow." He gave a feeble sigh and set his glass of Sprite on the table.

"Where are you going to stay?"

"I have a friend, a fellow townsman, who might agree to take me in."

"You know, you can always use my place. I'm on trips most of the time anyway." A small-framed woman of twenty-five with a sunny face, she was a flight attendant and often flew abroad. Sometimes she was away for a whole week.

"Thanks. I may be able to stay with my friend for the time being. To be honest, never have I felt this low—I can neither stay on nor go back."

"Why can't you live here?"

"Master Zong said I was already an illegal alien. He kept my passport."

"You shouldn't worry so much, sweetie. If worse comes to worst, you should consider marrying a woman, a U.S. citizen." She snickered, gazing at his lean face, her big eyes warm and brave.

He knew she was fond of him, but he said, "I'm a monk and can't think of anything like that."

"Why not return to this earthly life?"

"Well, I'm already trapped in the web of dust. People say the temple is a place without strife, worry, or greed. It's not true. Master Zong lives like a CEO. I guess he must spend more than ten thousand dollars a month just for his household expenses."

"I know. I saw him drive a brand-new car."

"That's why I am angry with him, for not paying me my salary."

"How much would be enough for you to go back?"

"At least twenty thousand dollars. He owes me forty thousand."

"I'm afraid he might never pay you that much."

Ganchin sighed. "I know. I'm upset but can't do a thing. He has a lot of pull back home. A cousin of his is the head of the municipal police. Sometimes I wish I were an illegal coolie here, so that I could restart my life and wouldn't have to deal with any crook. But I've never worked outside a temple and don't have any skill. I'm useless here."

"Come on—you can teach martial arts."

"For that I'll have to know some English, won't I?"

"You can always learn it."

"Also, I'll need a work permit."

"Don't worry so much. Try to get better. Once you're well, there'll be ways for you to get by here."

He didn't want to talk more, unable to imagine making a living in America.

When they were leaving the bar, she asked him to contact her whenever he needed help. She was going to fly to Tokyo and would be back the next week. The night was slightly hazy and most shops were closed. Some young couples strolled along the sidewalks hand in hand or arm in arm. A car honked about two hundred feet away. At the blast a linden sapling nearby shuddered a little, its leaves rustling. Ganchin had a fit of wheezing coughing and wiped his mouth with a tissue. Cindy patted him on the back and urged him to rest in bed for a few days. He grimaced, his face wry. They said good night, and in no time her sylphlike figure in its orange skirt faded into the dark.

Fanku wasn't really Ganchin's friend. They had come to know each other about six months ago at a celebration of the Spring Festival. Ganchin had been delighted to find the man to be a fellow townsman, from the same county. Fanku worked as a line cook at an eatery. When Ganchin asked to stay with him for a few days, Fanku welcomed him, saying he was proud to help a friend.

His studio apartment was in the basement of a nine-story tenement, close to downtown Flushing. It had a tiny bathroom but no kitchenette, and was furnished with only a cot and a pair of metal chairs standing on either side of a narrow table. When Ganchin had arrived, Fanku pulled a bundle out of the closet and spread the thin sponge mattress on the floor. "Here, you can sleep on this," he told the guest. "I hope this is all right."

"Very good, thanks," Ganchin replied.

In the morning he would roll up the mattress and stow it in the closet again. The sleeping arrangement satisfied both of them, but Ganchin's hacking cough troubled Fanku, who asked him several times about the true nature of his illness. Ganchin assured him that it was not tuberculosis, that he must have hurt his lungs during his kung fu practice, and that the illness had been aggravated by the anger and anguish he'd gone through lately. Even so, Fanku often examined the water in a pickle bottle—into which the monk spat—to see if there was blood. So far he'd found nothing abnormal. Still, Ganchin's constant coughing disturbed him, especially at night.

Fanku let his guest use whatever food he had in the studio

for free, while he himself ate at work. There were a few packs of ramen noodles and a half sack of jasmine rice in the cabinets, and he urged Ganchin to eat something more nutritious so that he could recuperate, but the monk had no money. He asked Fanku for a loan of two hundred dollars, but Fanku was almost as broke as Ganchin. He'd overstayed his business visa and had to pay horrendous attorney's fees, as he had been trying to get his illegal status changed. He lent Ganchin sixty dollars instead. Fanku often brought back food for Ganchin, a box of rice mixed with pork roast, or a bag of fish croquettes, or a bunch of egg rolls and spareribs. By now, Ganchin had started eating meat and seafood; it was hard to remain vegetarian when he had no idea where he would have his next meal. Fanku said he could get those food items at a discount, but Ganchin wondered if they were leftovers. Yet whenever the thought popped into his mind, he'd push it aside and remind himself to be grateful.

Then one morning Fanku said, "Look, Ganchin, I don't mean to pressure you, but I can't continue paying for the food I bring back. My lawyer asked me to give him thirty-five hundred dollars by the end of this month. I'm totally broke."

Lowering his eyes, Ganchin said, "Please keep a record of the money you've spent on me. I'll pay it back."

"You misunderstood me, brother. I simply don't have enough cash now. Goodness knows if my lawyer really can help me. A girl at Olivia Salon has spent more than eighty thousand dollars for attorney's fees but still can't get a green card. Sometimes I'm so desperate for cash that I feel like mugging someone. You know, I have to send money to my wife and daughter back home as well."

"Can you help me find work at your restaurant? I can wash dishes and mop floors."

"You're so ill, no place would dare to use you. The best you can do is rest well and try to recover."

Ganchin turned silent for a few seconds, then replied, "I'll try to get some money."

Fanku said no more. He yawned, having slept poorly since Ganchin had been here. Fanku was only forty-one but looked wizened like an old man with a pimpled bald crown. He must have lived in fear and worry all the time. He spread his hand towel on a clotheshorse in a corner and left for work.

After breakfast, which was two cold buns stuffed with red-bean paste and a cup of black tea, Ganchin set out for Gaolin Temple. His legs were a little shaky as he walked. A shower had descended the previous night, so the streets were clean and even the air smelled fresher, devoid of the stink of rotten fish and vegetables. He turned onto a side street. On the pavement seven plump sparrows were struggling with spilled popcorn, twittering fretfully and hardly able to break the fluffy kernels. Regardless of humans and automobiles, the birds were all working hard at the food. Approaching the temple, Ganchin heard people shouting and stamping their feet in unison inside the brick building. A new coach was teaching a kung fu class.

At the sight of Ganchin, Master Zong put on a smile and said, "You've gained some color. I hope you're well now." He led him to the back of the building, walking with a slight stoop.

Seated on a bamboo mat in the meditation room, Ganchin said, "Master, I came to see if there's some way you can pay me my salary. I can't stay on illegally—you know that—and neither can I go home without enough cash to clear my debts."

Zong's smile didn't stop, displaying a mouth of gleaming teeth, which had often made Ganchin wonder what kind of toothpaste the master used. Zong said, "Let me repeat, our temple doesn't owe you a thing."

"Master, you've pushed me to the edge of a cliff—I have no way out now and may have to follow Ganping's example." Ganping had been a monk at the temple, who, after three years' work, wouldn't go back on account of the unpaid salary. Master Zong had ordered him to leave, but the monk went to a park and hanged himself instead.

"You're not like Ganping," Zong said calmly, his fleshy face sleek. "He was insane and stupid, couldn't even do a clean job of hanging himself. That's why he is in jail now." People had spotted Ganping the moment he dangled from a piece of cloth tied to a bough of an oak, his legs kicking, and they'd called the police, who brought him back to the temple. Soon afterward he was sent back to China. But he went crazy because his girlfriend had taken a lover during his absence. He strangled the woman, with whom he ought not to have started a romantic relationship in the first place.

Ganchin felt like weeping but took hold of himself. He said, "Don't underestimate me, Master. If life is no longer worth living, one can end it without remorse."

"You have your old parents, who are looking forward to seeing you home. You shouldn't think of such a cowardly way out."

"If I went back empty-handed, I'd be a great disappointment to them. I'd prefer to die here."

"Don't talk about death. We monks must cherish every life. Life is given us only once, and it's a sin to destroy it. You know all this; no need for me to dwell on it."

"Master, farewell. See you in the next world."

"Stop bluffing. To be honest, according to my agreement with your monastery, I'm responsible for sending you home, but I won't force you. You can choose what to do." The master let out a huge burp.

"I only hope my soul can reach home. Good-bye now." Ganchin got up from the bamboo mat and made for the door.

"Pighead," Zong said.

Ganchin stepped out of the temple. Forks of lightning cracked the sky in the south, where dark clouds were billowing, piling on one another. The wind was rising as shop signs along the street were flapping. Pedestrians were rushing back and forth to avoid the thickening rain, a stocky woman running with a newspaper over her head, but Ganchin just strolled back to Fanku's place. Big raindrops pattered on tree leaves and on his face while his robe fluttered.

Cindy came to see him the next afternoon. His cough had turned harsher, thanks to the rain that had drenched him. He was also thinner than the previous week. She took him to Little Pepper, a Sichuan restaurant, and ordered a vegetarian firepot for both of them.

He had no appetite for vegetables and would have preferred meat or seafood. He spoke listlessly while she tried to cheer him up. "Don't think you're down and out," she said. "You're still young and can always restart."

"How do you mean?" He looked at her heart-shaped face blankly.

"I mean it's foolish to think you're done for. Lots of people here are illegal aliens. They live a hard life but still can manage. In a couple of years there might be an amnesty that allows them to become legal immigrants." She cut a cube of tofu in two with her chopsticks and put a half into her mouth, chewing it with her lips closed.

"I really don't know what to do. I hope I can go home soon."

"Continue to be a monk?" She gave a pixieish smile.

"I've never been someone else since I grew up."

"You can always change. This is America, where it's never too late to turn over a new page. That's why my parents came here. My mom hated her ex-mother-in-law—that's my grandmother—and wanted to restart her life far away from the old woman."

He grimaced again, having no idea what to say. He thought of borrowing money from Cindy to clear the debt of sixty dollars he owed Fanku, but refrained. He would prefer to leave her only good memories of him.

"You look better with your crew cut, you know." She pointed at his head, which used to be shaved bald.

"I didn't mean to keep it this way at all."

"You should let your hair grow longer. That will make your face look stronger—more masculine, I mean. Are you okay at your current place?"

He took a bite of a fake meatball made of minced mushroom and soy flour and answered, "It's all right for now. I don't know how long I can stay with Fanku. I might already be a burden to him."

"Keep in mind you can always use my place. I live on planes and in hotels these days."

"Thank you." His eyes went moist, but he averted his face and squeezed his lids. "If only I had been born here," he sighed.

"Except for the Indians, nobody's really a native in the United States. You mustn't think of yourself as a stranger—this country belongs to you if you live and work here."

"I'm too old to change."

"How can you say that? You're just twenty-eight!"

"But my heart is very, very old."

"You still have fifty years to go, at least." She giggled and patted his hand. He smiled and shook his head as if to admit he was beyond help.

After talking with Cindy, he realized that Master Zong had kept his passport with an eye to preventing him from changing his status, because illegal aliens had to produce their papers when the U.S. president issued an amnesty. It would be impossible to apply for a green card in good time if you couldn't prove your country of origin and your date of entry into the United States. Zong must be determined to get him back to China.

Fanku told Ganchin to stay in the next morning, because the superintendent of the tenement would come around eleven to check the smoke detector. Ganchin promised not to go out before the man showed up. He was lying on the cot, thinking about whether he should ask for a smaller amount of cash from Master Zong, say twenty-five thousand, since apparently the temple had never paid any monk a salary. How he regretted having tried so hard to come here! He'd been misled by the people who bragged about the opportunity found in America and wouldn't reveal the hardship they'd gone through here. They all wanted to appear rich and successful in their hometowns' eyes. Silly, how silly. If he went back, he would tell the truth—the American type of success was not for everyone. You must learn how to sell yourself there and must change yourself to live a new life.

As he was musing, someone knocked on the door. He got up to answer it. The instant he opened it a crack two men burst in. One was Master Zong and the other a brawny young fellow Ganchin had never met. They grabbed his arms.

"Don't resist," Zong hissed. "We won't hurt you. We're just helping you go home, to keep you from deteriorating into a bum."

"Where are you taking me?" Ganchin gasped.

"To the airport," Zong said, as they hauled him away. Ganchin was too weak to struggle and so he obeyed them.

They shoved him into the back of the BMW, buckled him up, and dropped on his lap two paper napkins for his phlegm. Then they got into the front seats, and the car pulled away. In a placid voice Zong explained to him, "Don't be upset. I bought the plane ticket for you and will give you some cash for your travel expenses. When you check in at the counter, I'll let you have your passport."

"You've kidnapped me. This is against the law."

The men both guffawed. The squint-eyed young fellow said, "Please don't accuse us like this. You're a Chinese and soon will board a plane for China."

"Yes, you can grouse as much as you like to the elders of your monastery," Zong told him.

Realizing it was useless to argue, Ganchin clammed up the rest of the way, though he was thinking hard about how to break loose.

They parked in a garage and then took him to Air China. A large uniformed black woman stood at the entrance to the ticketing counter; Ganchin wondered if he should shout to get her attention, but thought better of it. The three of them entered the zigzag cordoned lane filled with people. This wasn't personal, Master Zong kept telling him. They just didn't want to sully China's image by letting an ocher-robed monk roam the streets of New York. That would tarnish the temple's reputation as well.

What should Ganchin do? He could get rid of his robe as

he had slacks underneath. Should he go to the men's room and see if he could find a way to escape from there? No, they would see through him. How about calling to the fully armed security guards with the big German shepherd near the checkpoint? No. Master Zong might still be able to get him on the plane, claiming he was mentally ill, dangerous like a terrorist, and must be sent home for treatment.

As he was wondering, a passenger cart with three rows of seats on it was coming up, an old couple sitting in the first row. Ganchin glanced at his kidnappers—both of them were looking at the counter, where two young women were lugging a family's baggage onto the conveyor belt. Ganchin lifted the blue cordon beside him, slunk out of the lane, and leapt upon the last row of seats on the cart, then rolled down into the legroom. He pulled in his feet so his kidnappers couldn't see him. The battery-powered vehicle was running away when he heard Zong shout, "Ganchin, Ganchin, where are you?"

"Come here, Ganchin, you dickhead!" another voice barked.

"Ganchin, come over, please! We can negotiate," Zong cried.

Ganchin realized they didn't know he was on the vehicle, which veered off and headed for another terminal. He stayed put, letting it take him as far away as possible.

Finally the cart stopped, and he raised his head to look around. "Hey, this is for disability only," the black driver told him, flashing a smile while helping the old couple off.

Ganchin didn't know what the man meant, and just said, "Thank you." That was all the English he had besides "good-bye." He got off and went into a men's room, where he shed his robe. He dumped it into a trash can and came out wearing black slacks and an off-white sweatshirt.

• • •

He managed to get back to Flushing by a hotel shuttle, following the suggestion of a middle-aged Taiwanese woman. Terrified, he could not return to Fanku's place. Evidently that man and Master Zong were in cahoots. Where to go now? Where was a safe place? Never had Ganchin imagined that Zong would resort to force to fly him back. A pain tightened his chest and he coughed again.

He still had a few dollars in his pocket, so he slouched into Teng's Garden, which wasn't far from Gaolin Temple. A trim little man in shirtsleeves, apparently the owner of the restaurant, greeted him and, raising his forefinger, said heartily, "One?" He was about to take him into the interior.

"Just a minute. Can I use your phone?" Ganchin asked.

"There's a pay phone down the street. Why not use that one?" The man waved in the direction of the temple.

"I don't know how to use a pay phone."

"Similar to a regular one—drop in a quarter and dial the number you want to call. We're talking about a local call, right?"

"Actually, I don't have to use a phone. I'm Ganchin, a monk of Gaolin Temple, and I'd like to leave a word for Master Zong there. Can you pass it for me?"

"I don't know you."

"Look, this is me." Ganchin produced a laminated photo and showed it to the man. In it Ganchin, wearing black cloth shoes, struck a pose like an eagle about to hop off; above his shiny shaved head a golden banner was floating in a breeze; he looked like a movie star, a hero, full of spunk.

The little man squinted at the picture and then at him. "Yes, it's you. What do you want me to tell your master?"

"Tell him to say prayers and make offerings for my soul tomorrow morning before sunrise."

"What are you talking about? Like you're already a ghost."

"I'm going to die soon. Tell Master Zong to pray to redeem my soul before six o'clock tomorrow morning, all right?"

"Young brother, you shouldn't think like this. You mustn't give up so easily. Come with me, let's talk and see if this old man can be any help."

Ganchin followed him into an inner room; in its center stood a round dining table with a revolving, two-level tray on it. Apparently this was a place for banquets. The moment they sat down at the immense table, Ganchin said he'd decided to kill himself today. He was sick and penniless, while Master Zong tried to send him back to China without paying him the salary the temple owed him. The little man listened, wordless. The more Ganchin rambled, the more heartbroken he became, until he couldn't continue anymore and collapsed into sobbing.

The restaurant owner sighed and shook his broad head. He said, "You wait here and I'll be back in a minute."

By now Ganchin had calmed down some, though was still tearful. He believed this was his last day on earth. Thinking about his old parents, he felt his insides writhing. How devastated they would be by his death! And without him, their only son, how miserable their remaining years would become. But he simply had no way out. If he died here, at least some of the creditors might take pity on his parents and forgive the debts. Oh, this was the only way he could help his family!

The little man came back with a large bowl of rice topped with sautéed seafood and vegetables. He said to Ganchin, "Young brother, I can see you're hungry. Eat this and you might think differently afterward. Gosh, I totally forgot you're a monk, a vegetarian! Sorry about this. I'm gonna—"

"I eat seafood," Ganchin said.

"Then eat this. Keep in mind, yours is not the worst sorrow.

Life is precious and full of wonderful things in spite of all the bitterness and sufferings."

"Thank you, Uncle," he mumbled. "I will put in a good word for you when I meet the Buddha in the other world." He broke the connected chopsticks and began eating.

Oh, it tasted so good! This was the most delicious meal he'd had in recent years, and he picked up the shrimp and scallops one after another and swallowed them as if they did not require chewing. The snow peas were crisp, the bamboo shoots crunchy, and the portabella mushrooms succulent, perfectly done. He ate and ate, and in no time finished the whole thing. Then he lifted the bowl, about to drink up the remaining sauce, but caught himself and put it down.

"Uncle," he said, "I know you're kind and generous. You gave ear to a stranger's grievance, you didn't ask me but guessed I was hungry, and you have a compassionate soul. Here's a bit of cash. Please keep this." He pulled all the money out of his pants pocket and left it on the table, one five and three singles.

Waving his stubby fingers, the man protested, "I didn't mean to sell you any food. I don't want your money. Just think about all the good things in this life, okay? Don't let your grief crush you."

"Please tell Master Zong to pray for me before sunrise tomorrow morning. Good-bye, Uncle." Ganchin hurried out the door and dragged himself away, feeling the restaurateur's gaze at his back.

Where should he go? He wanted to find a building out of which he could jump and kill himself. How about the temple? No, it had only two stories. Too low. How about the elementary school? No, his ghost might frighten the children if he died there, and people would condemn him.

Having crossed Northern Boulevard, he saw a brick building to his right, partly boarded up. He took a brief measure of it—it was high enough, five stories. Also, this was a deserted spot and his death might not disturb many people in the neighborhood. So he decided to use this building, which must once have been a factory and still had metal ventilators on its roof.

As he was laboring up the sagging stairs, a flock of pigeons took off, their wings flickering explosively, and a few bats flitted about, catching mosquitoes while emitting tinny squeaks in the glow of the sinking sun. The distant houses and the spires of the churches were obscured, half hidden in the golden smog. At a landing the floor was strewn with needleless syringes, takeout containers, cigarette butts, beer cans. He wondered if some people lived in here at night. Well, if they did, they shouldn't continue using this place when it got cold. On the top floor he leaned over a few unboarded windows to survey the base of the building. Down there in the empty parking lot a lone seagull with black wing tips was wrestling with a paper bag, dragging out balled-up napkins and plastic cups and plates to pick up bits of fries. Ganchin decided to use the backyard to avoid the traffic on the front street. He propped two thick boards on a windowsill that had lost its wood and was just lined with bricks. He pictured himself running all the way up the boards and springing out of the building headfirst. That would do the job for sure. He backed up a dozen steps, ready to dash.

Suddenly his stomach churned and sent up a chunk of scallop and a few rice grains that he hadn't chewed thoroughly. Oh, they still tasted good! He swallowed the morsel while tears were trickling down his cheeks. He started running, up and up, until he hurled himself into the air. As he was falling facedown, somehow all the years of training in martial arts at once possessed him. His body instinctively adjusted itself and even his arms spread out, swinging to ensure that he wouldn't hurt himself fatally. With a thump his feet landed on the ground. "Ow!" he yelled, thunderstruck that he had just cheated death. A tearing pain shot up from his left thigh while his right leg twitched.

"Ow, help me! Help!" he hollered.

How ludicrous this whole thing turned out! He kept yelling, and some people came over, most of them high school students playing basketball nearby. A man dialed 911 and another comforted him, saying, "Don't move. Everything's cool, man. I know this hurts, must hurt like hell, but help's on the way."

"Oh, let me die, let me finish myself!" Eyes shut, Ganchin was screaming and shaking his head, but nobody understood his Mandarin.

In addition to a broken leg, the doctors found, he also suffered from tracheitis. No wonder he was running a temperature and coughing nonstop. They kept him in the hospital for three days until his fever was gone. Meanwhile, his attempted suicide had become news in the Chinese communities across North America, reported by numerous small newspapers; a charitable organization offered to pick up his medical bills; and even the owner of Teng's Garden got famous for a week, having appeared twice on local TV. Everyone knew that the master of Gaolin Temple had exploited young monks and pocketed their salaries. Many declared that they would never donate anything to the temple again. A pretty thirtysomething named Amy Lok, running for a seat in the state senate, paid Ganchin a visit and told him to contact her office if he needed any assistance. Several lawyers called, eager to represent him in a lawsuit against the temple. All the notoriety befuddled and unnerved Ganchin.

Cindy took him in after he was released from the hospital with a pair of crutches, and she persuaded him to let her speak with the attorneys on his behalf so that they might not take advantage of him. She urged him to use Jon Mah, an older man who spoke both Mandarin and Korean and was known for handling this kind of case. Ganchin was worried about the legal fee, but Mr. Mah told him, "You don't need to pay before you get the damages from the defendant."

Cindy said to Ganchin, "They'll get a third of the money the court awards you."

"This is America," Mr. Mah resumed, "a land ruled by law, and nobody is entitled to abuse others with impunity. Rest assured, you're in safe hands."

After the attorney left, Ganchin was still antsy. He asked Cindy, "What will the INS do to me? If they deport me, can I get enough money for the debts back home?"

"Now there'll be ways for you to avoid deportation—you can apply for political asylum, or marry a citizen or a legal resident. You know, you'll be rich, but not filthy rich like a millionaire who doesn't have to work."

Amazed, Ganchin thought about her words, then sighed. "I guess I'm not a monk anymore, and no temple will ever take me in."

"That also means you're free to date a girl." She giggled, rubbing her nose with a knuckle.

"Well, I hope that's something I can learn." He gazed at her and smiled.

ACKNOWLEDGMENTS

I'm grateful to the American Academy in Berlin for the Mary Ellen von der Heyden Fellowship for fiction and to Boston University for a sabbatical leave. The generous support from both institutions enabled me to complete this book.

I would like to thank Dan Frank for his comments and suggestions and Lane Zachary for her enthusiasm.

A NOTE ABOUT THE AUTHOR

Ha Jin left his native China in 1985 to attend Brandeis University. He is the author of the internationally best-selling novel *Waiting*, which won the PEN/Faulkner Award and the National Book Award, and *War Trash,* which won the PEN/Faulkner Award for Fiction; the story collections *The Bridegroom,* which won the Asian American Literary Award, *Under the Red Flag,* which won the Flannery O'Connor Award for Short Fiction, and *Ocean of Words,* which won the PEN/Hemingway Award; the novels *A Free Life, The Crazed,* and *In the Pond;* three books of poetry; and a book of essays, *The Writer as Migrant.*

A NOTE ON THE TYPE

This book was set in Caledonia, a Linotype face designed by W. A. Dwiggins (1880–1956). It belongs to the family of printing types called "modern face" by printers—a term used to mark the change in style of the type letters that occurred around 1800. Caledonia borders on the general design of Scotch Roman but it is more freely drawn than that letter.

COMPOSED BY
Creative Graphics, Allentown, Pennsylvania

PRINTED AND BOUND BY
RR Donnelley, Harrisonburg, Virginia

DESIGNED BY
Iris Weinstein